BLOOD
OF THE
MAJI

Book Eight of The Hayle Coven Destinies

PATTI LARSEN

ONE

He's falling again and I can't stop him. I reach for him with the desperation of one who will not survive without him. The earth swallows his tall, beautiful form, devouring his strawberry blond waves, his hazel eyes flecked with green, until only one hand reaches upward for me, the earth eating him alive.

I scream his name, dive for him. It takes forever to hit the ground. It vibrates under me, the tiny seedling bursting from the dark loam that smells of fabric softener and spring. I have to leap away as the oak tree explodes from that small, green bit of life, erupting as though it had been waiting for this moment. It looms over me, vast and powerful, before it turns to steel.

My hands grasp for the metal tree, tears soaking the now hard ground, but he's gone and only this monolith of cold remains. But no, it's hot, heating up under my desperate grasp, burning me as I cry out and fall away.

Falling, into darkness.

1

And then I'm flying. The armor I wear is heavy on my shoulders but I barely feel it, welcome its presence. It's kept me alive so far, saves me as I take a hit to the chest from the distance while my mount wheels and dives to protect us from attack. The pressure of building power pushes against me, burning through the metal and scorching my skin, bruising my damaged body. It crushes my chest so tight I have to fight for breath. I force my lungs to inflate out of sheer spite, scream a soundless yell of defiance, voice already parched and cracking, failing me.

But I will not fail.

My magic pulses, as weary as I am but refusing to quit as the massive wings of my drach friend sweep us forward, his power as unrelenting as my determination. We are together in the end, as we knew we would be and I will not falter for he is with me.

We must reach them before it's too late.

The glowing, white sword of light hangs over my head, weightless, brilliant, shining a beacon in our fore, casting shadows over the sharp, violent spikes that adorn his once smooth, scaled shoulders. He is a weapon from the tip of his snout to the sharp edged blade of his tail, all of his creation now made for war. Designed by Creator to do what must be done.

We both are, now.

I clench tight the sword's hilt in my gauntlet, sweat running from my hot palm down inside my suit of living metal. My mount's massive head arches backward, fire spouting in a cascade of heat and ash blowing past my cheek. I inhale fire, choke on it, searing my insides. The pain doesn't matter, won't stop me. Nothing will.

Another blow, this one to my head, carrying away the helm that guards my face. I shake off the blow, hair flying clear, ears ringing with the rush of impending death. I embrace it, suck it back like a draught of joy. We're almost there, the building juggernaut of destructive force between the armies hurtling toward each other narrowing by the instant.

We're almost too late. But Fate won't let us fall. Not now. Not ever.

We soar into the barest crack that remains, the bellow of my companion the trigger for the power that bursts from us, the sword over my head erupting into a massive outward explosion of white sorcery that devours everything. I revel in it even as I accept my true destiny. Doombringer. Light One. Wild Card of Creator.

Peace engulfs me while we die in the crushing press of the violent clash of their magic and ours.

I open my eyes in the darkness of my room, canopied bed quiet and empty save for me. I've curled into a ball, fetal position tight and rigid. It is impossible to unclasp, to release the tension. I need the support, holding myself together with this clasp of arms around knees, chest compressed to hold back my panting.

It is quiet in the house, oppressive and still. As lonely as my bed. Where is everyone? My magic reaches out, encounters nothing, not another soul. But that's not right, is it? The house should be full of people. Why then is it so empty?

But no, wait. There's another here. I feel myself unwind slowly, my hands unclenching from their grips on my arms to keep me in a ball, my legs relaxing, head turning toward the doorway of my room. And a faint light there.

He's smiling at me, his sweet face so kind and gentle. I smile back at my son only to find I can't, that I'm frozen, unable to move anymore, locked in position as he crosses to me and sits on the side of the bed.

I can't even muster a meep of protest, a whimper of my need to sit up, to hold him. Why can't I move? Panic grips me while he bends close, his young face now aged, his father's face. I weep silently as my darling Gabriel presses his warm lips to my cheek.

"Mom," he says, voice ringing like a bell in my head. "Wake up."

I sat upright, the bed shaking with the force of my waking, the room dim but faint light making it through the heavy curtains pulled tight over my bedroom windows. No canopy over me, just the silly, pink chandelier my mother once thought would endear her to me, a fixture, a piece of our history I never had the heart to remove.

My body trembled, breath coming in short, hitching pants as I did my best to unravel the dreams I'd just lived through. Crisp and clear, all three of them, blending one into the other, though the last felt the most real.

Why was I dreaming of Liam again? I'd hoped that one was gone. Same with the last battle precognition. It should have been over, yes? Max and I hadn't been forced to ride to the rescue and sacrifice our lives in the end. No, Gabriel—

My son.

My throat closed over a moment, forcing me to bend in half where I sat, forehead pressing to my knees while I unclogged my windpipe and managed to breathe again.

My son. Was gone. He'd saved Max, saved me from that final battle by becoming Creator.

Or, had he? Was there something I was missing? I sat up again, looked around the room that was mine when I was a teenager and wrinkled my nose at the scent of myself. Old sheets crinkled beneath me, tainted by the faint odor of sweat. I sniffed absently at one armpit and grunted. My mouth tasted like it hadn't been visited by a toothbrush in weeks, more likely a home for something that curled up and died. My shaking hands caught at the strings of my greasy hair, pushing them away from my clammy forehead. Suddenly disgusted with myself, I tossed back the covers.

Tried to. They seemed so heavy, I seemed so heavy, arms struggling to find the strength to perform such a simple act. All powerful, immortal and practically invulnerable to everything and this physical motion was beyond me.

Three minds sighed inside me, uncoiling as I felt myself uncoil, offering support. Enough I was able to shift the covers back, swing my legs over the side of the bed. And stare at my bare feet on the floor while sobs I couldn't control took over everything.

How long had I lain here? How much time did I lose to the comfort of the gray that devoured the grief I now expelled through my gaping mouth, from my burning eyes, coughed painfully from my aching chest? Did it matter? Maybe. If the dreams meant anything.

He came to me. It felt like he was really here. And though I knew no one else remembered him—aside from a choice few—Gabriel had come to me for a reason.

We'll figure out the details later, my vampire sent, faint but there.

First things first. Shaylee sagged within me.

Right. My demon's fire crackled, though without her usual vigor. *You stink.*

I nodded as I wiped at the ribbon of drool that hung from my lower lip, buried my face in the hem of my dirty t-shirt to absorb the last of my tears. And tried to stand. Took me three attempts. When I finally managed it I stood there in the dimness for a long moment, wavering on baby deer legs, feeling ancient.

A glance at the clock by my bed told me it had been three weeks since Gabriel chose to unite the two

Universes, since I did my Doombringer thing and let my son go be Creator. The date flashed at me as though with joy at my flinching understanding, beating me with glowing letters and numbers. October, autumn well begun.

It was almost Samhain.

Nothing had changed. I could easily sink back down onto the bed and retreat yet again. Felt the gray there waiting for me while the girls held still, silent and patient. Didn't seem like they were going to fight me if I chose to go back into retreat over taking action.

And yet, everything was different. I felt awakened, if that made sense. Like Gabriel's command had reached into my very soul and refused to let me go.

Okay then. Shower, change of clothes, food. And the real world again.

Each step took great effort, though by the time I reached the door on the other side of the room I was feeling a little stronger. The hall was empty but full of light. I blinked into the daylight streaming up from the downstairs, staggering across the hallway to the bathroom door, locking myself inside.

The hot water felt good on my skin, soap doing its job. I took the time to wash my hair thoroughly, adding a nice dose of conditioner and letting it sit as I stood under the stream of mostly steam and let it pound against me.

By the time I emerged and wiped the moisture from

the mirror, I felt more alive, the heavy, debilitating weakness fading. I knew that feeling, had been here before. And over Gabriel then, too. I'd let myself fall into the gray when I'd thought him dead, kidnapped in fact by Ameline Benoit so many years ago.

The woman who looked back at me from my reflection seemed old, face lined and weary. Dark circles added depth to my eyes, my mouth pulled downward as if I'd never smile again. Maybe I wouldn't. My cheeks had grown sunken, collar bone a sharp gash across my upper chest. I sagged against the counter and tried to recognize myself.

Gave up on that in favor of brushing my teeth three times in rapid succession, ignoring the haunted, grief filled stare behind my gaze. I'd survived worse, right? We'd see.

With fresh clothes draped over my lean frame, my son's need for me to rejoin the world keeping me going, I chose life.

And went downstairs.

TWO

Abnormal, this brightness beckoning me down the staircase into the real world. Upstairs felt surreal as I left it, as though the space above held time in its grasp and didn't want to let me go. I could feel them below, their power pulsing between them, the normal flow of emotion and, as I neared the middle of the stairs, the drone of their talk became words I could almost decipher with a little attention.

That made me waver, grasp the bannister, hold it tight with my left hand as I drew a breath that felt like the first in a long time. How had I missed the staleness of the air on the second floor? As if my lurking there, lost in the gray, tainted the very soul of the house. A wash of my power, cleansing and warm, evicted the lost sense of nothing I'd left behind. Magic swept open curtains and aired out the musk in my room, that space left to its own devices behind me.

My knees wobbled slightly when their power paused, sensing mine. Was I really ready to face them, to speak as though I cared what they had to say, to hear their troubles and make them mine as I always seemed to do? My socked foot touched down on the hardwood at the bottom of the staircase, slipping slightly as I pivoted away from the hall that led to the kitchen, eyes scanning over the living room and further as I continued to turn, staring down the narrow way past the door that had been Gram's. To the backyard on the other side of the screen and glass and wood at the end.

It called me as it always did. Solitude and quiet in the stillness of my favorite retreat. But I'd had enough loneliness I decided, my heart turning me back, pushing me off from the cool wood of the railing toward the light.

I drifted, as though still partially asleep, across the beam of sunlight cast over the wood beneath me through the front door. The formal one, the one we never used unless guests who didn't know us well came to visit. I'd met Quaid at that door for the first time, his adoptive, evil parents. Welcomed coven leaders and enemies through that doorway.

Passed it by, slowing my steps as the kitchen's light drew me on. I could see her in the periphery, waiting for me, her hip pressed to the countertop, dark hair threaded with gray pulled tightly back from her face. She'd abandoned her fuzzy socks, her worn housecoats and pastel dresses when she'd become a sorceress and then a witch and coven leader again. But my grandmother's soul had never changed and it was the essence of Ethpeal Hayle that finally drew me on.

Drew me home.

She moved forward the instant I passed from the hardwood to the tile, over the threshold, as though that boundary had kept us apart. Not my retreat from her, the one who knew me best. Silent, unjudging, supportive, she embraced me and held me close, with her body and her magic, Gram's love so much I choked on it.

I gasped into her hair, clung to her with hands so thin they hurt when I curled them around her, sagging into her strength. Used up, wasted, lost. How had I let myself fall so far?

She didn't speak or offer comforting words we both knew were useless and an insult to my hurt. Instead, she simply stood there, a rock of magic and flesh, the other half of my soul because I'd carried hers for so long.

When at last I managed to straighten, to cough through my pain, to pull myself back together enough I could stand on my own two feet without her, I leaned away and met her eyes. Blue, sharp and sparking with emotion so powerful it almost drove me to hug her again and never let her go.

"Girl." Gram cleared her throat, kissed my cheek to

hide her tears, though there was never hiding between us, not really. Not since she buried her magic in me when I was just a baby and lost it there for seventeen years. No walls between. "You look like hell."

The laugh was real, the pain of it, too. But I smiled as best I could, knowing it must have looked grotesque without truth behind it. She allowed me that falseness, nodded and wiped at her tears with a brusque efficiency that was all Gram.

"Thanks." I sounded as good as I looked, sandpaper voice rasping. "I smell coffee."

Someone moved, too fast, knocking into a chair, cursing softly while her red hair bounced around her. Tippy Meeks. I'd forgotten her, forgotten the dear girls who had been my college friends, who came to Wilding Springs to save me when Sashenka Hensley abandoned our coven and her place as my second to go to her hateful sister. Though, I couldn't abide hate right now, shedding it into the gray. At least it was still good for something, if only to be a hiding place for things I just didn't have the heart to face.

Tippy hurried forward, impressive chest straining inside a knitted sweater so tight I feared her endowments would pop free at any second. Made me grunt with familiarity, accept the hot cup of java from her as she skidded to a halt next to me. She smiled—Tippy always smiled—but with hurt and worry mixed in, washing over me.

Too much. My hand slipped, the mug falling in slow motion and I made no effort to retrieve it. Instead, I half spun, ready to run back upstairs. This I couldn't handle, not yet. Maybe never again.

Did Gram know? Clearly. Her power wrapped around the mug, saved it inches from the floor even as the coven leader of the Hayle family turned to Tippy, one hand outstretched.

"Give us a few minutes, would you, dear?" She forcibly led the redhead to the door, scooted her outside, closing it firmly behind her. I looked away, unable to watch, knowing Tippy would be staring. As soon as she was gone I exhaled, sank into a chair, knees buckling beneath me.

Gram sat next to me, sliding the mug toward me as if nothing had happened. Only then did he creep forward, silver Persian body crouched low on the tabletop, head drooping as he settled next to my hand and started to purr. I didn't have the willpower to stop his magic from doing its thing. Comforting, though. Acceptable.

I would need to shield when I had the time to think about it. The family prodded me gently, one at a time then in bunches, knowing I was awake, thanks to Tippy no doubt. I did my best not to be angry with her, sending that into the gray, too. The girls sighed inside me, their walls rising enough I didn't have to protect myself after all.

Thank you, I whispered to them.

For all of us, my demon sent.

"Tell me." That was a little better, not so harsh. I actually sounded human, if not yet myself. "What's happening." I couldn't even formulate it as a question, my words dropping like lead weights into my coffee cup.

"Everything is fine." Everything about that statement hit like an insult to the trauma I'd endured. Gram didn't force cheer into her tone, bless her. She simply sat back, arms crossed over her chest, shrugged.

I looked up, scrunching my nose at her tone. Best I could muster in protest. "Quaid," I said, accusing her with names. "Femke." Looked back down into my mug. A sweet little face I missed with a sudden ache wavered in my mind. I'd almost forgotten what my own daughter looked like. "Ethie."

Sass's purr faded, one paw reaching out to settle on my wrist. Where the black ribbon rested. It didn't twitch, held still, the soul of the drach that was Max in the Dark Universe still with me. I should wonder some things about him, needed answers still about his arrival, his ability to cross over to this Universe. But questions were too much work, I realized.

Gram sighed, nodded. But it was Sass who spoke. "Quaid is still alive," he said. I didn't feel relief. Should have, shouldn't I? It was beyond me yet, I guess. "Miriam is doing her best to delay the inevitable with old law and confusion."

My grandmother snorted softly. "I've never heard of half the crap she's digging up." Admiration for her daughter. How lovely. "Better than I'd have managed. Though I'd have broken the damned fool out by now and to hell with the consequences."

"He'd never allow it," Sass said, soft and somber. "We've tried to convince him. But he seems to want to see this through."

To die, Sass meant. For whatever reason, the idiot.

"As for Femke," Sass said, "she's devolving as Konstantin's soul takes her over. Syd, I can't imagine the battle going on inside her." He shivered. "She's hanging on, though. I think once she's gone completely we'll know it."

The black ribbon stirred and for the first time I felt queasy, as if someone walked over my final resting place. Discomfort and distortion made me flinch, lower my head to the table, the cool of the surface helping a bit as cold sweat rose and beaded on my skin.

"Syd." Sass sounded like he wanted to cry, might be crying. "What happened?"

I shook my head while I remained where I was, trying to shake the feeling that something was wrong. The dream I'd just had, the one that woke me at last, flickered in panels of images through my mind while my stomach turned over once more and finally stilled.

"It doesn't matter," I whispered. "It's over, now." Wasn't it?

Gram shifted in her chair while I slowly straightened, sat back. Met her blue eyes, now steely and worried. "Syd," she said. "Who is Gabriel?"

THREE

My upset stomach protested, grumbled its refusal to answer. My mouth filled with saliva, body threatening to reject the few sips of coffee that made it down my throat. "No one." Because he wasn't. He was everyone, and nothing and everything. And I had my daughter to think about now. But I couldn't forget him, knew he would live in my heart forever.

"He's someone," Gram said. "You've been saying his name in your sleep."

She'd been watching me, then. Not really surprising. I shrugged. "Ethie?" Repeating her name stirred guilt and shame.

"Coping," Gram said. "She's struggling a bit with the babies." Her grimace told me she wasn't surprised. Nor was I, come to think of it. Ethie always had possession and jealousy issues, even with her brother. It had to be hard on her. But I couldn't help thinking in my present state of mind I'd only make things worse if I interfered.

My daughter hated me and I dumped her on a woman who I never liked to raise while her father was slated for death while my son who no one remembered became Creator thanks to my choice. I really sucked as a mom.

I drew a breath so I wouldn't cry over how pathetic I was being and spoke again, choosing to ignore what I couldn't change. Typical Syd. "Charlotte and Danilo." Yes, focus on life and death issues, not on personal matters. That was better. They were out there looking for answers. Were they still?

Gram tsked and looked away while Sass spoke. "Still hunting the Black Souls," he said.

I frowned, confused and disoriented. "They still exist?"

Gram leaned toward me. "What does that mean?" Her question came out sharp, a weapon, demanding. "Still?"

So much to get used to, so much history to relearn. Gabriel's decision to combine the Universes had left me with memories no one else shared.

"Jean Marc." Easier to press on than to answer her. And it helped, focusing. Finding things of import to bring out of my mind. To remember I used to care about such events.

"Kristophe's tip about the Black Souls should have

helped." Gram's anger came through in her voice. "But even Piers is stumped. We did, however, finally track down Olena." Ah. The former regent of the werenation, Charlotte's mother, Olena Moreau. Who betrayed her people to the Russian mafia long after they'd been freed of that slavery. She'd fled, right? Yes, I recalled that. Showed no remorse the day Charlotte confronted her, the same day my friend became werequeen because there was no one else to take the throne.

"Let me guess." It made sense where she'd go. "She ran to the Black Souls."

Gram nodded, grim, so grim. "And so did Liander Belaisle and Eva Southway."

I shook my head, the cavern in my mind, his crushed form on the floor of the cave, Dark Brother's displeasure with Belaisle's failure written in his blood. "He's dead."

Both Gram and Sass twitched, exchanging a glance. "Since when?" They asked in tandem, would have been funny if humor was an option for me.

"Since..." Ah. So he'd survived Creator's sibling and His unhappiness? How fitting. I'd lost my son and kept my nemesis.

"Girl." Gram's tone had that no nonsense feel to it I knew far too well. And was in no shape to handle, not even from her. "We have to talk about this. Something happened to you." She paused, swallowed as though it hurt to do so. "Something you're not telling us. That makes no sense to anyone but you."

"You think I've finally cracked." That was funny, oddly, made me smile in what had to look like a grimace. "That I've borrowed a page from Ethpeal Hayle's book of nutters and will eventually spiral down into fuzzy socks, tequila, chocolate and screaming naked at the neighbors at three in the morning."

She actually blushed. I didn't mean to hurt her. Did she remember those days? How clearly? Clearly enough, it seemed, it embarrassed her to recall.

I should have reached out to her, offered an apology if only in a gesture. Tried to make it right, to laugh it off. Couldn't even lift my hand.

"You've obviously been through some kind of trauma," Sass said.

Trauma. "Which one?"

Sass paused, tilted his head, whiskers drooping. "I'm sorry?"

"Which trauma are you referring to?" I waited, knowing I was hurting him, too. "There's been so many, Sass. I lose track."

Neither of them spoke then, the tension in the room rising quickly, cutting off my air and my willingness to sit there and take it. No interrogation, not today. Not until I had time to work out what the world looked like now. And figured out how to handle the fact no one knew what happened.

Well, not no one. But I wasn't willing to hunt down the few who did. Not yet.

"Ethpeal." I'd missed her approach, didn't know Payten was there until she spoke. Of course she was still here. She'd been living in Gram's old room, her and the babies, since she had them. Quaid's new wife and daughters in my house, under my nose. "Sassafras." We all turned, stared up at her. She looked much better than the last time I'd seen her, three weeks ago. Shortly after giving birth prematurely to her twin girls. And who was I kidding? She'd looked amazing even then, even in agony, ready to die for her children.

I should have died for Gabriel.

That thought jabbed me, pushed my chair back, drew me abruptly to my feet while Payten shook and spoke again. "Leave her alone."

I wasn't expecting that from the woman I'd hated for a long time, had only recently learned to respect. My grandmother looked ready to tell her where to go, the silver Persian bristling, fur standing on end. But Payten had a spine, had found hers maybe in the last little while. Held out her hand to me without taking her eyes off them. I took it, felt her tug, stepped toward her then past her as she propelled me gently into the hall. Stood guard there. Let me go.

I stopped just out of sight, heard Gram draw a breath. And Payten, voice trembling, interrupted despite her obvious fear of my grandmother.

"Your questions can wait," she said. "Whatever happened, she's not ready. Even she has a point where she needs time to figure things out. And jumping on her when she's just come back to us isn't helping. At all."

"You step over a line you shouldn't cross, missy." But Gram sounded more testy and less authentic.

"She's right." Sass's despair was soft, almost lost as I started moving, away from them and from the unexpected understanding of the woman who I'd never believed capable of such an act.

The back yard beckoned, won out at last. Seemed I needed my loneliness after all. I left them to their discussion of me, not caring what they would say. Likely they'd been saying their piece for three weeks. Another few hours wouldn't hurt. And Payten was right.

Time to figure things out.

FOUR

The bench. The chill of the October air. The morning sunlight washing, weak but present, across the dying grass. I reached for the gray place, hoping it might offer some comfort, a place to retreat for a little while, and found it gone along with the emotions I'd buried in it.

Whatever my son had done to wake me, he'd taken my ability to hide from reality. How kind of him. It was hard not to feel bitter about that, and yet I thanked him at the same time. Not like me to turn my back on what had to be done. Not the first time, sure. But I'd always come home to the truth. That I had a destiny, a particular set of evolutionary and magical skills, a fate like no other. Light One, Doombringer, Creator's Wild Card.

I like the last one best, my demon sent. *Makes me feel powerful.*

How is that? Shaylee seemed frustrated and restless, pacing inside me. The normally quiet yet emotional princess was more demon than her sister at the moment.

Those who follow fate are sheep, my demon snarled back. *Being a wild card means we have choices.*

Does it? My vampire seemed unconvinced and I was with her on that. *We seem to be on a set path despite your belief.*

I don't know about that, my demon sent. *We had a choice.*

No real choice, though. Shaylee hugged us all with her earth magic, suddenly sad. *Creator knew us well enough to know we'd do as She'd made us.*

Give up our son to save the Universe. My vampire's words surprised me.

You think of Gabriel as your son? It seemed odd to me until all three of them smacked me as one.

How dare you? My demon's mental voice vibrated, the scent of smoke powerful in my nostrils.

You did not *just say that out loud.* Shaylee's power rumbled under my feet.

We will attempt to forgive you that slip, my vampire finished for them, cold and hurt. She so rarely expressed emotion of that nature I instantly felt horrible for speaking up.

He's ours too, Syd. My demon's anger shifted to pain so sharp I hugged myself physically to hold her with both my arms and my power.

We carried him with you, Shaylee sent. *Nine months of him.*

Nine months of grief about Liam.

And we raised him, as part of you. My vampire's pain was gone, hidden perhaps. Her coldness had turned to quiet. *We miss him so much.*

I didn't cry, a miracle. I guess I was teared out. But they did, the three of them and, for the first time, I supported them instead of the other way around. Amazing, really. They'd been here for me in the thick of things, for a very long time. And I'd only ever drawn on their strength. It made me feel better, sitting there, holding them as they wept inside me, my soul healing as they grieved at last.

Depression took its toll. And yes, I was more than willing to admit I'd fallen victim to it, with good cause. Had battled it before, over Liam, over Gabriel. Likely had other moments in my life when I beat myself up for being weak when it was honest to goodness depression that had me in its grip. Allowing the girls to wallow in theirs while I was the one who offered the shoulder to cry on showed me just how far down the hole into the gray I'd allowed myself to fall.

When they finished, I relaxed my arms, sitting limp and emotionally spent but much more Sydlynn Hayle than I'd been in a long time. Awake, aware. But more. Willing and able to pay attention, to find curiosity again. To crawl out of the metaphorical—and physical—covers and face the world and the fact Gabriel wasn't in it the way I wanted him to be.

I've been acting like he's dead, I sent to them. *We all have. But he's not. And Trill was right. He's here. In every rock and blade of grass and wind's whisper. He's right here. And always will be.*

Okay, so I couldn't hold him. But I could smile into the pale October morning and send love to my son. Creator. It wasn't enough for us, for the three souls inside me. I had to know, now I was willing to find out. If he was there.

The veil welcomed me. Gone was the hurting, desperate space between planes that begged me to save it. Instead, it embraced me, hugged me tight with excitement and exuberance, felt young and new again. Did it remember? The vastness of it was impossible to communicate with. We simply didn't have the language to speak to each other. But the warmth of its joy and the way it carried me with extra care to my destination told me it at least understood part of what happened.

The cave entrance was unblocked, gaping and dark, mocking me when I stepped out into the clearing. I'd have to seal it up again. Though, as I passed through from the brightness of day and allowed the tunnel's dim to engulf me, I realized the power that had protected this place was gone. No more the deadening pressure that took away my access to elemental power. Lost the bandage seal Creator made from the exact moment in time Max divided the magicks in this precise spot and used it to seal off the Dark Universe from ours. Just a cave, then. A hole in rock that sighed with the heartbeat of our plane. The duskiness inside was now permanent, vanished the magical permalight that used to wash this giant space in a cold, white glow from above.

I lit it with my own power, though my demon's sight didn't need the help. Slowly, painfully, knowing what I'd find as I turned, I scanned the entire space, finally stopping at the spot where Gabriel—giant and towering in power and looking like his father perfected—had held Creator in one hand and Dark Brother in the other. Deciding both Universes deserved to be.

I'd hoped there might be a statue, some indicator of his presence. But no, nothing. Just an empty cave and the moist scent of dirt and damp. Unremarkable in its beauty and natural formation.

Where there should have been proof, some showing of the immense and Universe shifting events that happened here, there was nothing. That truth hit me like a blow, drove me back toward the entrance. Why did it hurt so much? Because there should have been something to commemorate what he'd done. To save us all.

The boulder made a dull boom as I slammed it shut over the entry and sealed the cave behind me.

FIVE

I couldn't go home, not with questions and tension waiting for me. Instead, my heart heavy but my choice to live again driving me onward, I picked a conflict to tackle and stepped into the veil.

While she'd given me permission to enter the palace directly, old habit let me out in a patch of snow on the edge of the lawn. The werepalace in Ukraine towered overhead, sprawling left and right, stately in the coating of white left behind by their early winter. I shivered despite not really feeling the cold at the sight of the evergreens weighted down by snow and ice, the still, calm perfection of the afternoon on the other side of the world. So peaceful here, so calm. I loved snow and the pure whiteness it blanketed over everything, as if all sins no longer existed under a soft, fluffy coating of white. Forget that shortly that white would crust over, become thick and suffocating as true winter took hold.

Another shiver. I shook off my dark thoughts, striding through the wet flakes to the driveway and across to the front door. My socks had soaked through, slipping on the marble steps. I'd forgotten to put on shoes when I'd left home, my body's lack of care for temperature failing to register the icy wet coating my feet. The wereguards who observed me seemed confused and concerned. I must have looked rather wretched to them. Frightening, even? Maybe. Whatever. They said nothing, did nothing as I passed between them and through the towering wooden front doors.

I shed the moisture in my socks at the entry with a push of magic, feet sinking into the plush, purple carpet on the other side. Soft sounds echoed back to me as those who called this place home went about their business, their voices and footsteps carried upward to the vaulting ceiling painted with gold and cherubs with vast, soft wings. The interior of the foyer always made me feel like I had stepped into history, as though a giant Fabergé egg had come to life around me. I stood for the first time ever, staring up in awe at the pure creative power that had been poured into making this place.

How had I failed in the past to see just how beautiful it was? I'd never once taken the time to admire the craftsmanship of the arching ceiling, the perfection of lines and the creative genius of its art. Yes, it was overdone, maybe tacky to some. But the utter devotion to creativity took my breath away.

I felt her approaching, descending the stairs at her stalking pace, her mind and magic shuttered from me. No change, not really. Charlotte Girard—Queen Sharlotta Moreau of the werenation—had never been an open book to me, unless she chose. It happened so rarely I was used to her silence, to her stoic nature and the way she watched me with hooded, blue eyes with her wolf behind them.

But this was different, enough so I looked down from my peaceful and joyful examination of her home to sigh out an exhale of regret. Her, too? Yes, of course Charlotte would worry. And want to fix me, fix what happened to me. Because that was her nature.

Oh, she wasn't so blatant about it, of course not. That wouldn't be my werefriend at all. But the subtle way she altered her approach, her physical carriage, told me she saw me as a frail thing that had to be handled with great care.

We knew each other well enough, I think, she saw my anger as it snapped onto my face. With her, at least, I didn't have to hide how I felt. Charlotte would never take it personally. As if I was good at it anyway. She came to a halt, an entire conversation passing between us in the time it took her to reach me, our body language sorting out exactly how each of us felt because we didn't need words.

Charlotte hugged me. And I hugged her back.

Enough said.

"Come." She turned, hand grasping mine in her firm, warm grip, her wolf not allowing me to say no. I followed, obedient. It did nothing to protest against her bossiness, I'd learned. And besides, having someone take control and tell me what to do actually helped. Removed my need to find a path in a pathless world.

I climbed the stairs, feeling weak by the top, forcing Charlotte to slow as I panted softly at the exertion. She didn't comment, though the faintest of frowns formed between her eyes. That was Charlotte worried about me all over again.

"I'm fine." I moved on, forcing myself to breathe slowly and steadily and had my wind back by the time she drew me through the door to her private quarters.

Sage rose from the desk where he poured over what looked like an old map, came to my side. My former martial arts teacher hugged me as his mate had hugged me, strong body as much a wolf's as hers. Sea green eyes showed concern hers never would. Sage America hadn't been a were long enough to perfect that solid, bluff outer coating of pride and *сан*. I hoped he never would.

"We've been worried about you." Sage was brave enough to just come out and say it. Charlotte chuffed softly in protest but he ignored her, led me to a chair and sat me down. Poured me a cup of strong coffee. I cupped the delicate porcelain and inhaled the heavenly aroma before speaking.

"I don't want to talk about it."

Neither of them seemed willing to argue. "You're here about the Black Souls." I didn't need to look up, to acknowledge he was there. I already felt Danilo Moreau lurking in the shadows. Charlotte's brother came forward, the former wereking's hulking form filled out once again. His heavy, black beard and thick brows always stirred images of a bear, not a wolf. And his temper was far more violent than any werewolf I'd ever known. But his focus was lupine, the drive burning in his dark eyes familiar.

"I am." I sipped the coffee, sighed in small pleasure at the heat sliding down my throat. I'd had so little at home, and no time to enjoy it. The delicious brew hit the spot. I took one more taste and nodded. "There are loose ends to tie up." As if Femke's problem could be called a loose end. Or Quaid's pending death. But, compared to what I'd gone through lately, it felt that way.

Charlotte sat, regal and powerful in her red silk blouse and black pencil skirt, one shapely eyebrow arching as she crossed her legs, hands resting on the arms of her plush wingback. "I've failed you," she said in a no-nonsense, won't accept comfort or denial tone of voice. "We've uncovered nothing."

"Not true," I said. "You found your mother."

Charlotte flinched ever so slightly in reaction while Danilo grunted as though I'd punched him.

"We've tried using our connection to her to trace them," Charlotte said. "And done the same with Jean Marc." She'd spent her entire childhood and early adulthood with the Dumont family. If anyone could find the oldest son of that defunct coven, it would be her. "As I said. I've failed you."

I knew better than to argue. Besides, she was right. If only she knew her failure wasn't even a blip on my radar of crushing personal guilt. Let her carry hers. Mine was heavy enough, thank you.

"Just keep looking," I said, weary with all of this suddenly. I set my cup aside, rose to my feet. Wariness passed through her magic, touched me. "What, you expected me to berate you? To find a solution, drop it in your lap?" I shook my head, looked away from her. "I'm just here to touch base, Charlotte. Nothing more."

She hesitated and I waited out of love and courtesy for her. When she finally spoke, it was directly into my mind and with so much caring, so much concern I blinked through tears at her gift.

I love you, she sent. *I'm here for you as you were for me.* I knew what she was talking about. She'd needed to unburden her story, to share it and, in doing so, maybe halved it or released it. I think it worked, was happy to take it on for her. *No judgement*, she went on. *No doubt. Just a wolf's ear and compassion.*

I swayed, fighting my lip tremble, the temptation to unload on her. And shrugged.

Thank you, I sent. *But I'll be okay.*

Disappointment but acceptance. The way of the wolf.

I left them, returning the way I'd come instead of stepping into the veil in her quarters, needing the time of retreat to gather myself. This felt like a wasted effort, like everything I did, was about to do, had no meaning. Would amount to nothing. Was that some kind of foreshadowing of the rest of my life?

The chill of late October in the North of Europe turned to warmth and amber sky filled with moons as I exited my plane and crossed to Demonicon. Fire sizzled along the edges of the veil at my entry, my demon grandmother's spirit welcoming me with subdued magic. She didn't speak, rarely did to me these days. Ahbi Sanghamitra's connection to the Node of this collection of planes seemed to be the culmination of her reign as Ruler here. She felt satisfied to me, confident and happy.

I could be so lucky to have that kind of an ending.

My sister rose from her desk, tall and imposing, red tinted skin dark in the low light of her office, polished black horns curving elegantly back from her gorgeous face. Amber eyes watched me carefully, flickering with flames, wide, full lips pursing. I don't think she realized she looked so striking and yet so cautious at the same time. Knee length black curls foamed around her in a lush, loose cloak as she nodded to me, perfect body tight and muscular under her slick, black cat suit.

"I'm here to fight," I said, realizing it was true.

Meira grinned suddenly, nodded. "Then let's fight."

SIX

It wasn't the kind of fight I expected. I'd planned, in that split second I understood I needed to let out all of my hurt in a burst of anger, to just scream at her and have her yell at me and cause a general verbal disturbance that might or might not make me feel better.

Instead, a few minutes later, I found myself standing in the amphitheater half a dozen levels below her office, in the battle training ground of the Seat used to teach and as a testing facility for demons to vent, rehearse and generally puff themselves up in prep for plane battles. It had been a long time since I stood in this place, since learning to fight was a matter of life and death. Trapped here with the tall, stunning demon before me, with our silver Persian for backup, we were forced by our Ruler grandmother to fight for the ranks she'd given us.

So long ago. And so much had changed, physical

appearances notwithstanding. Meira was no longer the small, sweet faced girl I'd tried so hard to protect. Nor was I the frustrated, innocent young woman who thought she could fight her way out of anything. I trembled as I faced off with Meira, hands shaking at my sides, though not out of fear. Out of despair at how far we'd come and who I was now.

Someone I didn't really know at all.

She'd chased off the small cluster of demons—mostly extended family—who'd tried to linger, to watch our battle, and I was just as glad. I felt her seal off the space, though the touch of the odd demon mind, well hidden, told me we weren't alone here. That the Daeva, the private assassin order with their own timeless agenda, likely observed as they always did. Let them, as long as they stayed out of this.

"Rules," my sister said, staring me down with those amber eyes, jaw tight, face grim. "No killing."

I waited for more. Felt hysterical giggles bubble. "Nice list," I said. "No wonder you're Ruler with all that wisdom and stuff."

She grinned, white teeth a stark contrast to her dark red lips. "Shut up and fight."

I'd never fought my sister before, at least not when she was in full control of herself. Sure, she'd come after me when she'd been hooked on nectar, controlled and manipulated by Sass's mom, Sekaniphestat. But that hadn't been Meira. Nor had she been Ruler then, come through her own trial by fire to own completely her role, her life.

I should have known she'd hit first, striking with the power of Demonicon behind her. And didn't pull her blow, either, forcing me to slam up a shield of white sorcery. The ball of amber fire blew apart when it hit inches from my face, sending smoke and sparks cascading around me to fizzle out on the sandy floor.

"Nice try," I growled, fury rising. I let it, drawing on it. Anger had never let me down, my constant friend and companion. Time to let it out. I hit her, as hard as she'd hit me, relishing the release of magic in a slice like a blade aimed at her ankles. Not to hurt her, just to drop her to her knees. Meira's own white sorcery countered, the two powers thudding together before dispersing in a flare of light.

"You thuck, Thyd the Thquid." Meira's magic encompassed me, squeezed with all the might of the Node, trying to crush me where I stood. A flick of my own power sent it back at her, crashing into her shields. Did she waver? Maybe. I grinned in return, embracing the thrill of expelling my rage at someone I didn't have to be afraid I'd hurt. And struck again.

And again.

And again.

Meira took everything I had to throw at her and came

back with more, the two of us pounding each other into submission. Failing utterly. By the time I wiped sweat from my brow, hair hanging limp around me from the moisture in the air, the sizzle of sparks and the stench of burned sand choking me she was equally worn out. My sister panted, hands curled into fists before her, wide spread feet embedded to her ankles in the hard packed sand. My socks were full of it, too.

The need to fight left me in a rush. But I couldn't back down, not now. Sheer stubbornness and old ego pride held me in place, facing off with the demon queen I loved more than my own life.

She laughed then, cascading curls rippling as she tossed them back. "Done?"

I shrugged. "If you are."

Another laugh. "That was fun." Amber eyes flared with fire. "Did it help?"

I nodded, rubbed my hands over my face, sighed and released my shields even as she did the same. No worry she'd try to best me now, that this was a trick. She was the only person I would ever trust to stand down at a time like this.

"Thank you." I shook my feet loose of the ground, staring with forlorn regret at my sodden, filthy socks. She waved at them, made clean and bright again. And led the way out, back to her office.

By the time we reached it, I was ready to talk.

Grateful that her husband, Rameranselot, and daughter, Zuza, kept their distance. Sinking into a leather chair overstuffed with soft cushioning, I opened my soul to my sister and told her everything.

It took a while, an hour at least, while the moons over Ostrogotho spun in their orbits and my sister filled us glasses of sweet, amber wine. Mine went mostly untouched, though she emptied the bottle as she listened and didn't speak. When I finished, admitting my retreat was an attempt to escape yet again, that I ran away just as she'd accused me last time when I left to be with the drach, she finally interrupted.

"I can hear myself saying that," she said, sitting forward with her elbows on her knees, nodding and frowning. "I can only imagine. But it's pretty easy, listening to you, hearing what you did, to get into that headspace. To be pissed at you for running. But Syd." She looked up then, eyes on fire, "I will tell you one thing you need to hear right now. And get through that thick, stubborn skull of Hayleness we both carry around." I drew a breath, held it. Waited for the inevitable hit. "Nothing about what you did the last three weeks was running away."

No, she didn't understand. I did run. I hid in the gray.

My sister sat back, staring at the fire now dim in the gigantic hearth next to us. "I can't even begin to imagine how hard it is to live with this alone." Sadness in her voice, but no pity. I couldn't have dealt with pity. "Of course I believe you, have zero doubt everything you just said happened exactly as you say." She turned back again, jaw jumping. "If I was forced to choose between the Universe and Zuze... well, the Universe wouldn't be here."

I choked on a sob, stared down into my wine.

"I'm sorry," she said. "That I don't remember him."

That did it. The dam broke and all the sorrow came out. She joined me on the chair where I sat, squishing me sideways so she could hug me and rock me. Stroked my hair and rested her cheek on the top of my head as if I were the younger sister and she the elder. She didn't try to comfort me beyond that, stayed silent while I wept, her physical touch enough.

When I was done making a mess of myself, she handed me a handkerchief and sat back, still sharing my personal space while I blew my nose and wiped my cheeks.

"It's hard not being home," she said. "Mom had me convinced you were ready to kill yourself."

She *what*? I stared in shock at my sister before swallowing hard. Had that crossed my mind? Silly Syd, of course it did.

"I knew better." Meira leaned in and kissed my cheek. "But you have to understand how different and difficult this has been for us." I hadn't considered their feelings, not really. "One minute you were fine, Sydlynn Hayle, kick ass favorite of all creation. And the next." She patted my knee. "The next Mom found you lying in the back yard looking like you'd been through hell and babbling about stuff none of us understood."

Okay, yeah. That had to have looked bad.

"You might want to talk to Mom," Meira said. "I'll come with you, if you want. But she's worried, Syd. Enough you know what that might mean."

Mom worried about any of us meant she was on the cusp of doing something I'd hate to try to fix me.

I stood at last, hugged my sister. "I'd better go."

Meira nodded, released me with her arms but not her magic. "Like it or not," she said, "you did it again, Syd. Saved the Universe, put things right. And did it so we'd all be okay even though you knew you wouldn't be." Tears rose in her eyes, tightened her voice. She cleared her throat with a soft sound then nodded brusquely, once. "I'm proud of you."

She'd gone there at last, pushed me over the edge. With a low cry of denial, just not able to accept such things, I fled. And Meira let me go.

SEVEN

I stood in the veil, letting its warmth embrace me as my sister just had, doing my best not to run. Because I wanted to run very badly. The fight with her had taken the anger out of me, left me calmer at least, without the franticness I'd felt building inside me since I'd woken up. I only now recognized it was gone, that seeing Gram and Sass, Charlotte and Sage and Danilo and, finally, Meira, had brought all of that anxiety about the future forward.

What future, exactly? Meems was right. I'd done it, saved the Universe. Done what I had to do in order to make sure they all survived another day. And now? Now?

Now what?

Femke. Quaid. The Black Souls. Ethie. All things the magical people in my life could handle on their own. Without giant, imposing, messy power like mine getting in the way. I was a weapon without a war. A soldier no longer needed after the last battle had ended.

Maybe I should rest? Find somewhere to go and take a… what? A vacation? The very idea was laughable, horribly wasteful. No, not a vacation. As I hovered there, the girls within me holding their collective breath, I knew.

It was time at last. To go. But I'd made a promise. And I wouldn't back out on that, not this time. Though he wouldn't remember I'd made it, would he? Sassafras wouldn't recall I'd sworn to take him with me when I left. Because I hadn't gone before, not to him. My time with the drach had been erased with the combining of the Universes.

I could go, now. And he'd never know.

He had Jiao now, too. His heart would heal. So why then did I find myself stepping through into my bedroom in Wilding Springs? And why was I not surprised to find the fluffy, silver Persian perched on the end of my bed, one paw raised, whiskers hanging low, waiting for me with hope in his amber eyes?

"I promised you," I said through more tears, knowing I was mumbling, rambling, talking too fast and with too much emotion. "I swore to you when I left again I'd take you with me. But you don't remember. You'll never remember." I clutched at my ribs, the aching inside. "I'm here and I'm upholding my end of the bargain. If you want to come."

Sass seemed lost a moment before he spoke. "Of

course I'm coming with you," he said. "But what about Ethie, Syd?"

My daughter. Could I leave her? Could I afford not to? I'd already messed her up so badly, abandoning her to pursue Creator's need, Fate's path. And yet not, right? She wouldn't remember either. So confusing, so painful to try to decipher what was real and what wasn't anymore.

I gave up trying, sank to the edge of the bed. Allowed him to crawl into my lap and purr, kneading my knee with his front paws and rubbing his head against my chin.

"Gram will do a better job with her now," I said, voice dull as I realized it was true. "She won't forgive me for not saving her father. When Quaid dies—" I choked. He would die if I didn't do something. "When that happens, she'll be lost to me forever." And Gram wasn't alone in the mothering department. "And she has Payten now, the twins." I bit my lower lip, hating myself. "I don't know if I can be her mom anymore, Sass. Not without Gabriel."

He looked up at me, purr gone. "Syd, you need to talk to me. Who is Gabriel?"

I shook my head. "It doesn't matter now, cat."

"It does." He stood up on his hind legs, front paws on my shoulders so we were at eye level. "We're afraid for you. And want to understand."

I opened my mouth to answer and felt the ribbon flex

at the same time. That same instant my stomach flipped over, heaved a bit. I had to clench my teeth against bile, feeling it burn the back of my throat, the world wobbling around me as if a distortion passed through the plane. Sass didn't seem to notice, though his amber eyes flickered with more concern. So the reaction had to have shown on my face.

Something was off. I didn't want to go there, to think that the things I'd done, the sacrifices I'd made might not have been enough. No. I was imagining things, I was sure of it. The distortion, the discomfort, just a byproduct of my own head. Maybe they were right to worry about me. Perhaps I was cracking down the middle after all.

"Let's sleep on it," Sass said, purring again, his magic urging me to lie down. It was only late afternoon by then, but a wave of weariness washed over me and let it take me, sighing into rest with the power of my oldest friend luring me into peace.

He falls and I follow dressed in shining armor dented and battered, helmet gone, screaming his name as the earth swallows him and a blazing sword flares to life in my hand. It's tinted red, sticky and smoking as the coating of heavy darkness burns away. And I see for the first time, I'm covered in that same stuff, drenching my legs, my arms, washing over the armor I wear in a flood of crimson. The life of a race carrying me away in a tide of red so heavy and dense it's drowning me and I don't have the strength to pull free.

Wings beat overhead. And I weep.
Their blood is on my hands.

My entire night was plagued by dreams, of falling and Liam. Of oak trees bursting from dark earth and turning to steel columns etched with images and faces too muddled for me to make out clearly. And, inevitably, my final ride on the back of a drach into light and death.

Over and over my mind spun out the same sequence, drawing me deep into the darkness. And yet, when I woke fully in the morning, sunlight penetrating the room at last between partially opened curtains, I felt refreshed, awake and aware. As if dreaming so constantly had fed something inside me.

Sassafras's warm, furred weight was missing, though only by moments from the indent of his body by my head, the faint scent of his fur, the vanishing heat from where he'd curled up on my pillow. I stroked one hand over the place where he had been and sighed into the dust motes curling their happy way through the sunbeam casting itself across the foot of my bed.

Peace hugged me, pressed me down into the mattress. Awake I might have been but the allure of remaining under the covers a little bit longer, enjoying fresh sheets and warmth from head to toe, of cuddling my pillow and pretending nothing outside this space mattered felt right. Good. Joyful, even. I had so little of those emotions lately

I luxuriated in them and found myself smiling when I finally climbed out of bed, stretching up on my toes.

And froze at the tightness of my cheeks, the way my heart felt. I shouldn't be happy. My son was gone, no one remembered him. I should be suffering still, shouldn't I?

Oh, Syd, my vampire sent with a sigh so full of frustration I giggled. *Can't you just accept the gift of this and stop being so hardheaded for once?*

Like that will ever happen, my demon snorted.

Well, I for one like the change of pace, Shaylee sent. *We've earned a little peace.*

No argument from me.

Another shower, long and delicious. Clean clothes and a fresh ponytail. The woman in the mirror didn't look quite so abandoned, broken. Thin, sure. But the dark circles were kind of gone and I didn't see endless loss in my eyes anymore.

I felt Mom as I exited the bathroom, her presence clear as she rather pointedly alerted me to her arrival. Not that she needed to. I would have sensed her regardless. Why the politeness? Whatever her reason, I descended to the first floor with some trepidation, considering the conversation I'd had with my sister yesterday. She'd warned me Mom was worried and that meant she wasn't thinking straight. Mind you, she had no idea I was planning to leave again, either.

Wasn't I? I paused in the hallway, feet stuttering to a

halt. I'd been determined to go yesterday. Was sure it was the right thing to do. But now… the ribbon on my wrist twitched, sighed. As if the Max from the other Universe was relieved I finally stopped reacting and started thinking.

The fog was gone completely now, my heart still heavy but no longer shattered. My lips ached a little from smiling, cheeks tingling from it. And my whole body felt lighter, my soul optimistic despite it all. And, not for the first time, I hugged myself and wondered where this resilience came from. Creator? Maybe. She'd designed me, hadn't She? From DNA to experiences to fate. I wasn't sure if I should be grateful for the ability to move past things that would likely be the end of others, giant, devouring things that would eat another's soul. Or if I should be furious I wasn't allowed to be normal.

My demon laughed. *I thought you'd given up on wanting that a long time ago.*

She didn't mean "normal" normal, Shaylee sent.

Maybe I did, I sent.

You're as normal as the rest of us. My vampire sounded amused. That was about as good as it was going to get.

Are you all right? The cold spirit magic of her power prodded me gently. *With being able to move past this?*

I don't know. I shivered, shrugged. *Part of me wants to feel guilty still, to wallow. Because of what I did.*

You saved all of us by making that choice, Shaylee sent.

And, if you recall, he's still here.

Everywhere. My demon sounded awed, as if she'd only just processed that truth.

Watching us. My vampire sent. *Protecting us. It could be he who soothes you, Syd. Have you thought of that?*

Tears burned the corners of my eyes, forcing me to blink over and over to keep them from spilling. I was smiling again. *You think?*

That would be like him, Shaylee sent.

Indeed. My vampire shrugged herself. *Regardless the reason, whether written into your very soul or just a byproduct of facing so much trauma, I'm grateful to be back.*

Whole again. My demon's fire flared. *Together.*

I'd take it. And sent love to my son, to Creator out there, and chose gratitude. To believe they were right, that my darling sweets was behind my recovery. And would have my back for as long as I needed him.

Feeling the most upbeat and comforted I had in a long time, I resumed my journey and stepped across the wooden threshold into the kitchen with a smile for my mother.

To find she wasn't alone. That my grandmother was absent, Tippy and Donalda and the other girls, too. Just Mom and a strange witch I'd never seen before sitting at my kitchen table, waiting for me.

Why did I suddenly feel like Meira's premonition about Mom was about to come true?

EIGHT

"Syd, sweetheart." Mom stood abruptly, smiling in return, offering her hands to me. My own smile faded rapidly, disappearing as I hugged her and kissed her cheek. "You look wonderful."

What's going on? I shot that question directly into her head but she shook it off and turned, still smiling that Council Leader smile I knew so well, gesturing to the woman sitting at the table.

"I'd like you to meet someone." Mom's voice shook, imperceptible to someone who didn't know her. But I knew her oh, so well, didn't I? She sounded like she knew what she was about to do was going to set me off but couldn't stop herself. I clenched my teeth against my need to overreact before she could actually commit the deed and nodded to the dark haired witch with quiet, green eyes who waited with a smile of her own. Middle age but hard to guess exactly how old, attractive but not overly so. Softly ordinary. "This is Theria Mills, of the Mills coven." I'd never met her, didn't know the Mills family very well. She wasn't their leader, though, I knew that much. "She's on special assignment to the Council."

How nice for her. I didn't move, holding very still, waiting for the giant, pointy toed witch shoe to drop. Instead, Mom sat again, hands folded in front of her coffee cup while Theria smiled at me.

"It's lovely to finally meet you, Syd," she said in a voice like soft marshmallow cream. Magic. She was using magic to augment her voice. Why? "I've long wished the chance to introduce myself to such an incredible young woman." I wasn't sensing any animosity, no judgment, nothing. Just the sweetness that bordered on just a bit too much but not enough I could protest.

Okay then. "Nice to meet you." I turned my back, went to the coffee maker and helped myself while Mom spoke again, voice a little too loud, too cheerful.

"We wanted to check in and see how you're doing." Mom paused when I half turned and raised one eyebrow at her.

What is she up to? My demon's musing thought held no fire, just curiosity.

She only has our best interest at heart, Shaylee sent.

Of course you'd defend Miriam. Demon's anger was back with a snap, suspicion growing.

52

Children, my vampire murmured. *Pay attention.*

"I'm fine," I said as if there weren't three alternate egos carrying on a conversation in my head.

"You look much better." Mom seemed to hesitate, glanced at Theria, as if doubting something. Who was this woman? And why did Mom bring her here? "I'm so glad to see you up and around again, sweetheart."

I shrugged, dolloping cream and sugar into my mug. And decided rather than walking out I'd give Mom the benefit of the doubt and play out her little one woman show. Just to see what she was thinking.

The chair creaked softly beneath me as I sat across from them and sipped. "Cut the crap, Mom," I said in the exact tone I knew would set her off. "What is this?"

Her jaw jumped. And then she smiled again, all controlled and stuff. Well now.

She's worried we're going to crack again, Shaylee sent. *That has to be it.*

I could have fun with this, I sent.

Syd. My vampire's chastisement rang so heavy with disappointment I almost laughed out loud.

Mom turned her head slightly, a tell. They were talking between themselves, cutting me out. So tempting to just barge in and see what they were saying. But I waited it out, almost amused by this whole farcical whatever it was.

When my mother stood abruptly I started at the

unexpected motion. She continued to smile, easing sideways toward the basement door.

"I just need to talk to your grandmother," she said in a rush before hurrying through and down the stairs. Leaving me alone with the kindly smiling Theria.

Hmmm.

"Your mother is a remarkable woman." Nice of her to notice. "And she loves you very much." Like I needed a stranger to tell me that. Funny, but her voice magic was working, lulling me a little, almost like Sass's purr. I didn't bother shaking it off, confident the girls and I were aware enough not to let it affect us while I let her go on. She sipped her coffee, set it down again with precision in exactly the same spot, radiating soft sweetness from every pore. *Trust me*, her magic whispered while she went on. "You're not a slouch yourself, Syd." A tighter smile, one that pulled at the corners of her eyes. She felt genuine enough, if practiced at it. Which made no sense when I tried to unravel that conundrum.

Oh dear, my vampire sighed. *I know what this is. And you're not going to like it.*

Well, that went without saying. Still, I didn't prod her for answers. I really, really wanted to figure this out on my own. So I could fully appreciate the rage that would take over when I told Mom off.

"We're all so grateful for everything you've done." She leaned slightly forward, one hand touching mine, just brushing me with her fingertips, before she sat back again. "All that you've sacrificed for our benefit. You're an amazing woman, Syd. Not many people would come through so much intact and balanced."

Oh no, she did not. Shaylee's confidence in Mom shattered suddenly. *Tell me she didn't.*

Another sigh from my vampire while my demon and I still waited for enlightenment.

Was this fun? Dear elements. It was. I really had something seriously wrong with me.

The instant I had that thought, my demon grunted and gasped. But I cut her off. Savored my own understanding moment. Wanted it. Needed it to feel alive. Had no qualms I was the last to know. Liked that fact, actually, while the three of them simmered and grumbled and argued among themselves.

"I never had a choice," I said. "Fate didn't give me one." Or Creator.

Theria nodded. "I understand," she said. "How does knowing you didn't make you feel?"

Flash. Insight. Awareness. Clarity.

And the terrible, brilliant joy that came with catching up to what the girls already knew. I smiled back at the witch before me, leaned in, showing teeth and a flash of power in my eyes as I prodded Theria Mills ever so gently. Not enough to be a threat, not yet. Just enough she would know it was time for her to go.

Her green eyes widened, but she held her ground, bless her heart. Didn't know me well enough yet. Nor would her little therapist heart get the chance to. Because that's exactly what she was. A witch shrink. Because my mother thought I had finally cracked my nut and lost it.

"You have five seconds," I said in my own sweet voice, "to get the hell out of my house."

"I'm here to help you." Wow, she really had no idea what I was capable of.

"How nice for you," I said. "Four seconds."

She gaped at me, her sweet magic fading, faint fear showing along with fine lines around her mouth. "You might not like it," she said, "but your wellbeing is important to all of us, Syd." She paused. "And threatening me won't change that. It only makes me concerned your mother's fears are correct."

Did she just analyze me? My smile widened. "Three seconds."

Theria stood, slowly and calmly, though I could feel the tension in her. "When you're ready to talk to someone," she said.

"It won't be you." I opened the veil to Harvard for her. Prodded her with power while my demon snarled, Shaylee rumbled and my vampire shook her head. "Two seconds."

Theria waited. Brave of her or stupid, whatever. Gained a bit of respect, I have to admit. She didn't scurry when she finally turned, didn't run. Left as if it was her idea to go. And paused one last moment to level her green eyes at me, voice still soft but full of warmth I wasn't expecting.

"Take care of yourself, Syd." And then she was gone.

I snapped the veil shut behind her the same instant I reached for my mother. And realized, yet again, she wasn't alone. Only this time it wasn't a stranger next to her.

The basement below was full of people. She'd smuggled them in while I was talking to Theria, obviously, using white and black sorcery to mask their arrival. They trooped upstairs one at a time, grim, nervous, filling the kitchen with their dark expressions and stooped shoulders, their worry washing over me like a bad smell.

Mom. Dad. Gram and Piers. Charlotte and Sage. The Zornov boys. Demetrius and Tippy Donalda. Josie and Nicci. Even Karyn Barrett, leader of the Barrett coven and someone I considered a friend. Sebastian, Sunny, Uncle Frank. No sign of Mabel, though. Or Oliver. The Order soldier was long gone, I guessed.

Finally, Payten and her twins, though she looked unhappy to be part of whatever this was.

Oh, come on, Syd, my demon snapped. *You know what this is.*

An intervention. Shaylee's offense to the word shook

the ground under the house.

Girls. My vampire rarely showed her temper, but she silenced them with a sharp word. *Patience.*

Sassafras leaped up on the table, huddling next to me, amber eyes full of tears. "We're so afraid for you," he said.

Traitor, I shot at him.

You were going to leave. He shook, whiskers drooping. *You were going to* leave.

Right, he'd missed the whole drachness six months.

"Sydlynn." Mom's voice shook, her hands, too. "You have always been there for us when we needed you. It's our turn, now." Everyone nodded, all the faces I loved, all the people who cared about me most. "We're worried about your mental state. You've been babbling about things that never happened, cracked without warning or cause we can see." She paused, shook her head, long, dark hair threaded with more white than I remembered. "And now you've told Sassafras you're going to leave us." She tossed her hands. "We need to know why. And how to help you, if we can."

I should have been angry. Fought this. Told them all off. But there was so much love in the room, so much need to fix me I sagged under the weight of their fierce protectiveness and pushed my coffee away before standing.

"Tell me something," I said, voice quiet. It was the

best I could manage. Didn't matter. The room had fallen into total, deathly silence so I doubt they missed a word. "Have I ever crumbled without cause?"

Head shakes, mutters.

"Have I ever been wrong when my instincts have guided me?"

More negatives.

"And do you think I would actually just lose my crap for no good reason?" Now my voice was rising. Couldn't help that, either. Because frustration drove my words and I needed it to finish this for me. My heart wasn't in it. "Can you please, for once, just believe me when I say something happened that you might not know about? That you can't comprehend or understand? That you're not part of?"

They stared, silent, as one.

I tossed my hands. "You have no idea what happened," I said. "And Creator wants it to stay that way. For some reason, I'm meant to carry this alone." Not alone. Time maybe to reach out to those who knew, too. I was ready for that at last. "But can you just cut me a little damned slack already?"

Gram cleared her throat. "Okay," she said.

Mom looked around, desperate, hurt they'd abandon her as, one at a time, they nodded. Piers winked, Charlotte's flat expression softened. Uncle Frank blew me a kiss while Sunny's face calmed. Even Dad seemed to relax a little. All but my stubborn, terrified mother.

"No." She stepped toward me, eyes glassy, face crumpling in grief. "I won't accept that. I can't. You mean too much to me."

"Mom." I grasped her shoulders, stared into her eyes. "I'm okay. I promise. And I'm not going anywhere." I glared down at Sass a moment before sighing. "You're stuck with me for a while yet."

She hugged me fiercely. *Don't you dare hate me for this*, she sent. *For loving you this much.*

Oh, Mom, I sent. Almost wept from the joy of it. *Don't ever do anything like this again.*

Don't tell me what to do. She pulled away, sniffed delicately. Tried a brave little smile.

I left them in the kitchen to figure out what to say to me in their own time, to talk among themselves in their slight embarrassment and relief I wasn't about to explode into a million Sydpieces.

Sass followed me, paused on the threshold of the back door, letting me go outside alone into the yard.

"Did I really make you promise not to leave me behind?" His voice quavered.

I nodded into the morning air, chuckled. "Stubborn cat."

"Well," he whispered. "I meant it." I turned to find him gone.

When I spun back, I wasn't alone anymore. Oliver

stood, grim and stiff, a few feet from me. I forgot how delicious he was, tall and broad shouldered, dark blond hair shaggy around his high cheekbones, his wide jaw and full mouth. But it was those eyes, gray and quiet, that watched me with a mix of humor and respect.

Not so much at the moment. Instead, wrinkles had formed at the corners of his gaze, stress balling his big hands into fists at his hips. Tension hummed between us and I immediately felt my stomach knot, the world spinning sideways a moment, disorientation back again.

I shook it off, gulped air past the wobbliness, to find him doing the same. And caught my breath.

"Something's wrong," he said. "And no one else will listen to me."

NINE

I don't go looking for trouble, I swear. It has a habit of finding me. You must know that by now. But I have to admit that little thrill of relief I felt at Oliver's words told me more about myself than anything else I'd accepted in my thirty years.

"I know," I said, calm washing through me as though I'd been waiting for someone else to say it first. And watched that same relief pass over his handsome face.

"Dizziness," he said while I nodded, "disorientation. The feeling that something is out of sync." My head bobbed agreement so much and so rapidly I was getting a headache. Oliver tossed his hands at his sides, a faint smile on his wide mouth. Sunlight caught the scruff of his unshaven cheeks, the gray of his eyes. We stood there in the quiet of my back yard, absorbing the fact neither of us judged the other for what we were feeling. What a novelty that was.

And, like nothing had changed, as if I hadn't sent him out of my life with harsh words and purposeful hurt, he came to me and embraced me, pulling me against the thin fabric of his plaid button up, the faint scent of fabric softener weakening my resolve not to reciprocate. I sagged against him, arms around his chest, cheek pressed to solid muscle and soft shirt while his big, generous heart beat in my ear slow and confident and present.

Da-dum.

"It took me a long time to come to you." His voice rumbled in his chest, vibrated through my body, the two of us still holding each other while he spoke, low and deep. "You'd been through so much and I didn't want to bring this to you if it was nothing." Doubt and concern, so familiar to me, colored his magic, his tone. I held onto him, clinging and listening. "But I can't deny it anymore, Syd. Something's going on. Something that's not supposed to happen." He hesitated and I looked up at last, cheek missing the warmth of him, a cool breeze rising in that moment to waft over my face. But my arms held tight, refused to let go and I didn't fight them. Not even when he tipped his chin down, looked into my eyes, so close I could feel his breath on my lips, see the sparks of light in his gaze. "You're better at this than I am," he said. "I'm new to the Universe saving game. So what's happening?"

I shrugged, not caring at the moment. Should have, right? He hit the nail square and true. This was my gig, what Creator made me for. The best way I'd found to shake off grief and hurt was to dive into trouble with both feet. But standing there holding him seemed more important at the moment.

"I don't know," I said.

"But I'm not crazy." Another smile, slow and on the edge of a smirk. His eyes held only caring.

"Well," I said, "I wouldn't go that far." My sense of humor was back. Awesome. I sighed then, finally stepped away though his arms closed reflexively for a moment as if his entire body rejected the idea of letting me go. He did though, crossed biceps bulging as he seemed to force his arms to cross over his chest. "I've been feeling it too, but…"

He nodded, didn't look away even when my eyes burned, when my throat tightened and I struggled to keep my lower lip from shaking. Oliver stood there, strong and present. Exactly what I needed.

The moment of weakness passed. "They think I'm the crazy one." I gestured at the house. Oliver glanced back over his shoulder, brow furrowed before meeting my eyes again.

"What happened?"

I told him, briefly and quietly and wasn't all that surprised when he laughed. Found myself grinning somewhat sheepishly as he slapped both thighs with his big hands and bent over to let out his amusement.

"It's not that funny," I said.

Oliver's mirth faded to chuckles then the odd snort. "I'm sorry," he said. "It really isn't. But I would have loved to see your face when you realized what she was."

My demon chuffed while Shaylee giggled and my vampire simply sighed.

Perhaps we can get to the important task at hand? Why did she sound so irritated?

Oliver arched one eyebrow at me and bowed at the waist. Wait, he heard her?

Of course he did, she sniffed at me, suddenly prim and sharp. *You two aren't taking this nearly seriously enough.*

I've had my share of serious for the last three weeks, I sent to her as softly as possible. *I think a moment of levity is in order.*

She sighed again and I felt her nod within. *Forgive me*, she sent. *But Syd, I've been feeling it, too. We all have. And now that we're awake again, I can sense this isn't something that's going to go away on its own.*

Agreed, Oliver sent directly to her, eyes never leaving mine. His own good humor remained but he added weight to his mental voice with a dose of magic that showed all of us just how worried he'd been. About what he was feeling and about me. *It feels almost like I'm living in a dream sometimes.* He shook his head, frowning. *Wavering between realities.*

I reached out with power, linking automatically to his. The veil was there, as always, happy and contented. Not a trace of its previous hurt anywhere to be found. The plane I stood on was as stable as any other, the Universe turning as it was wont to do.

"I don't feel anything." I let him go but Oliver held onto me this time, linking our magic, tying us together without asking, without apology. I could have severed the connection at any time but found myself hesitating to do so. It felt so good to have him there.

"Neither do I." He gestured at me as he spoke next. "The bond should keep us both in the loop when the disorientation happens again."

Right. Logical. Not for purely emotional reasons or because he cared about me or anything.

The back door creaked, the fat cat Persian emerging, sashaying his way toward us. I held still as Sass settled next to me, misery clear on his expressive face while his whiskers sank low, ears flat to the sides of his head. His tail curled around his body, body hunching forward, one paw settling on my foot.

"I'm sorry," he said.

I bent and scooped him into my arms, snuggling him close. "You did what you thought was best," I said. "I keep forgetting you don't have the memories I do."

He shivered in my arms. "Something's wrong." I looked down at him, waited. Did he feel it, too? But no, he glanced over at Oliver next, his words telling me otherwise. "You two are sensing something." Sass sounded like it hurt him he was left out of the loop.

Oliver nodded, one hand settling to stroke the Persian's ears and cheeks. Sass's purr emerged instantly. Habit, I suppose.

"We're just trying to figure out if the two of us are right or if we've both cracked our nut." The big soldier winked at me.

Sass's purr stilled. "You might want to talk to Jiao," he said. Was that guilt in his voice?

I didn't get a chance to call her. The instant the cat spoke the air beside me parted and the slim *lóng* stepped through. She'd grown out her short, precise bob, black hair now hanging over her shoulders, though her dark eyes were as focused and serious as ever. She glanced at Sass but didn't address him directly and when the cat half turned in my arms, his unhappiness radiating from him, I realized his relationship with Jiao was struggling.

And, from the tight, angry look on her normally expressionless face, I knew what they'd been arguing over.

"Tell me," she said, voice a growl that held the timbre of her race's magic, "I'm not the only one."

Oliver nodded instantly even as Sass exhaled in sadness.

"Syd and myself," the Order soldier said. "You're

feeling it, too." Not a question.

Jiao exhaled sharply with a tsk at the end. Her gaze flickered to the distraught cat and, before I could stop her, she liberated him from my arms, holding him up so their gazes met, black snapping anger to amber regret.

"You will learn to trust," she said, voice vibrating with hurt, "or we are through."

He nodded hastily, body transforming so fast I blinked and he was a young man, the afterimage of the silver Persian gone a moment later.

"I'm sorry," he said.

She grasped his face in her hands and kissed him, so intimately, so powerfully I found myself blushing. Worse when I looked away and caught Oliver looking at me with a grin on his face.

Jiao released Sass who tucked himself against her instantly, arm around her waist, hers around him. Like they'd locked together now their argument was through. I envied them that closeness while Oliver broke the uncomfortable quiet.

"So," he said, "not to ask the obvious. But why us?"

I knew before the words were out of his mouth, before he was done speaking. Turned to Jiao to ask her, though I didn't need to do so to know the truth. "Gabriel," I said, voice low, controlled.

She nodded, glanced at Oliver who nodded back. "I remember."

TEN

I almost hugged her. I would have if Sass hadn't been right there. Still debated wrapping my arms around both of them as my vampire spoke up.

There is one other we must consult then, she sent. To all of us, clearly, as the rest of the gathering nodded to me. *Surely he will have information for us. His experience and wisdom is necessary, I'm thinking, to solve this mystery.*

I hadn't seen Max in weeks, knew he'd stepped down as leader of the drach when the dust settled, left Mabel to run the show. I'd lost track of him after that, though the flash of worry on Jiao's face before it settled into her more natural poise concerned me I'd failed to have the back of a dear friend again.

I did that sometimes. And usually came to regret it.

"He may not be able to help," she said. Rather delicately, for Jiao. Just made my anxiety crank up. And stirred my anger.

"We'll see about that." No way was Max abdicating responsibly now. Not after all the stuff we'd come through, lived through. Yes, he'd lost his wings to Dark Brother. But he had them back now, didn't he? Or did he? I couldn't remember if the combining of the Universes reversed that terrible act or not.

It must have. Because the Max I rode in my dream had wings. That thought made me pause and gasp. I know my face must have drained of color because Oliver reached for me, hand holding my elbow as I exhaled and shook my head at him.

"I'm okay," I said. Even while I accepted my death was still to come.

I didn't wait for them to respond, to question my assurance, but made a way to the Stronghold and stepped through the veil gap with a huge load on my mind. The instant I touched down, the massive intelligence on the other side settled against me.

Light One, the Stronghold sent, his mental voice grinding stone turned to powder. *Welcome back.* He genuinely sounded happy to see me. I always found it odd to talk to a building, though he had a bigger heart and soul than some people I knew. But his thought process was different, overwhelming if I let myself look too closely. *You are well?*

His question choked me up and I felt his confusion at

what he obviously thought was a common greeting.

Yes, thanks, I sent, trying for cheery and hitting brave. *So happy to hear your voice.* He'd been gone for a while, the heart of Creator's statue's theft taking his soul with it. I still wondered why he'd remained though the heart and statue both were long gone. But I wasn't going to look that gift dragon down its throat. Probably find fire at the bottom and I'd been burned more than enough lately.

And yours. His mind settled into bedrocky happiness. *You've come to see the drach?*

Max, I sent even as Mabel appeared in the large foyer of the Stronghold's main entry, the shimmering mirror that was the more pedestrian form of travel to and from shimmering with her reflection as she crossed to us in her slow, stately pace. Her long, thick hair hung to her feet, the dark braid swinging over the gray robe she wore, diamond eyes glittering in welcome.

The Stronghold fell silent though I felt him listening as the lady of the drach bent to kiss my cheek.

"Your presence has been greatly missed," she said.

More tears. I really had to find a spell or something to cut off the waterworks. At this rate I'd spend eternity crying my eyes out.

Oh wait. Right. I was going to die soon. Okay then.

"Hi, Mabel," I said, then cut off the usual preamble. "Where's Max?" She was used to me being to the point, at least. The sad twist of her lips told me I wasn't going to like her answer.

"I thought you'd come to see him eventually," she said, diamond eyes glistening with moisture of her own. "I'm afraid, however, you've come too late."

She might as well have punched me in the stomach. "Too late?" For what? "I need to talk to him, Mabel. It's important."

The drach leader hesitated then shrugged. "Of course you can try," she said, the sadness in her making me stumble as I followed her when she turned and walked away. "But I fear he won't hear you."

Oh, he'd hear me. Damn right he would.

I wasn't expecting her to lead me where she did, and found myself falling numb with worry when we descended to the familiar space I hoped I'd never have to visit again. Oliver's hand slid over mine, big fingers squeezing kindly, keeping me locked into the present though the past tried over and over to devour me. I touched down at the bottom of the stairs into the underchamber, where the column of stone that was the soul of the Stronghold soared overhead. And stumbled to a halt, staring in shock at the statue sitting on the throne at its base.

Gabriel! Had he replaced Creator on that throne, made a statue of his own? His name was on my lips, screamed in my head before I realized the stone figure wasn't my son. Not even close. My hand freed itself from Oliver as I ran and wept, falling at the feet of the giant, bald figure in the gray robe now a frozen replica of my drach friend.

Even his diamond eyes were grayed over, his form rigid, unmoving. And, as I tried to see past my tears, to catch a glimpse of the drach he used to be, his dragon form appeared, faint, distant.

Wingless.

Sobs wrenched themselves from my shaking body, my heart pounding so fast I could barely breathe as I stared up from where my knees had buckled and carried me to the floor. Up into the still, silent face of one I'd never thought would give up on me.

"Max," I whispered, all I could manage out loud. *MAX!* My mind did a better job. But neither attempt stirred a response. I spun on Mabel, wiping the hot tears on my cheeks, anger awakening again, surging, saving me from my wretched grief. "What's happening to him?"

My ancestress bowed her head, tears on her own gray skin. "He has chosen at last to depart this existence," she said. But there was no acceptance in her tone, just flat sorrow. When she looked up again there was hurt so deep in her diamond eyes I couldn't comprehend what his leaving was doing to her. Millennia of friendship and trust turning to stone before her eyes. "This is how our race dies of natural causes. Once his soul has completed its transformation, he will emerge in the ribbon form you're familiar with." She gestured at my wrist and only then did

I notice how tightly the black strip of drach soul hugged my arm, how it shivered and wept its own sorrow. Mabel's voice was dull, the song of her people gone as she finished. "When he rises, his soul will depart for its final home."

I gaped at her, struggling to comprehend what she was telling me. "He's killing himself."

She hesitated as if wanting to protest my crude description but shrugged at last, looked away. "It's his choice."

Yeah, I didn't agree with it, either.

"Without his wings," she said, voice cracking at last, "he felt it was his time to go."

I should have felt bad. Should have hugged him and whispered to what was left of Max I understood, I got it. That this was my fault and it was okay, he could let go.

Should have, maybe. Didn't. Oh, *hell* no.

Fury burst out of me, hit his statue in the chest, firing sparks of white and green, amber and red, blue and black. They cascaded down, pooling in his lap, making the pale, gray stone glow a moment. Wisps of smoke rose from him while I pounded him with all the rage I had in my heart, teeth clenched, letting loose my emotions at last.

"You do *NOT* get to leave me." I hit him again, the stone rocking slightly on the throne, color flickering through the casing. A shell yet, thick and heavy, but he was in there still. I felt the trickle of who he'd been remaining inside. "You don't get to run, Max. We don't get to choose how we die." Another blow, but I couldn't crack the stone shell, couldn't break through the crust. "How can you abandon me now?" Not fair, you say? To hell with that. "I need you, damn it, Max." Weakness returned, the rage in me draining away as my blows failed, as the force I needed to bring him back to me waned, paled, died. "Something's wrong," I finally whispered, shoulders sagging forward, heart broken. "I need you."

The sudden silence in the space hurt more than the fact he'd quit on me in the end. Just when I needed him most.

I turned to Mabel at last. "Gabriel," I said, knowing what she'd answer with.

Confusion. "Who?"

I had my answer. And, in an instant, a breath of him once more as the voice I loved so well whispered in the air: *Gateway.*

But that was the last of him, the final breath of who he had been. I spun back, reached out. And found him gone. Gone.

Goodbye, Max.

ELEVEN

No one moved, said anything, not for a long time. Though I held out a tiny breath of hope since no ribbon appeared and the former drach leader's soul didn't rise as I'd seen others do when we returned the pieces of Creator. For all I knew, though, these things would happen differently now. And no amount of searching and calling out could reach him.

Mabel's sorrow softened, eased as she bowed to him and then to me. "Whatever you need of the drach," she said, "we are here to assist. I am, personally."

I shook my head at her, dashing at cooling tears, chest tight and painful as I turned from her. I'd already decided the price I'd asked others to pay was far too great. "I've taken one leader from the drach," I said, choking on the words. "I won't take another."

She didn't protest. So she felt the same way. Didn't

make me feel any better.

I looked up and into dark eyes that hovered on the edge of grief of her own, something I'd never seen in Jiao. I'd forgotten she'd been Max's apprentice, bound to him with magic. How must she be feeling? A surge of protectiveness took me, aimed at her, and I shrugged. "Jiao will do."

Her eyes flickered with emotion, her power with gratitude for the distraction as she arched an eyebrow at me. "Thanks a lot."

"What do you want to do now?" Oliver sounded like he had his own ideas, but I wasn't in the right headspace—or place—to make any kind of decision about the future. Not with my dead—or still dying—friend perched on the throne that Creator once used, or with the living staring at me like I should know what I was doing.

"I need a minute." Without explanation, I parted the veil and left them there, breathing my overwhelm of emotion into the rubber membrane as I dove into it and hovered there on the literal edge of the Universe. Nice of me? Not really. But I couldn't deal with people right now, and it wasn't like they didn't have their own means of transport. Abandoning them was more metaphorical than physical. I just needed a damned second to pull my crap together without other voices in my head.

Thanks a lot, my demon snorted.

Okay then. Max was gone. I hadn't planned on that. The steady, powerful and always caring presence wasn't mine to access anymore. The ribbon on my wrist flexed and I stroked it once, as an apology. But even he knew it just wasn't the same, that the Max from the other Universe wasn't the soul I longed for.

I drifted in the quiet, felt myself being pulled out of the veil and, trusting my instincts, parted the way. Found myself standing once again in the cavern in Wilding Springs, in the cool, damp mustiness that had once held so much power.

Was this my new go to place? Somewhere to hide from my troubles, more private than the back yard, a melancholy space now devoid of the things that had made it special? I shook myself physically, jaw clenching. I did this, clung to stuff, to people that were no longer who or what they had been to me. Tried to return to what I knew, to comfort myself with what was already long gone.

No more.

Things had changed. Gabriel was gone. Max was gone. Life as I knew it had shifted into new normal. And I just had to get used to it. And move the hell on.

That meant taking action. A sliver of hope perked inside me and I offered a wry smile to the cavern's dull air.

"Sweets," I said into the stillness. "I figure Creator

being my son and all, I should have an inside track on what to do next, right?" I waited, not really expecting a conversation but hoping for something, at least. A sign, a whisper. "You know I hate rules and games and all that crap. So, if you can, just give me something."

Nothing, only the dark and the chill damp. And yet, he was trying to reach me, wasn't he? What was the dream that woke me about if not? The discomfort and distortion? I clung to that as I breathed in and out in steady rhythm, until I believed it.

"I'm here," I said. "I'm listening. You got through, Gabriel. I'm ready to act when you need me."

Again nothing, except... wait. Was that a faint sigh? The tiniest of embraces hugging my power, warming me? Imagination played tricks, I got that. But I took it as a sign anyway. Because I needed to just then.

"He can't help you." Her voice was soft enough it didn't jar me, her entry into the cavern a whisper of her own. I turned and managed a smile for Trill despite everything.

"I know," I said. "I just thought I'd give it a go anyway." My head tilted on its own accord at the frown on her face, the way she seemed uncomfortable with being here, though she didn't leave. "You can, though?" A guess. Why else was she here?

Trill's hands rubbed briskly at her upper arms before she tossed them, irritation plain on her face. "We're not done," she said, gruff and a little angry. "But you know that already."

I nodded. Accepted. Felt calm descend and welcomed it as the girls settled inside me, content. This was what we were made for, after all. And it was time I understood the only moments of peace I felt were when I had some action to take, some giant disaster to correct. That any other sense of calm was a lie, a construct of me trying to pretend I was like everyone else.

"Okay then," I said. Smiled again.

Trill wept, hung her head. I could have offered comfort, but instead she shared her own. "He's doing great," she whispered. "I'm so proud of him, and you should be, too." Her dark eyes met mine, hands rising to rub at her tears with her jacket sleeves, the denim darkening from the moisture. So much guilt in her. I recognized it easily, had my own to carry. "He has such a huge job to do, Syd. To balance what he did."

I drew that in, absorbed it. "So the Fates were right." Both had protested the moment of his choice, when Gabriel combined the two Universes instead of picking one and one alone. "What are the consequences?"

Because there would be consequences. And maybe I was experiencing some of them with the discomfort of my own.

Trill shrugged. She drew herself up, jaw a firm line, eyes heavy lidded and still. "He had no choice," she said.

"He did the only thing he could. Bought us time." She hesitated. I'd always known she had far more information about what was going on than I did, and I used to be furious with her for keeping it to herself. But, oddly, standing there in the quiet cave, in the dark and stillness, I just felt sorry for her. Calm and at peace and full of patience that wasn't my norm. Waiting for her to go on without judgment, without pushing. Finally, utterly trusting Creator. And accepting who I was.

Trill seemed to sense the shift in me, relaxed slightly, nodded. "Syd." She paused at my name, exhaled. "It's time to find those who remember but for their own reasons." Trill swayed slightly and then, with a shake of her head, vanished.

Leaving me alone to ponder, though with a chill of nerves. I knew who she meant, or at least thought I did. Only one race had disappeared seemingly of their own accord during the collapse of the Universe. One race whose lack of action frustrated me to no end from the moment we met, their ultimate flight and abandonment of us when we needed them always stirring my anger and disdain.

And, in that instant, it happened again. Dizziness overcame me, pushed me down to my knees, a pattern of disorientation knocking my breath out of my chest, stirring bile in my stomach. It was over in less than five seconds, but seemed to me to last forever.

When it was done, I gasped into the dull air and pulled myself to my feet.

The veil parted before me with precision, the Stronghold underchamber appearing instantly on the other side. Mabel and the others turned, Oliver and Jiao both appearing a little green around the edges. They'd gone through it, too. I stepped over, absently sealing the way behind me as I frowned up at the new leader of the drach.

I had a focus, someone to blame. Because I had no doubt in my mind the second race's disappearance had everything to do with what was wrong in the Universe.

"Where," I said, "are the maji?"

TWELVE

I should have known better than to ask her. Mabel looked at me with a mix of confusion and concern.

"Who?"

There was that dazed and worried expression I'd come to expect from those I cared about. Lovely to see it on my ancestress, too. Seriously.

"Never mind," I sighed. "Just trust me on this. There is a second race, one that came after Max split the magicks."

More stunned wonder. Right.

"Okay, let's start from the beginning. Time you had a bit of an education in what the hell really happened." In as short and succinct a time and with as much patience as I could muster, I told Mabel and Sassafras—Jiao and Oliver nodding along and murmuring their agreement— everything that happened from the moment the

Brotherhood attacked the coven to the point when Gabriel combined the Universes. Despite my attempt to be brief, it wasn't long before we found ourselves in the massive cafeteria upstairs, drinking coffee and eating through the conversation while the two listened with more care and attention than I'd ever hoped for.

By the time I finished, the sun was setting outside the Stronghold, the drach quietly going about their evening business while I fell into silence, throat parched and body drained from telling the convoluted and hurtful tale. Oliver's hand had found mine again and I squeezed when I realized it, welcoming the warmth of his skin and the silent support it offered.

Mabel exhaled softly, sat back, Sassafras frowning into his glass. But it was a deep and resonating voice that broke the stillness fallen over us.

I feel your truth. The Stronghold's mental touch swept over us. *While I do not remember such events, I trust and believe in you, Light One. What momentous shifts in power, and what a burden to carry alone.*

Didn't cry. Barely.

"And so it is Trillia Zornov's belief these maji are to blame for what is happening right now?" Mabel's voice held no doubt, only her query.

"I think so." I shrugged away my own hazy worries I was off the mark. What other explanation could there be? "She gave me that impression. Or, at least, that they might know what we don't about what's going on."

"So, how do we find a race missing entirely from the collective knowledge of almost every soul in the Universe?" The drach leader didn't sound discouraged. More eagerly curious.

Good question. "I have no idea," I said. "But they have to be somewhere. Trill is alive, right? So the maji blood remains." I bit my lower lip. "There are some people I need to see. To check if they still exist or not." That sounded so weird, but bless them, my friends didn't make me feel like I'd stepped into crazy or anything by saying it. I stood, still holding Oliver's hand and he rose with me, Sass and Jiao joining us. The grim unhappiness in Mabel's magic told me she hated being left out but I shook my head to her, held up my free hand in farewell.

"We'll keep you posted," I said. "For now, protect the Universe, as you always have. And if there's any change with Max…" Choke.

She let us go, me leading us into the veil and out again. Underground, in a sandy, golden cavern deep beneath the shifting dunes of Egypt. Only to have the veil reject my choice, show me instead a wall of amber earth, the cavern that held the elder council no longer in existence.

No, had never existed. This was really going to take a lot of getting used to.

Instead, I shifted our goal, landed us on a staircase at

the peak of a tall mountain, the towering spires of a castle overhead as the cold wind whipped past us. Nepal was never my favorite place, nor this winding, narrow stairway to the home of the Empress of vampires. It always stirred my old vertigo despite my invulnerability and enough power to protect me from falling. I shivered despite myself, ascended the metal steps to the arching entry.

I usually deposited myself right into Moa's bedchamber. But somehow it felt wrong this time. She didn't know me the way I knew her. Everything had changed, hadn't it? Instead, I took the diplomatic route, though using the word diplomatic to describe how I pushed my way past her guards and the other vampires turned Order of a sort was stretching things just a bit.

Snort.

They knew to get out of my way at least, not a single one of them challenging me, bowing their heads, stunning faces still ageless and beautiful, long hair and elaborate clothing remaining. Oliver frowned, a faint smile that had no humor in it pulling at the corners of his mouth as he observed them.

My people, he sent, *would never dress like that.*

Maybe once, I sent back with a prod of mirth. *I'm sure the Empress could spare you a doublet and tights if you're interested.*

No answer outside a flare of horror.

Double snort.

She sat on her throne where I was so used to seeing

her, though in her massive main room and not in her private bedchamber. Moa felt the same to me, less Order and more vampire and, as the essence that made her absorbed her presence, I understood why.

She never joined them, my vampire sent. *She's still a vampire.*

How was that possible? I didn't have time to find out. And did it really matter?

"I assume," she spoke in her young woman's voice, so odd as usual from the wrinkled, mummified mouth of the tiny, withered creature she was, "there's a reason for your visit, Sydlynn Hayle."

Coldness, bitterness, fear. So, we had a far different relationship now, did we?

Moa, my vampire sent. *We must speak plainly.*

She seemed surprised, twitching physically when the essence spoke to her. The tiny black beads of her eyes flared with white power a moment, not sorcery but spirit magic called up in answer to her startled response.

Mother, she sent, suddenly humble. *You've never spoken to me before.*

Sadness woke in me, compassion though I knew the Empress didn't want or deserve it. It was my vampire's soul that woke those emotions in me.

We seek those who wish ill to this Universe, she sent to Moa. *The maji.*

The Empress seemed as confused as Mabel, though

87

she hid it better. "I know not of these maji," she said out loud while her people stared.

Hardly a shocker. "And the drachmor?" The *lóng*, as she knew them. Jiao twitched beside me.

"What of them?" Moa's anger was back, her reclusive bitterness. "You ask questions that make no sense, Sydlynn Hayle. The rumors of your madness must be true."

My demon snarled, Shaylee huffing in anger, but it was my vampire who spoke through my lips, her dry voice cutting away Moa's attempt to shame me.

"Hear me, child," she said as the ancient vampire, the first of her race, flinched. "Such disdain is beneath you. The Universe is in danger and remains so for as long as those in power refuse to acknowledge they must work together to save it."

"The Universe." Moa's snappish tone only made her sound younger despite her ancient appearance. Petulant, even. "What care has it for me? For my people, abandoned and cast off for choosing our own path and not that of the Order?" Is that what happened? "Locked away here, on this barren mountain by *his* kind." She jabbed a sharpened nail at Oliver who didn't even twitch at the accusation. "And the drachmor." She spit into the air. "Cowards who vanish when their alliances no longer serve them."

Vanished, hmmm? To where?

Moa had no more answers, only simmering frustration. And, despite my vampire's attempts to speak to her further, we were shut out, cut off, the old Empress turning herself physically from me, waving us away.

After another few futile minutes trying to make her speak, I tossed my hands and left, the others trailing after me.

This makes no sense, I sent to Oliver and Jiao, to Sass. *Where are the drachmor?*

I don't know, Oliver sent, sounding worried now. *Honestly, I haven't encountered any of them in weeks.*

Nor have I, come to think of it. Jiao's own concern surfaced. *They left the Stronghold. I've been so absorbed in how I've been feeling I failed to realize they seem to have gone.* She paused, her power pushing outward and I felt her despair the moment it encountered nothing. I knew because she let me piggyback, let us all feel her desperate search turn to nothing. *Where did they go?*

I didn't know, not for certain. But I had a very bad feeling they weren't alone. And that the others I sought might have had something to do with their disappearance.

What the hell were the maji up to?

THIRTEEN

I paused at the exit, mind still struggling to process all the changes in the world—the Universe—around me, when movement from the shadows near the doors caught my attention. Sass hissed like the cat he'd been, putting himself instantly between me and the lurking vampire who cackled at him for his attempt at protection. I kindly moved him aside, not only because I didn't need anyone to look after me but also out of the sudden need I felt to face this particular past head on.

"Batsheva Moromond." I kept my tone light but hollow, not wanting her to read anything into the greeting as the former queen of the Wilhelm Blood Clan slunk closer. She, like the other vampires in the castle, dressed in an elaborate gown, hers crushed crimson velvet with heavy lace at her wrists and plunging neckline. But, unlike the rest, she seemed disheveled, coiled blonde hair frizzy with escaped pieces, eyes wild around the edges.

She's mad, my vampire sent without regret.

Nothing new there, Shaylee sniffed.

And yet, there was something shifted in my old enemy. The last time I'd seen her she'd been as cracked as she was now, but still mostly in control of herself. From the shaking of this incarnation of Batsheva's pale hands, the way she smiled in a dazed and absent way while she giggled and curtsied to Oliver before sticking her tongue out at me, she'd fallen all the way down the rabbit hole at last.

"Let's go." Sass's discomfort wasn't misplaced, but I felt a morbid curiosity as Batsheva flicked her fingers in his direction, palsy trembling them at the tips.

"Run off then, pussy cat," she said in a singsong voice. "Clean your whiskers and sip some cream." She laughed, wide lips gaping to show her white teeth.

I really should have just put her out of her misery. There were so many reasons why she needed to die. But I stood there, hesitant, sad. Not my usual reaction to Batsheva, not after she tried so many times to hurt me, kill me, ruin my mother and my family. Seeing her like this reminded me just how much things had changed, how many roads I'd travelled and, oddly, how much I'd lost.

Oliver seemed confused but didn't reject her when she drifted closer, one hand sliding over his chest. She winked as though that act had to be appealing, tongue running over her lips while she staggered slightly. The Order soldier caught her, supported her with care and concern while Sass snorted his disgust.

"Let her fall," my friend snapped. "She's not worth the effort."

Batsheva snarled back at Sassafras, shifting from coquettish to hate filled in a flicker of an instant. "You know nothing, wretched boy," she said. Her eyes met mine, evil unmasked there, naked and roiling with the need to hurt. "And I know everything." She leaned closer and I was unable to retreat, caught in her gaze and the sorrow still holding me in place. She was no threat to me, not really. Not physically. But my soul shriveled a little as she went on. "Everything. You know what I find truly the most amazing thing, Sydlynn?" Bright, painful, with clarity she'd regained as the darkness inside her took control. "The most perfect and beautiful truth of all the things you've bungled through over the years?" She leaned closer, almost nose to nose with me. "You've failed in the end." She smiled, sweet and fresh, youth in her gaze, in her delight. "Your best, my dear, wasn't enough. And the blood of the maji will be on your hands." Another cackle escaped her, turning to a full blown attack of laughter. I held still, heart pounding, while she doubled over, unable to breathe—she didn't need to, though, did she?—as the fit took her over.

She's wrong, my vampire whispered.

Of course she is, my demon sent, flare of fire and whiff of smoke her response.

Just kill her already, Shaylee sent in a bored tone.

Wait. "You remember the maji." Not a question. How was it this creature remembered?

Batsheva's laughter cut off like a switch being thrown. She staggered into me, talons of her right hand slicing through the thin fabric of my t-shirt and leaving bloody tracks behind. I winced from the cuts on my bicep but waved Sass off when he tried to stop her. Oliver and Jiao glared, but held their distance, too, while I pinned the old witch turned vampire with my power at last and shook her.

"Tell me," I said, "what you know of what's to come."

"Or else what?" She spit in my direction but I was ready for her, blocked the wad and sent it to the ground in a sizzle of flame. My vampire reacted without my participation, her power grasping Batsheva's firmly. Her eyes bulged as the spirit magic within her contracted at the touch.

"Or else," I said. "I'll kill you slowly. Instead of giving you a quick ending."

She laughed again, this time with bitterness and bile. "I've suffered long enough at your hand," she said. "Trapped in this body in the darkness of your basement.

Or did you forget that torture?"

She was right and guilt rose for the first time. Yes, she'd been the source of a lot of pain and grief for me. But I wasn't any better, was I?

Enough, my demon sent, though not unkindly. *It's time to end her at last.*

I didn't get the chance. Sass's second hiss drew my attention. I looked up, realized only then we were surrounded and that Moa was watching. She and her vampires had created a circle of power around us, the ancient Empress observing with more than a little curiosity and guile.

"It's time for you to go," she said.

"Not without Batsheva." I was already planning to take her by force if necessary, the hardening of Moa's features at my demand enough to inform me we'd not be leaving without a fight. Until my vampire sighed.

There will be another time, she sent while my demon growled and Shaylee sniped a few choice curse words. *We have things to do and a battle with Moa over this isn't on the agenda.*

Always next time, my demon grumbled. *How many times has that come back to bite us in the ass?*

Enough we should just have done with it, Shaylee sent.

For the first time, though, I disagreed with them. There was nothing Batsheva Moromond could to do hurt me, not anymore. The madness returned, the evil within her devouring her clearly, visibly. I shook my head and backed off, shrugging as I cut a hole in the veil.

"I'll be in touch," I said before leaving like I wasn't just bullied into going.

The veil embraced us as I selected our next destination.

You can't just leave her there. Sass's anger matched my demon's. *Syd.*

I spun on him in the dimness of the veil and let out a bit of my anger. *Can you give it a rest?* He had no idea how tired I'd become of being told what to do. By Fate, by Creator, by life. He wasn't helping any. *I'm not an idiot, Sass. If she was a threat, I'd take care of it.*

He pointed at my arm. I looked down as he spoke, the blood congealing in thin lines at my elbow. I'd forgotten she'd hurt me, the pain gone, wounds already healing. *She's a loose end. And a loose cannon.*

Then you go kill her, I snapped before tearing at the veil again. It whispered to me and I apologized, remembering my time as a drach, that the membrane between worlds felt pain when I opened the way. Its instant forgiveness only made me feel worse. *I have work to do.*

Sass fell silent while we stepped out into the chapel at Sanctuary. I was already calling out for Zoe Helios as we did, and she appeared instantly with her Fate sister beside her. So odd to see Mia Dumont alive and well. And whole. More than whole, in complete and utter control of herself. The Mia I knew had been first an angst riddled teenager who went by the name Pain. Then, later, when we discovered who she really was, her emotional state deteriorated into her own madness, ending in her death at the stake.

I wasn't expecting to find her here, the Mia I'd met in the other Universe. But, then again, where else would she be? It made sense now the two were combined that the Fates would be together, much as Bellanca and Thanos had been. So much information to balance and confirm or deny. I took a stab at things and greeted them both by name.

At least they didn't react badly. In fact, Zoe smiled and hugged me, kissing my cheek.

"Syd," she said. "I'm so happy to see you."

Mia's smile was as kind, if more guarded. "You're looking well," she said and left it hanging. Both seemed aware I'd been out of sorts, but how much did they know?

"How's Piers?" I wasn't quite ready to dump the heavy duty stuff on them just yet. Best to feel them out first.

Zoe seemed confused. "Southway? The Sorcerers League leader?"

I knew in that instant how much had changed between them and felt tears rise, my chest tight. Her genuine lack of emotion toward him came through loud and clear. Whatever happened in this timeline, my two friends had never fallen in love and that broke my heart almost as much as losing Gabriel.

I swallowed past the lump in my throat while Oliver spoke up, smoothing out the silence as though knowing I couldn't do it myself.

"We're after information," he said. "About a race known as the maji."

The Fates exchanged frowns, head shakes, before Mia spoke.

"We've no knowledge of such a people," she said. "Something we should worry about?"

I managed to snort, shake off my grief. "You have no idea," I whispered. "You really don't, do you?"

This makes no sense, Oliver sent. *They should remember, shouldn't they?*

And yet, they are oblivious, Jiao sent.

No comment on that, Sass sent. *So, why you three—and Max, apparently—in the loop, but no one else?*

There's one other, I sent as I nodded sadly to the Fates. "Have you seen Trill?"

Zoe shook her head, answered for them this time. "Not in some days," she said. "Is there a reason the young Zornov witch should be on our radar?"

Both she and Mia seemed disturbed, shaken a little. Made sense, I guess. I was asking them questions they, Fate, couldn't answer. Had to be uncomfortable for the two people in the Universe who were supposed to know everything.

Hang on. "Witch?" Right. No maji. So, her second race blood wouldn't exist. And yet, I was sure it did. Honestly, if I had to think about this any further, dig any deeper, my head was going to explode.

"Sorry to trouble you." I opened the veil again, could tell the Fates were about to stop us. I blocked them, pushing my companions through the gap with power, forcing a smile at the two women who relented at last. "See you later."

Syd. Oliver's mental voice held laughter. *Did you really just tell the two Fates of the Universe you'd see them later?*

How common, Sass sent.

Fine, you two deal with them next time. I huffed as I led us home to Wilding Springs. *I've got a lot on my mind.*

Now what? Sass stepped out onto the grass, though not at the house. I had one last stop to make, one last assurance everything in my perception had changed. Gone was the beat up trailer from the driveway, though I could feel her presence in the house.

I left them on the walkway at the street and went to the door of the small bungalow, knocking softly, shaking inside, clenching my hands against my thighs as it opened and a sweet, wrinkled face appeared, smiling in welcome.

"Nona," I said. Choked on her name as the truth hit me.

"Syd, dear," she said, not a trace of maji in her, elemental witch magic all she held. "The boys aren't here. Can I offer you tea?"

FOURTEEN

I made a quick retreat from Nona, unable to handle the change in her. Yes, I knew intellectually the maji had somehow erased themselves from existence. Logically, I understood what happened when my son combined the two Universes together. And yet, it made no sense to me where the maji had gone, or how it was they removed awareness of their creation from the mass consciousness.

That is, with a few exceptions. Sass slipped one arm around my shoulders as I rejoined him on the sidewalk, Jiao tucked in on my other side, Oliver trailing us with a forlorn expression I caught out of the corner of my eye when I glanced back, as though he felt left out of our circle of knowing. Not sure why it was important, I paused and held out one hand, pulling him in with us. And, despite the tightness of the space, we almost huddled together on the walk home, layered in pairs down the narrow path.

"Where," I found myself whispering a moment before my house came into sight around the corner, "have they gone?" No need to give voice to who I spoke of. All three of my companions nodded as I went on, more questions falling from my numbed lips at the implications of what I wondered. "How did they go? The Universes combined, Gabriel saw to that." I shivered, hugged myself even as Sass's hand hooked around my bicep, Oliver's arm now draped over my shoulder. "Where does an entire race hide from Creator?"

The massiveness of the question made my heart skip a beat before restarting with a painful thud.

"And," Jiao said in her cool, blunt way, "if the drachmor are also truly gone, did they join the maji? If so, why is it everyone remembers them and not the second race?" She shook her head, black hair shining in the daylight. She looked out of place in the midmorning sun, like a porcelain doll who would be damaged by too much illumination. "So, does that mean they are elsewhere?"

"But where?" I stopped on the sidewalk, hands sliding into my pockets. "Surely there aren't two impossible places to find in the Universe now?"

"Who knows what kind of damage was done when the two became one." Oliver winced a bit but shrugged at my lower lip bite of anxiety.

That was a possibility, unfortunately. "The Fates

weren't very happy with Gabriel's choice," I said, hating to admit my son could do anything wrong. He was Creator, for the element's sake. And my kid. Gone from me or not, I was still Proud Momma. Still. "They seemed afraid of his decision to combine the two Universes instead of choosing one."

"Which means," Oliver said in his deep, caring voice, refusing to let me back away from facing all possible truths, "there's a chance this is less a direct act of the maji than a glitch in the system."

But Sass was shaking his head, dark hair hanging over his bronzed skin, brown eyes flashing amber a moment. "You told us they were gone before the Universes combined," he said. "Remember?"

He was right. Breath of relief my son hadn't screwed up about as badly as his mother managed on a daily basis.

Oliver smiled then, shrugged. "I'm happy to be proven wrong," he said. "However, that leaves us back where we started."

"Where are they," Jiao said, "and how did they do it?"

"Bellanca and Thanos had to have something to do with it." I had little doubt of that. The two fallen Fates weren't happy with their new circumstances, though the former Light Fate seemed the most damaged by the new order of things and her return to ordinary maji status.

"Possibly," Oliver said. "The new Fates know nothing?"

I shook my head. "They're not deceiving us," I said, bouncing on the toes of my sneakers a little as stress drove me to move. "Whatever the reason, we won't find it here in the middle of the street. Let's go inside and talk this out."

The general consensus agreement, I led them up the driveway to the kitchen door and into the warm interior of the familiar house that always made me feel at home.

I sat back in my chair and listened to them debate, offering occasional grunts and nods to their discussion but now lost in my own thoughts as I sipped my rapidly cooling coffee. Bless Tippy for keeping my mug full, but she seemed out of place and uncomfortable with our conversation and quickly left when I waved her off. It had to be hard to try to decipher something that sounded like nonsense. I could only imagine, putting myself briefly in her place.

How much simpler life would have been if I could just step away from what happened, forget and forgive, move on and live instead of fighting so hard to figure out how to save the Universe yet again. At least, I assumed it would come to that. I had the premonition of my dream as warning enough something huge was still pending.

As if you'd ever want to be on the sidelines. My demon snorted softly.

For once, Shaylee murmured, *it might be nice.*

Liar, my demon sent.

Shaylee surprised me by laughing. *Yes*, she sent.

I don't know where this fatalistic attitude comes from, my vampire sent, ignoring them and focusing on me.

The dream is pretty specific. I shivered slightly, remembering the weight of the sword in my hand, the burning smoke in my lungs. *So real.*

And yet, like all precog, my vampire sent, *is up to interpretation and manipulation if you know what you're going into.*

That's the problem though, isn't it? I sighed and rubbed my face with one hand, aware the other three at the table now turned to me with expectant faces, like I'd come up with some amazing solution to answer the issue at hand. Instead, I pointed at my temple with my index finger and rolled my eyes. They all smiled, Oliver winking, and went back to their talk while I went on. *We have no idea what's coming, not really. Outside of me riding a now as close to dead as he's ever been drach into a fight where I die myself in a flash of light.*

Worrying about that will get us nowhere, my vampire sent. *Perhaps you need a fresh perspective, someone who will listen and offer alternatives without judgment.* She flashed me a familiar face, one I used to dream about in other ways. I flushed at the memory of the times I'd considered Sebastian DeWinter as a possible partner, and the one circumstance long ago when I'd seen him dressed in tatters and little else.

My demon chuckled. *She's right, though*, she sent. *He's Order now, or our version of it. And he's always been willing to listen to you.* She snorted. *Why, I have no idea.*

Actually, I sent, standing up so abruptly Oliver leaped to his feet with his hands forming a ball of power between them before he grinned with sheepish apology and let the white sorcery die. *That's an excellent idea.* "We're going to the mansion," I said.

I really was lucky to have these amazing people in my life. Not one of them questioned my reasoning as I opened the veil and stepped out into the vast foyer of the former vampire stronghold.

As luck would have it, Sebastian and Sunny stood only a few feet away, talking in hushed voices with the tall, red haired Shonya Opal. Oliver saluted his commander mother who nodded back, tilting her head to one side, wrinkles forming around her eyes as she frowned a little at our small group of travelers.

"Sydlynn." Sebastian came to my side, embraced me with the warmth I was accustomed to, lips pressing to my cheek before he leaned away, blue eyes as deep and engulfing as ever. I felt my skin heat at the contact but refused to pull away. There was something delicious about the former Blood Clan turned Order leader I had always adored and I wasn't about to let myself let go of that now. Especially considering he'd been gone much of the last year or so, vanished into the void with the rest of the vampires. While that might not have happened in the new blended Universe timeline, it was real enough to me.

"Sebastian." I finally released him, hugging Sunny who laughed softly in my ear, throaty and full of understanding. So, he had this effect on her, too? Despite her love and dedication to my darling Uncle Frank? Nice to know at last this was Sebastian's superpower. "Sunny."

"Darling Syd," she said, full lips smiling, pale blue eyes full of happiness. "I've missed you lately." *You look well.* She wasn't prodding, that was never Sunny's way. But she had worried, that much was obvious. I flinched inwardly that I'd let her suffer and squeezed her hand. I'd missed her, too, though she had no idea why.

I'm okay, I sent before turning to Commander Opal. "Shonya," I said with a nod, not waiting for her to acknowledge me before returning my attention to Sebastian. "I need to go downstairs."

He frowned around his smile, even more yumtastic than ever. "My basement is your basement…?"

I frowned myself before offering an internal kick to my own behind. "Crap," I said. "It might not be here."

Sebastian exchanged a look with Sunny, though neither seemed particularly worried I was muttering to myself. Maybe the fact Oliver, Sass and Jiao weren't treating me like I'd cracked my cauldron helped.

"You're looking for something specific?" Sebastian gently took my elbow but I shrugged him off.

"You could say that. Just follow me." I strode across the foyer, now worried I'd wasted yet another trip. The red carpeted hallway I entered was the same, the wooden doors lining the stone corridor familiar. Light filtered in through the tall, narrow stained glass windows, dappling everything in unearthly illumination, making me a bit dizzy. By the time we reached the door to the library I was feeling like I'd walked out of the real world and into some kind of surreal version of my life.

Okay, so that wasn't really new. Just accentuated times a million.

They followed me into the large room, the air heavy with the scent of old books. It reminded me instantly of the Gate archive, which stirred images of Liam and then, naturally, Gabriel. I pinched at the inside of my arm hard enough to hurt, blinking at the tears that seemed to well at the least provocation.

The back wall loomed, stones interlocking in a seemingly flawless pattern. I bit my lower lip as I tried to remember the combination, then took the plunge and hit the first one.

What do you know? The grinding sound greeted me instantly, floor panel retreating, exposing the stone steps leading down under the mansion. I grinned like an idiot, feeling utterly and completely vindicated, relieved. Yes, I knew I wasn't crazy. I had three other people willing to back that up. But physical proof, hard, substantive evidence? Crushed the last bits of worry I carried I'd truly lost my mind and this was all some fabrication of delusion.

Still could be, you know, my demon sent.

Don't be cruel, Shaylee snipped at her.

Girls, my vampire sighed. *Honestly.*

"Sydlynn." Sebastian sounded completely flustered. I turned to him and shrugged as he stared first at the hole in the floor then at me.

"I know," I said. "There was a time you would have remembered this place. And now that I'm here, I'm kind of shocked it's still around. But there should be answers below, if you want to come."

He nodded without question and followed as I led the way into the dark.

FIFTEEN

The underground was exactly as I remembered it. Talk about a walk down memory lane. Ghosts lingered with me, though only those of my own making. Of finding my grandmother down here with Pender Tremere, summoning Alison's echo and trapping her in the living world again. Liam with me next, finding the upper chamber to the maji depository below. I ran one hand over the stone wall as I felt the way open for me, crossing into the round room of stone carved with the history of the Universe. Was it different now? Likely though I'd never had time to study it. Liam meant to, but time was never on our side.

The podium in the middle remained, calling to me and my hand. I pressed my fingers down into the stone where carved depressions waited, feeling the warmth of magic tingle from me into the rock. Maji power. I'd given it up when I'd joined the drach, but regardless my blood still ran with their lineage and the pedestal recognized me as one of them.

So, they did exist once, as I remembered them. Confidence returned, confidence I hadn't known I'd lost or had shaken so badly until just that instant. I almost bounced to the second set of descending stairs, skipping with light feet down the circular steps and into the pale, white light of the maji chamber below.

I didn't take the time to observe Sebastian's gaping or to register Sunny's gasp of surprise. I was just too excited to have this proof in my grasp. The instant my feet touched down I summoned her, feeling for Ameline Benoit in the quiet and stillness, the pulse of maji magic light and almost dissipated but present. Here. Real.

"It feels different." Sass rubbed at his upper arms, frowning into the permalight that illuminated the carvings in the rock. My gaze skimmed over my family tree as I turned slowly in a circle. The center slab remained empty, the air quieting further while we stood and listened as one, barely breathing.

"It does," I said, reaching further into the power of the maji for Ameline, worry returning when she didn't appear. I could feel them here, if barely. Had they somehow found a way to hide themselves here and in the other maji chambers around the globe? But if so, why and how? But no, that wasn't the answer. They weren't here per se. Still, their magic was linked here.

And if there was a link, I could follow it. I did, diving after the thin thread left behind, the chamber itself seeming to assist me, as though starved for what it had lost. Within moments I felt her flutter against me and drew her to me, Ameline appearing at last before me with a stricken look of fear on her face.

Syd. Her lips moved but no sound emerged, just the mouthed version of my name.

I pumped power into her, felt her flicker further, solidify. Her hands grasped for me, gripped mine an instant before sliding through my skin with a shudder like her echo had passed over me. Frustration twisted her beautiful face.

I felt him next to me before he spoke, his deep voice full of wonder.

"Don't you feel it?" Oliver's big hand passed through Ameline. She glared at him before sighing visibly and tossing her hand in the air, still unable to communicate vocally. "She's not here. But she is."

I nodded, reached for her with a concentrated boost of maji power. Ameline gasped, this time audibly, though when she spoke again there was nothing.

"This is a gateway." Oliver turned from her, white sorcery bleeding from his hands, leaking toward Ameline and being sucked into her, through her, past her, disappearing while she shook her head at him. He stopped even as I tried to follow the departure of his power with my mind.

And ran smack into a rubbery bubble of nothing.

"A gateway." Gabriel? Had my son done this? But Ameline was mouthing with exaggeration, her red lips forming two syllables that I easily deciphered.

Maji.

"She's not here," Oliver said. "She's no longer in this Universe."

That couldn't be right. And yet, there it was again when I pushed up against the magic within her. That squishy, bubble feeling. Like the rubber membrane of the veil only thinner, softer, without its own life. A construct.

A construct…? "I know what they did," I said, dread in my stomach as I tried to work out the details and stumble over explaining at the same time. Ameline's desperate expression watched me while I went on, tumbling words over each other in my haste to speak and make sense of this. "This is like the realm, isn't it? The Sidhe realm?" She nodded quickly, excited suddenly, wringing her hands at me. *More*, she mouthed. Yes, more. "A pocket of a plane carved from the veil," I said. "Outside this plane but connected to it."

She shook her head this time, held up one hand. I could see through her, feel the thread and took it to the last step.

"They detached it, didn't they?" That was the only

thing that made sense. "From everything. From the Universe itself. They made themselves their own little Universe."

Ameline's relief practically poured over me as she flickered in and out before solidifying briefly again. My mind boggled, chest aching from holding my breath at the utter insanity of what they'd done.

"I don't understand." Nor would Sebastian. Or any of them. I barely understood, and I was a child of the Universe.

"When the Sidhe made their realm," I said, my voice falling to almost deadpan as I continued to think things through while talking, "they used this plane as an anchor point and bubbled out their own little space still attached but walled off. You understand?" He nodded, they all did. "The maji," I waved off their confusion, "just listen. The maji are the second race of the Universe, created after Max split the magicks." Another wave to silence them. I just didn't have time to go over the whole story right now. "Trust me this is the truth, okay?" More nods, though tentative. "So, Max splits sorcery into the elemental powers and shifts everything. A second Universe was created to protect that instant in time from destroying us all." Not quite accurate but it would have to do. "Creator's sibling, Dark Brother, took over on the other side where only sorcery existed." I jabbed a finger at Shonya then at Oliver. "Your Universe. Meanwhile,

Creator split Herself into a bunch of pieces and scattered them through our Universe to protect us from ever combining the two. Only, that's exactly what happened not so long ago." I ignored their clear need to ask questions, grateful Oliver, Sass and Jiao were there as buffers to such incredulousness. "So, my son, who you don't remember, was the Gateway." I wasn't even going to try to explain that one. "He found and replaced all of Creator's pieces which triggered a choice." Skimming much? They had a lot of catching up to do and there was so much more to the story, but I had a nutshell's amount of time to fill them in and I was still working out the final bits and pieces. This bought me time to do it. "Gabriel became Creator, was told to choose between the Universes." I shrugged. "He didn't. Instead, he combined the two. But," I focused on Ameline, "before that final choice was made, the maji vanished from Core and Center. I can only assume they knew what was coming and were hiding from it?"

She nodded though she seemed to think there was more to it. Okay then.

"They created a bubble like the Sidhe did, only this time, instead of anchoring it to a plane they severed the connection and set themselves adrift. Correct?" Firm nod that time. "And then, I can only assume, they found a way to take themselves out of the Universe entirely." There was the piece I still hadn't worked out, though it made sense despite making zero sense, honestly.

"By removing themselves," Sass said, slow and considering, "they literally removed themselves."

"That's why no one remembers them," Oliver said, nodding himself. "Outside of us."

"I don't understand," Sebastian said in the quiet that followed, but held off my protest with one raised hand and a smile. "But I have always, always trusted you, witch girl." He hadn't called me that in years. "And I'm not about to stop now. So, all things being equal, is there a threat involved with these maji being absent from our Universe?"

That was an excellent question. I turned on Ameline who nodded so fast her dark hair whipped around her face.

"They are detached," I said, "and outside the Universe. Where, in the void?" That might make sense. The nowhere the Universe fell into might work to insulate them and their little realm from the rest of us.

Creator, Ameline mouthed.

And then it made sense, clicked together like puzzle pieces mounted on magnets. "They did what Creator did when She split the Universes." That had to be bad. The deep, roiling feeling in the pit of my stomach told me as much. "They started the mess all over again."

She seemed to relax at last, sagging, head falling forward. When Ameline looked up again, there were shining tears on her face but she clasped her hands under her chin and smiled at me like the sun rising in the East.

The whole point of losing Gabriel was to save us from having to go through this again. And the damned stubborn, asshat, greedy, hardheaded, idiotic maji had just dragged us all back into the fire.

"Ameline." I drew a breath, fighting panic. "Dark Brother?"

She shook her head. So we didn't have Him to worry about. That helped a little. But she was anxious all over again, pushing the touch of the thread at me. I grasped it, felt it and remembered the doorway Trill left me to cross into the other Universe, to retrieve the heart. It had been subtly done, almost perfect, really. Had held back the Order for as long as we needed. This doorway, this gate as Oliver aptly named it, had none of that finesse. If anything, as I stood there with my former enemy staring into my eyes with her fear written all over her face, the gateway the maji created felt like a child's finger poke through a thin piece of paper compared to the powerful door I'd used.

"This is bad, isn't it?" Of course it was. I didn't need Ameline to tell me. "Gabriel knows?" She shrugged, seemed at a loss. He had to know. Why wasn't he fixing it? "What happens now?" The worst part was her uncertainty. She had no idea. But it was pretty clear from her continuing concern I needed to figure this out sooner rather than later.

"We have to get over there." Sassafras nudged past Oliver, stood next to me. "Get them to cross back and destroy the new Universe."

Ameline seemed to think that wouldn't work. She stepped to one side, hand out. As if to say good luck.

"How do you plan to do so?" Oliver clearly didn't mean to sound teasing, though his tone remained light. "Without the Gateway," without Gabriel, "we have no way of crossing." He met my eyes, question in his. "Do we?"

I shrugged, shook my head as I realized he was right. "Maybe me," I said. "Maybe. But I gave up my maji status, remember? I'm more drach now. Enough their power recognizes me, sure." I poked at the thread and felt it rebound my power again. "Not enough to let me through without a fight."

"And a fight might make things worse." Sass nodded, backed down. "Now what?"

There was one other person I could turn to. But the likelihood of her actually talking to me was slim to none. If Trill Zornov knew about this and left me to find out on my own, I'd kick her butt.

No amount of calling for her did any good. And, at last, I had to let Ameline go. She held up one hand, waving to me as she disappeared while the rest of us stood and stared at the place where she'd been.

Sebastian again broke the silence, voice quiet and without the normal rich lilt that made him sound so seductive even in normal conversation. "I will have my people monitor this place," he said. "Day and night until a solution is found."

I thanked him absently, fear driving me inward to my spinning mind and the girls arguing on their own over what to do next. Oliver's hand on my elbow was a welcome distraction and guide as he turned me toward the exit.

Syd. Mom's voice reached me, weary and clearly upset. I perked instantly, relief at the distraction making me over eager.

Mom, what's wrong? I reached for the veil even as she sighed in my head, sorrow pouring over me while she let it out.

I'm so sorry, she sent. *I've tried everything. But the last of my stalling has failed.*

What was she talking about…? I paused before crossing to her, chest tight though I couldn't put my finger on why. I could see her on the other side, watched her struggle with her emotions as she met my eyes through the veil.

Quaid, she sent. *He burns at dawn.* And burst into tears.

SIXTEEN

I stumbled through the veil and into Mom's office, into her arms. She wept on my shoulder while my friends piled in after me. Maybe I should have been crying, too, but I just couldn't past the numbness. Being lost in the gray place seemed to have given me a buffer against Quaid's predicament, I suppose.

From the worry and sorrow on Sass's face, he knew exactly what was going on. "Miriam," he said, taking Mom from me, hugging her. "You did everything you could."

I mouthed *Quaid* to Oliver and Jiao and both nodded.

"There has to be more," she said, desperation in her voice as she turned to me while still holding onto Sass like a lifeline. I knew the feeling. He'd been that for so many Hayle witches. Just because he was in humanoid form again didn't mean he stopped being our rock, clearly.

"But I've already pushed so hard, Syd. From here on in, if I keep going, I put the whole North American Witches Council at risk." She hiccupped softly, sagged. "I can't do it. I'm sorry, I just can't."

"No one wants you to," I said as firmly as possible, feeling anger bubble up inside me. "Quaid still won't offer any help in his own defense?"

Mom wiped at her nose delicately with a tissue retrieved from inside her sleeve. How could she look so beautiful after crying like that? I might have inherited a lot from her, but weeping and staying pretty wasn't on the list. "He refuses to let me help him aside from what I've been doing." She'd run out of old laws to throw into Femke's path, obviously. Mom's shoulders tensed as she squared her jaw. "I'm prepared to resign as council leader," she said. "And push on."

"Oh, hell *no*, you're not," I said. Ground my teeth together in frustration. I did not have time for this. For Quaid and his martyr attitude. He might have killed Tallah Hensley but, damn him, there were people who needed him. Were Femke in her right mind and not under the control of the soul of Konstantin, I was sure she would have commuted his sentence by now or found a way to quietly shunt him off to serve out his time with his family. But, thanks to her possession, this issue remained front and center and, if I had to guess from Mom's stress, was being used as some kind of leverage against her in the world witch stage.

Well, you know what? I was sick and bloody tired of the whole damned thing. Of Quaid, of Femke, of witches and councils and feeling stuck in one place. Like it or not, this problem I could handle with a little brute force even if Quaid hated me for the rest of his miserable life.

"I'll be right back." My words may or may not have emerged in a growl. Sass tried to follow me, but I blocked him, keeping Oliver at bay, too. *Let me handle my ex*, I shot at the Order soldier. He backed down instantly, smirking at me as I crossed from Mom's office to the prison in Ireland.

I'd broken out a prisoner before from this place of white hallways and normal security tied to magic. Danilo Moreau had been happy to come when he realized he was needed, that some kind of redemption was in order. My ex-husband, on the other hand, simply glared at me over his crossed arms as the door to his cell blew inward in a controlled explosion of magic.

"Get up." I smacked him in the chest with more power, hearing him grunt, watching his face darken at the blow, ignoring the irritating flashing lights and wailing siren that warned his captors I was there without an invitation. "Now."

"Leave me alone." Petulance, how delightful. It didn't suit his dark handsomeness. Made me think of him as the teenager he'd been, the one who couldn't commit to me.

Maybe a little lesson in commitment was a good thing.

"Quaid," I snarled, jerking him to his feet as my demon's power latched onto him and pulled him upright from the narrow bench he sat on. "I have had it with the entire Universe let alone your little attempt at nobility." He stumbled as my magic pulled him toward me, a blast from the line of Enforcers who appeared in the hallway behind me impacting the shielding I'd raised. It was a nice try. But I came prepared and the drach in me, while dormant, still lingered.

I spun and roared at them, fire erupting from my throat, smoke filling the corridor and sending them back, choking and yelling at each other to stand firm. Like it mattered what they did. My hands settled around Quaid's shoulders as he opened his own mouth to yell at me, too late.

The veil parted and I pushed him through, backward. He staggered away, through into the cool quiet of the room on the other side while I strode after him and turned, purposely sealing the veil in the face of the Enforcers who tried to follow.

"That was stupid." Quaid's words sounded loud in the sudden silence of the upstairs bedroom. Our old bedroom. I didn't know why I brought us here. Habit? Maybe. He battered against me with magic, trying to escape. "They're going to come after me. You've put the entire coven at risk. Miriam. The council." Desperate worry crossed his handsome face. "I have to go back."

"And die. For no good reason." My demon snorted while I rolled my eyes at him.

"I murdered Tallah Hensley, Syd." He said it like I wasn't there when it happened, that I'd missed this detail somehow.

Power fluttered against the barriers around Wilding Springs. *Syd*, Gram sent, tight but controlled, not panicked, just firm and prepared. Of course she was. *You want me to seal off our territory, girl?*

That would be lovely, I sent. *And warn Mom, could you? This will be over soon.*

She cackled in my head. *Tell me I get to kick Femke's ass.*

Just call Mom, I sent and cut her off. Quaid opened his mouth, more protesting prepared, probably. I held up one index finger for silence and reached for Charlotte.

Here, she sent instantly. *Did you just do what I think you did?*

News travels fast, I sent.

I've been waiting for this. Her wolf sounded amused. *About damned time.*

Quaid tried to push past me, blue flames flickering at his feet. I doused them and snarled. *Sit and stay.* Scowling, he backed down, but he didn't look happy. Good for him.

I'm done with all of this, Charlotte, I sent. *I want the Black Souls. Now.*

So do I, she sent back. *If you'd like to find them for us, that would be lovely. Because all of our searching has turned up nothing.* Now her irritation showed through. *And if I find out you can locate them and sent me out here on a wild goose chase for the last several weeks when you could have saved me the effort I'm going to be very, very disappointed in you.*

I laughed out loud. Couldn't help myself. *Love you*, I sent.

Hrumph, she answered. *Seriously. I'm not kidding, Syd.*

Any idea where Konstantin's bones are buried? I could get Gram to try the necromancy thing, with me as backup. She had far more experience with it than I did.

Gone, Charlotte sent while Gram slammed down the family defenses just as I felt something impact the edge of the territory. Femke was here, clearly. I really had to go give my grandmother a hand. *You're thinking of raising his echo?*

That was a thought, I sent.

Do you need him? She paused, her wolf panting softly. *He's inside Femke.*

True. But that was part of his soul. And the whole problem. If it was a simple echo possession this would have been over ages ago. But a soul possession was something else entirely.

Or was it?

That's it then, I said, jabbing a finger at Quaid and jerking it forward, telling him silently to follow me to the door as I stomped my way out and into the hall, down the stairs and to the kitchen. *We need access to Femke.*

You mean, Charlotte sent at her most dry, *you want to kidnap the leader of the World Paranormal Council.*

Hell yeah.

Gram waited in the kitchen. I wasn't surprised to find Mom with her, Oliver, Sass and Jiao also in attendance.

"You all know Captain Crankypants," I said, jerking my thumb at Quaid.

He opened his mouth to say something, likely to tell me off or be an idiot all over again. But he didn't get a chance. Not when Payten burst into the room, sobbing, hugging him with so much need I had to turn my back on their reunion.

Was worth it. Had to be. He was hers now. They'd keep each other safe and loved. And he'd stop fighting this. Because she needed him, his twins needed him.

When I turned around again, composed, and met his eyes, I read the anger there and the acceptance. He'd stay.

The family wards vibrated under an attack. Gram sipped a cup of coffee and winked at me over the rim of the cup. "Those new wards sure are strong," she said in a cheery tone.

I grinned back at her.

"So," I said, "who wants to commit treason?"

"I think we already have." Even Mom seemed more relaxed. Was it the house, the familiar family environment? Or just the relief Quaid was safe? Didn't matter. I often had the feeling when we all worked as one nothing could stand in our way. And today was no different. Arrogant, maybe. But we were Hayles. And not even the destruction of the Universe could keep us down.

"We could depose Femke." Gram set her mug aside, eyebrows arched at Mom. "Is there a law you could dig up to make that happen?"

Mom shook her head, sinking into a chair. Payten's sobbing slowed, Quaid easing her into a chair next to him, holding her hand and murmuring to her. I ignored them, feeding more power into the new lattice of shielding I'd helped Gram create before the Universe had even collapsed while Femke did her best to break inside.

And had a moment of gratitude I'd done so in this new combined Universe. Cold sweat time. I could have left the family open to some serious trouble. I really had to get a handle on what was real and what wasn't.

"She's done nothing to warrant it," Mom said, not knowing I was now shaking internally from the aftershock of understanding. "She's been careful to keep her actions within the law." She sighed, waved her hand over her shoulder at outside the house in general. "Even now."

"We could talk to my superiors," Oliver said. "I'm sure my mother could come up with some kind of charge to at least take her into custody temporarily."

"The Order's reach is more Universal than local,

Oliver," Mom said, sounding tired now. "Still, it might be worth a try."

"I'd rather we came across as the criminals in this," I said. "Me specifically. Femke isn't responsible for her actions right now and once we've found a way to fix her I want to be sure she doesn't suffer for what Konstantin did to her." Despite it all, she was still my friend. Loyalty was everything.

"You could give me back." Quaid barely had those stupid words out of his mouth when Payten smacked him. Hard.

"No," she snapped. Looked to me. "Syd risked everything to save you, you big jerk. We're all just a little bit tired of the whole poor me act, too." Wow. Talk about a shocker. I had no idea Payten had a backbone. "Now, you get your sorry ass into the nursery and say hello to your baby daughters before I kick you where it hurts." And then, as if that outburst was the most she had in her, she burst into more tears.

Quaid stood, face now sunken in wonder and sorrow. "Our daughters?" So no one had told him? Seriously. Had he not noticed the fact her stomach was no longer the size of a small mountain? He met my eyes, hesitated, mouth open.

"Just go," I said. Smiled to make it okay.

And, with his arm around his wife, he did. Not ashamed to admit it hurt to watch him leave.

Saved by the punishing blow of Enforcer magic on the shields. I grinned at Oliver and nodded. "Do it."

"Might I suggest," he said softly but with humor in his voice, "you stay out of it this time?" His gaze took on a distant look for a moment and I knew he was talking to Shonya before he refocused and grinned. "Let the Order handle it."

Fine. Whatever. I have no idea what he said to his mother in such a short time, but it seemed like it was only an instant later the bombardment of our territory suddenly and completely ended. With a satisfied look on his face, Oliver bowed to Mom, then to Gram.

"Well," my grandmother said, a bit breathless. "You're useful."

Oliver laughed.

Syd. Dear elements, what now? Zoe's intensity didn't allow me an instant to enjoy this seeming victory. *You must come. Now.*

On my way. "You lot have this in hand?" I backed away, feeling for Zoe's location, surprised to find she wasn't in Sanctuary. Latched onto her and opened the veil, half through it while Mom waved me on.

"Go," she smiled. "And thank you." I had to trust they had things well in hand as I crossed from my plane—the sunny, happy kitchen I loved and would always call home—to one of the least happy places I could think of.

Center was as quiet and abandoned feeling as I remembered, though as I appeared at the entry to Fate's grotto, I realized I wasn't alone with Fate. That Zoe had brought me here for a reason. She turned, a stricken look on her young face, kneeling over a fallen form in a white robe.

"Syd," she said through her tears. "Help her. For I cannot."

I hurried forward, stumbling to a halt as I realized who lay at her side.

Iepa. Pale as death. I reached for her with power even as Zoe disappeared, leaving me to fight to keep the fallen maji alive.

SEVENTEEN

My former maji guide didn't respond when I reached for her with magic, unconscious and fading quickly. That couldn't be right. She was second race, powerful beyond measure, a bottomless well of rainbow magic. And yet, she lay prone and near empty, the barest whisper of her essence all the remained to her.

I poured power into her, gasped for breath as a wash of weariness took me. She felt like the void, the dark space outside the veil, her very soul a shard of that dark place that had almost devoured me several times. Again I fed her strength, white sorcery this time, only to have it disappear into a bottomless hole deep inside her.

There was nothing I could do to help her. At least, not alone. Desperation drove me home, taking her still form with me, the kitchen at Wilding Springs suddenly too bright, too cheerful as I staggered out of the gap in the veil and dumped Iepa on the tile floor at my feet.

"Help," I gasped. "She's dying."

Gram acted first, pouring power into the silent second race woman while I lashed out into the coven for two minds linked by blood and magic. The Kennecotts reacted instantly, though their brief flare of reluctance made me angry enough I jerked free of them with a tsk of irritation.

My grandmother's blue eyes met mine as she guided Iepa's magically suspended body out of the kitchen toward the hall into the main house. *Gently*, she sent.

No time for gentle. The door slammed open, Phon and Lula rushing in, their pale complexions flushed pink. Due to embarrassment at their initial delay or the exertion of their run I had no idea. And didn't care.

Iepa, the maji who guided me, who did her best to protect me despite my lack of confidence in her, the only person in that misbegotten race who had ever really shown me a scrap of kindness… was *dying*.

Steady, my vampire sent as I stood in the doorway of Gram's old bedroom, Payten and the babies now nowhere to be seen. *What's wrong with her?*

I can't tell, Shaylee sent as I clutched at my t-shirt with one hand, the other clenched into a fist at my side. *But her power is nearly depleted.*

Sucked dry, my demon sent. *By whom?*

No, what. I shuddered, sent the image of the void to

Lula and Phon. Both looked up, startled, confused. I let them feel the weakness in me, the draw of the darkness. They finally nodded, faces grim. *Somehow she's been linked to the void.*

It has to be the other maji. I was leaning toward agreeing with my demon's snarl of anger. I could think of no one else who could have managed it.

Or the drach?

As if Mabel or any of her people would do such a thing. Shaylee sighed at me.

There's the Order, my demon sent with grim rage.

And the drachmor, my vampire sent. *None of whom matter right now.*

We have to help. Shaylee wrung her metaphysical hands inside my head.

We already tried, remember? My demon's frustration bubbled like a cauldron of magma in my chest. *We can't even feel her she's so far down the gap.*

The Kennecotts, faces paler than usual, freckles standing out against whitened skin, turned to me as one yet again and shook their heads.

No. I would *not* accept failure. Not now.

Syd. Gram's mind met mine. *Whatever's happening to her, it's past our power to stop it.*

A hand slid into mine, handsome face above me twisted into a deep frown. *I can't feel her either,* Oliver sent, quiet, almost ashamed. *What do we do?*

Damn them, why were they all looking at me?

I pushed Phon physically aside, sat down on the bed next to the maji woman. Took her hand in mine, feeling tears rise. Why did Zoe call on me only to abandon Iepa to this fate?

It's possible, my vampire sent, *she had no other choice.*

I'll never accept that, my demon snarled. *Even Fate has been messing around with power and recent proceedings. Pushing boundaries. Zoe herself was being misled by Bellanca.*

True enough. I ignored them further, chest tightening against the inevitable as Iepa faded further and further from me, the void that existed within her devouring her very soul.

The air beside me stirred, tanned hands taking mine and Iepa's while a few voices gasped in recognition. I looked up, blinking through tears and the most helpless I'd felt since I'd lost my son to find Trill beside me, her brown eyes full of sorrow.

"I'm not supposed to interfere," she whispered. "Too freaking bad."

She took me with her, deep into the crevasse inside Iepa. Showed me the hole her attacker opened in the very heart of who she was, connected it through her blood and magic to the bubble plane the maji created to cut themselves off from the Universe. Watched as she was cast out, her connection incomplete, damaged. They'd kicked her out of their new little commune, left her to drift in the void. And, somehow, she'd escaped, at least managing to make it this far.

To Center. To Zoe.

To me.

There had been a time I'd found Trill Zornov frustrating and a little amusing, a long time ago. And then had considered her a good friend. Turned traitor. Finally, I'd come to understand she had a far bigger role to play in Fate and the downfall of the Universe than anyone had ever expected. But I still had holes in my knowledge, knew there was so much more yet to come.

I shouldn't have been surprised to feel her magic fill Iepa easily, her power forming a patch across the gap in her soul, pulling her back into her body, capping off the exodus and allowing Iepa to live. Shouldn't have been. Still gaped at Trill like I'd never seen her before or even heard of magic.

Trill shrugged, a tiny sparkle in her eye as if she was trying not to feel too good about breaking whatever rules she seemed to think she was breaking.

And vanished.

I didn't have time to chase her, not when the maji on the bed gasped a shaking breath, her hand now clinging to mine instead of the other way around. Iepa opened her eyes at last, looked up at me. And wept silently if passionately in the deepest hurt I'd ever felt from another living being.

Bless Gram for shooing out the onlookers, though I didn't get a chance to thank Lula and Phon for coming so quickly, for trying despite knowing there was nothing they could do. Oliver lurked, as always, Sass and Jiao and my grandmother. And Quaid of all people, arms crossed over his chest, scowling at no one in particular. Part of me wanted to send him away, to Payten and the babies, hating the sight of his judging stare. Shouldn't he be with his family and minding his own damned business? But I was too busy to deal with his attitude.

Later. I'd chew him out later. If only to make myself feel better and let off some steam.

A soft, silver bundle landed on the end of the bed, my demon friend returning to cat form. He curled up against Iepa, purring heavily, the amber power of his magic soothing the crying maji until she coughed softly through the last of her tears, free hand stroking his fur as she smiled through her sorrow.

"Thank you," she whispered, fixing her gaze on me before repeating those words in a voice that choked off. "Thank you." She cleared her throat, sighed. "I wasn't sure I could even renter this Universe let alone escape the void. But I had to try." She blinked a few times. "Your contact with Ameline's soul was the only thing that made it possible for me to find my way home."

Like my trip to the maji chamber was fate. How appropriate.

She'd just confirmed what I already knew. "How did they do it?" The bubble of reality had to have been a massive undertaking.

Iepa shrugged, shifted so she could scratch Sass's ear before letting her heavy arm fall with a thump at her side. "Zeon and Bellanca drew on the power of both maji people," she said. "They claimed it was the only way, Syd. I tried to argue, but no one would listen to me. And in order for the erasure of our kind to be complete, everyone had to go."

"You were a prisoner." That made sense.

She nodded. "There were a few of us who were taken into custody," she said, bitterness rising, free hand twitching on the quilt beneath her as if she were trying to scrabble for freedom from the memory. Tears flooded her eyes again. "I tried to warn you, but by the time I knew what they were doing it was too late."

"You know what happened after?" How much did they know? That could be an advantage. But Iepa's frown and small head shake told me that hope was futile.

"Bellanca seems able to transfer herself through the void," she said. "I have a feeling it has to do with her once being Fate. Though, I have suspicions about her brother."

"Thanos is helping her." That seemed logical.

"Maybe not on purpose." Iepa sighed again. "I don't have proof, but he's been absent for weeks. No one has seen him. I fear she's using him somehow. Like a bridge."

"Is that what she tried to do to you?" Oliver's gentle tone didn't intrude. In fact, if anything, it seemed to calm Iepa further.

"No," she said. "She was just trying to kill me." She closed her eyes a minute, lips twisting into a wry smile. "I made her believe I was on her side and then betrayed her." She met my eyes again, hers angry but determined. "Long story and of no matter right now. Needless to say, I failed in returning here on my own recognizance, at least with my power intact."

"How long before the fall did they remove themselves?" I guess it didn't really matter, but I needed to clear up my own timeline if only to settle my mind.

"About two of your weeks," she said. "Bellanca knew what was coming, we all did. But we had no idea Gabriel would decide to combine the Universes." She seemed oddly proud of that choice. "He was supposed to pick one or the other."

"I know," I whispered, grateful to know another soul who remembered my son.

She squeezed my hand, sympathy all over her face, in her renewed power. "I'm sorry, Syd," she said. "But he did the right thing, the one thing Bellanca never expected. It took her weeks to recover from the confusion he created." Iepa's laugh wasn't kind. "It's part of the reason I was able to trick her, at least temporarily."

The Fates hadn't liked it, either. But, as Trill had just said, too freaking bad.

"Because we were outside the two Universes," she said, "nothing has changed for us." So the maji had memories of all that happened, did they? "And yet, everything has changed." Fear washed over her expression, her long, narrow fingers clinging to me. "At first, dark and light banded together, retreated as one. Bellanca made sure to combine us so we would have the power to create the pocket Universe. But that's shifting, Syd." Her throat worked as she swallowed past her rising terror. "It's the reason I needed to return, to warn you."

But I already knew what she was going to say, didn't I? I'd been hearing it over and over again, in different ways, from different sources. Still, it all came down to this.

The blood of the maji. The dream. The uncomfortable feeling something was wrong. It woke in me again, the disorientation, only this time it settled and refused to go away.

"The dark maji have fully embraced the new white sorcery that was Creator's gift," Iepa said, intensity drawing me closer to her until I huddled over her, both of her hands now grasped in mine. It was as though she thought more contact would make me pay attention. She had no idea just how focused I was on what she said, despite the dizziness of my discomfort. If anything,

138

listening to her helped me adapt to the steady buzzing of awareness inside. "But the light refused, calling it a curse, a tainted result of the evil that has taken over since the Gateway woke Dark Brother."

Zeon had always blamed Gabriel for the inevitable. I nodded for her to go on, mouth so dry in anticipation of her words I couldn't have spoken if I tried.

"Zeon claims Gabriel is a false Creator and refuses to accept the new way of things." She panted for breath, as if unable to calm herself now she was able to deliver her message. "It's his intention to put everything back the way it was."

But how? Gabriel was Creator, like it or not. And yet... my worry about the bubble the maji made, taking themselves outside the Universe, clung to me like the maji woman before me.

Oliver sat behind me, leaning over to stroke hair from Iepa's sweating face. His touch calmed her, the warmth of him against my back doing the same for me. Did he feel the wrongness, too? Or was I the only one to carry that burden? Amazing how quickly I could adjust to this shift within. Already the girls had shuffled themselves sufficiently the discomfort was less painfully disorienting and more a dull ache of reminder I had work left to do.

"He must know that's impossible." So reasonable. But didn't Oliver know by now reasonable had no place in this Universe?

Iepa's eyes blinked slowly, tears leaking from the edges. "I wish that were so," she said, finally voicing my fears. Though, oddly, as she went on I started feeling better, lighter despite the now steady pressure of the feeling something was off, as though this were happening at a great distance, to someone else. "But they plan to use their last connection to this Universe to rejoin it, to recreate the barrier Creator made between the old Universes, and return things to the way they had been for millennia."

I floated above myself, the scent of smoke in my senses, the ghostly feeling of a drach between my legs, flare from a burning sword in my hand as I screamed defiance at the charging armies before me.

"He will trigger a maji war," Iepa said while I dove on drachback into the slender way between them and burst into light. "And use that power to make their Universe the only Universe."

Except he didn't know, didn't understand as I did just what that war would mean.

The end of everything at last.

EIGHTEEN

I slammed back into my body, exhaling as Iepa stared at me with shock and more than a little terror.

"You knew," she choked out.

"The blood of the maji is on my hands," I said, like that meant something.

Iepa meeped in fear, freeing her fingers from mine, hugging herself. "You have to stop it," she said.

I laughed, empty and hopeless. "How?"

Oliver's hands settled on my shoulders, Sass's blinking amber eyes fixed on me. "You need to reach the maji," the Order soldier said like that was as simple as a walk in the park next door.

"We already talked about this," I said, not turning to him, staring down at Iepa. "No Gateway. No Gate." I paused, frowned at her. "The maji chamber?"

Iepa shook her head. "I don't know," she said. "I

planned to use that connection, but was cast into the void before I could try it. Only when you fed power to Ameline was I able to find a way out."

Well, it was an option then, maybe. I loved maybes so much. So much. But I had no desire to land in the void or on the other side as drained as Iepa now was. And without a drach beneath me and armor and a sword to defend me.

"Tell me," Oliver said, calm and resilient and making me a little irritated with his attitude of rationality, frankly, "are the drachmor indeed with your people?"

Iepa seemed startled, then nodded quickly, wiping at her tears with trembling hands. She struggled to sit up and I helped her, absently, wishing she'd get on with it already. Patience, Syd.

"They appeared some weeks ago," Iepa said. "Though I don't know how. Bellanca was with them, so it's possible she was the catalyst of their arrival."

"She's found some kind of keyhole," he said, more to me than anyone else. I finally turned and half faced him, perched on the edge of the bed, looking up into his gray eyes and their flashes of light. "The drachmor entered my Universe at one point, remember?" I nodded at that, heart stilling as I willed him to work it out and tell me what I needed to know so I didn't have to think about it anymore. "And, somehow, the soul of Max from my side," his gaze dropped to my wrist a moment then returned to mine, "did the opposite." Right. I ran one hand over the black ribbon that twitched and sighed before falling still. Listening, too? Maybe. "We never found out how that was possible."

"Trill's doorway," I said. "The one we used to cross."

He shook his head, frowning. "I get the feeling that was meant to be a one use gap," he said. "With Gabriel's help, remember?" Oliver looked away. "I feel like I'm missing something important."

So did I. And yet, the inevitable seemed to be rushing toward me like the oncoming armies I was destined to fight.

Sydlynn. I wasn't expecting to be interrupted, especially not by that voice. I perked, disoriented by the touch of Danilo Moreau and sent a brief wash of confused greeting before he rushed on. *We need to talk.*

I'm a little busy. Or was I? Iepa was safe, we still didn't know how to get to Bellanca and despite the fact the maji war was pending I didn't have a drach to ride into battle, did I? The one I was sure would be my partner had gone and done himself in.

Unfair, my vampire whispered.

The Order are questioning Femke and the WPC, Danilo went on as if I hadn't tried to shut him down a second ago. *But their delay tactics won't hold her forever.*

I know that, I sent. *I just wanted her off my back for a bit so I could figure out what to do with Quaid.*

While I'm personally grateful jailbreaking is a favorite pastime of yours, he sent with enough amusement I knew he'd be okay again someday, *it's a bad habit we really have to talk about at some point.*

That glimpse into the return of my friend made me grin, despite everything. *What do you need?*

I have a plan, he said, brusque and commanding. *But Charlotte won't like it. And neither, my friend, will you.*

What else was new? *Just tell me and I'll freak out at you and then we'll sit down and talk about it like reasonable people, okay?*

Danilo's chuckle sounded lighthearted, almost as though he'd found peace at last. While I wasn't against him forgiving himself, I had a feeling what he was about to propose to me had a lot to do with that newfound peace. And would likely, knowing the werewolf's sense of justice and reparation, mean he'd be putting himself into harm's way.

Oh. I had no idea. Not until he spoke again with excitement and eagerness in his mental voice.

We can't fight Konstantin, he sent. *Not inside Femke. But we can give him someone else to wrestle with. Someone prepared for his occupation.*

He might as well have slapped me. *Danilo. Tell me you didn't just suggest what I think you suggested.*

I did, he sent, firm, resolute now, truly at peace. *I want to take on the evil to save Femke.*

NINETEEN

I stood from Iepa's bedside, gesturing for Gram to join me, leaving the maji to Sassafras as Oliver followed into the hallway and listened in on our mental conversation. *Danilo*, I sent, tense and trying not to feel excited by the prospect considering what he suggested might be a terrible idea, *tell me again.*

It's simple, he sent as if it really could be. *Femke was in no condition to handle the invasion of Konstantin's soul when it happened. She'd been tortured and drugged, correct?* I had no idea of the full details, really, but assumed as much from the terrible condition she'd been in. The former wereking went on when I didn't answer. *But I'm prepared. And in full control of my power.* He paused then. *And I have a singular advantage, being a werewolf. A creation of the Black Souls. I understand them and their magic.*

I turned to Gram who stared at the floor, plucking

her lower lip with her index finger and thumb while she mulled it over. When she finally looked up again, tossing her hands with a huff of breath, she shrugged.

I have no idea if it will even work, she sent. *Necromancy typically deals with echoes, not true souls. It might destroy you, Danilo. And Femke at the same time.*

Brother. Charlotte's crisp mental tone cut in. *You are not bringing this foolhardy idea to Syd.* Now, I adored the werequeen and considered her one of my closest friends. But if she'd spoken to me in that particular tone even I'd be a bit nervous.

Danilo, on the other hand, mentally shrugged, giving me a flash of an image. He sat before a fire at the werepalace, his sternly glaring sister standing behind him.

We have sought out the Black Souls to no avail, he sent, quiet this time but still determined. *No amount of seeking has helped, not even with Iosif's agreement.* Charlotte's old Mafia contact had done his best, I guess, still not good enough. *Femke is dying, losing her battle with Konstantin. And I am meant to be a life's prisoner for the betrayal of my people.* Danilo's gentle tone appealed directly to me. *I care about her, too*, he sent. *Femke always treated the werenation family. She's my friend, as much as yours. Her kindness and understanding prevented my death when I should have been put out of my misery. It is the only way. Let me do this for you, for her. For all of us.*

And if it kills you? Charlotte's sharp demand did nothing to break her brother's resolve.

Then it does, he sent. *And if it also kills Femke, we are releasing her from a fate worse than the death her freedom will bring.*

I hate to agree with him, Gram sent in a tight, private thought, *but he's right, Syd. Femke won't last much longer. We have to try something. And this might be her only shot.*

You knew he was going to suggest this. Not a question. Leave it to Gram to work this out behind my back.

He might have brought it up, she sent.

Grumble, mumble.

Piers. I reached for the leader of the Sorcerers League, and then his second. Demetrius. Both registered my call immediately. From the flicker of insight I was allowed on connecting, they were together anyway, at the castle in Scotland. I prodded Danilo who filled them in while I struggled between worry about him and Femke and growing hope this might actually save her.

We're in, Piers sent while Demetrius murmured his agreement. *You realize though we'll have to have access to her to try this.*

Which means taking her into custody, Oliver sent.

Kidnapping her, you mean, I shot at him, at all of them.

No one argued with my terminology.

Well, we discussed the possibility, I sent. *So, what are we waiting for? Let's go nab us a World Paranormal Council Leader already.*

Let me talk to my mother, Oliver sent. *She might be able to get us access with minimal fuss.*

147

The Order won't like us using them to further our own purpose, Piers sent.

Let them lump it, I shot at him. *Shonya Opal might not remember, but she owes me.* Okay, not really. And yet they all did, didn't they?

Oliver chuckled but didn't comment. Even as my vampire spoke.

You know we can't involve them.

I hate it when she's right, my demon sent. *But she's right, Syd.*

Trouble we can handle, Shaylee sent. *We're made for it.*

Damn them. *Fine.* Like I didn't know already we'd be on our own yet again.

I sighed then, shook my head. *Like it or not*, I sent, *this can't be on the Order. Or the Sorcerers League.* I squared myself as I stepped back from Oliver and saluted my grandmother. *If this is on anyone, it's got to be on me.*

Syd, Charlotte sent, tense and low. *You need backup.*

Since when? I flashed her the image of the cavern in Wilding Springs. *Meet me there. I won't be long.*

I'm coming with you. Oliver seemed to forget he was in my head despite being right in front of me, reaching for me with one big hand, worry on his handsome face.

Not this time, I sent, blocking him with power. *See you shortly.*

The veil parted with a sigh, as if knowing where I was going. *Mom*, I sent. *Be prepared for anything.*

She spluttered back at me before I cut her off and stepped through the gap into Femke's office in Hong Kong.

She stood behind her desk, blonde hair grown to her shoulders now, blue eyes cold, washed briefly with black as the soul of Konstantin woke and pushed itself to the forefront. I hadn't expected to have to deal with Shonya Opal, however, the Order commander greeting me with a blank expression and an eyebrow raise that was her outward show of surprise.

"Sydlynn," she said.

"Commander." *Oliver*, I sent. *Distract your mom, would you?*

I'll do my best. He hesitated while I slowly made my way closer to Femke. I'd have to get my hands on her to make this work. *Be careful.*

I didn't bother responding as the tall commander straightened, her armor gleaming, nodding to Femke.

"I understand there's been a conflict over the removal of a prisoner." She sounded irritated through the level of her normal tone. So, Oliver hadn't been entirely forthcoming with his mother when he asked her to call off Femke, then.

I shrugged, smiled. "We're working out the details," I said.

Femke snorted, crossing her arms over her chest, glaring at me while I casually kept coming, only ten feet from her now. The night sky behind her glittered with stars and the lights of the city, tall, glass windows towering over us, making the room feel like it hovered on the edge of a cliff. Only the two lamps on her desk cast full illumination, the overheads on dim. Eerie, quiet, white carpet whispering under my sneakers. Like a dream unfolding.

Eight feet. Six.

"Details," Femke said. "There are no details. You illegally removed a murderer from confinement and are presently harboring him in your territory." Her smile seemed grotesque, the glimpse of the soul within her showing through. Danilo was right. Femke was almost done. I had to act now or lose her forever, even if that meant the Order came after me, too. Shonya twitched, frowned. Oliver must have been talking to her, my distraction.

"I was informed," Shonya said, "your territory was being unlawfully attacked. Information from one of my soldiers." She stated the last through clenched teeth. "The same soldier who is right now trying to convince me not to arrest you for false accusations against your own WPC leader."

I winked at Shonya. "Alleged false accusations," I said. And smiled at Femke as I closed the last of the distance, within touching distance. "But I'm happy to talk about it," I said. "However, this is a private conversation, between me and Femke. Right?"

She spluttered, flickered her gaze at Shonya. Even as my friend—my powerful, brave, battling friend who was dying before my eyes—surfaced long enough when I reached out and grasped her hand she took it. And whispered, "Syd."

That was all the encouragement I needed. In a flare of white sorcery I dragged her on shining fire from her office directly to the cavern in Wilding Springs. No veil, not this time. Not with the Order out there, just in case. Instead, I pulled a trick from the Enforcer's book and rode my power directly to my destination before sealing off the outside of the cave with a burst of magic.

Let them try to break through.

SYD. LET ME IN. Gram's power hit the outside of the shielding while I turned slowly to find Charlotte and Danilo waiting for me. The werequeen nodded even as Femke stumbled at my side, collapsing against me a moment.

Stay out of this, Gram, I sent. *You and Mom. You can claim deniability this way. I told you—this is on me.*

SYDLYNN THADDEA HAYLE, YOU OPEN THIS SHIELD RIGHT NOW. Whether Mom was putting on a show for the wave of Enforcers who'd just arrived or the Order soldiers I felt layering themselves against my wards, or was genuinely pissed at me I had no idea. Didn't care. Gritted my teeth against the pressure building outside and gestured at Danilo while ignoring the flickering image of the clearing filling with bodies. Lots and lots of bodies. Black robes and shining armor piled on top of each other. I firmly and completely blocked that view out and nodded to the werewolves.

"I hate to rush you," I said.

There is nothing I can do to protect you. Mom sounded terrified.

If this works, I sent, *you won't have to. Just buy me some time.*

Syd—

Mom. This is our last shot to save her. I didn't need to tell her who I was talking about, not with half the Universe now outside the shields and trying to get in. *I'm tired of losing this fight. If we save her, she'll call off the dogs.*

And if you don't?

I guess I'll be relocating to the Stronghold with the drach. That was, if the Order didn't come for me. Let them try. *Give us a few minutes.*

I don't think you have that long, girl. Gram's tight message preceded another hit. I staggered under the weight of it, knowing Shonya was behind that strike and was pulling her punches. But not for much longer.

Sydlynn Hayle. Return Femke Svennson immediately. This is your final warning. Shonya's voice echoed in my head, in the cavern itself. *Oliver told me what you're trying to do,* she sent privately. *Hurry the hell up already.*

So, a little leeway. I spun on Danilo and snarled in his general direction while he grasped Femke's upper arms in his hands. But I didn't have to tell him to get to work. From the strained expression on his face, he was already at it.

Whatever control Femke had wrested back from Konstantin failed as Danilo made his move.

I think I knew as soon as the Black Soul sorcerer surfaced we'd failed. This was a terrible idea. Danilo's power was no match for Konstantin, not because the sorcerer was stronger, but because he had control of Femke and the WPC magic. What the hell were we thinking? Maybe if I knocked her out, didn't give him a chance to resurface—

Danilo shrieked, the howl of a wolf. And Konstantin laughed, surging forward and taking over, at last, the woman who had been my friend.

TWENTY

No. Failure was not an option. Give up on this amazing woman who had only ever been my friend? Never. I threw power at Danilo, pouring it into him as I had Iepa, feeling the strain of the loss of my magic so soon after encountering the void again but not caring, not even a little bit.

They could have it all. She could have every last scrap if it meant saving Femke Svennson from a fate worse than death.

But she was dying still, her mind falling from mine, grasping for me as I panted out the seemingly infinite power at my disposal, knowing then no matter how much magic I had access to it wasn't enough. I wasn't enough. I just didn't know what I was doing. Without the tools to separate her from Konstantin, she was doomed.

Her head turned, lolling back on her long, thin neck,

eyes returning to that blue I knew so well. And, in the final instant Femke had, she surfaced like a drowning victim one last time, gasping for air, knowing she was through.

"Syd," she whispered. "Kill me."

The piercing scream that followed those words made my ears ache, goosebumps leaping to the surface of my skin. I lunged for her, for Danilo who still grasped her tightly despite his failing strength, the wolf in him leaping to the fore, body shifting half into form, snout dripping drool as he panted over her.

We have no choice now, my vampire sent, soft and kind but full of knowing. *Syd, we must let her go. Before it's too late.*

And to hell with the consequences. My demon grunted as she took her turn reinforcing the shields keeping us safe for now. We'd lose any semblance of safety though if we took Femke's life. That would be it.

We'll be fugitives, I sent to them, feeling drained of emotion, of caring and power and everything else that mattered right now.

So be it. Shaylee hugged me with earth magic, shaking the ground beneath me a moment.

She deserves our best, my vampire sent. *And the best we can offer is peace.*

Okay, I sent. And reached for Femke with my magic, my power settling around her heart even as she sank beyond my reach, Konstantin taking over. One squeeze, one quick reflexive motion and my friend would be dead.

No, not my friend. The evil that had finally won.

A tear tracked down my cheek, tickling my skin, as I clenched my fist of magic with a silent whisper of love to Femke's lost soul.

Only to feel someone block that mercy. Damn it, had I failed her in this, too? But no, it wasn't Konstantin who still battled against the werewolf holding him pinned as best he could with power and claws. No, it was a tall, blonde woman in a white robe suddenly standing next to me, Iepa's calm gaze as familiar as Femke's blue eyes. She smiled gently at me and shook her head.

Allow me, she sent. And turned to the battling sorcerer and werewolf.

Syd, Oliver sent, tight and tense. *Mother is running out of time and excuses.*

Just one more minute, I sent back, a whisper as I tried to follow Iepa's power into Femke. I succeeded, but whatever she did was a blur to me, a mixture of rainbow magic and pressure linked to some kind of transfer of energy that felt so absolutely fundamental I finally retreated and shivered at the massiveness of it.

Some things, Iepa sent, *even you aren't meant to know.* She sounded happy again. *Allow me this, Syd. As my thanks to you.*

Considering it was Trill who saved her, I didn't argue. I needed this, we needed it. A victory, especially the return of Femke…

It was over in a moment, but not before I had a flash of insight. And shared through the surface of the shield just exactly what we were up to in the cavern. With every single soul beating themselves against my failing wards.

That shut them up. Especially when, a moment later, the visible soul of Konstantin lifted free of Femke, struggling and spitting in a black wave of materializing features and fury, hovering a moment between my friend and the former wereking.

I can't simply destroy him, Iepa sent. *He has created a permanent loop of this fragment of his soul. Left to his own, he will simply infect another. But any attempt to extinguish him will rebound on the one who attacks.* She sounded confused and a little sad. *What is your wish?*

Silence from outside. Only then did I realize Iepa had followed my lead, was sharing with everyone what exactly was happening.

Danilo Moreau has agreed to take on the infection of the Black Soul, I sent as formally as possible. Like this had been the plan all along, that the ones observing were intended to stand there beyond the wards as witness. While I hadn't figured that part out initially, it seemed to work so I ran with it. *As part of his punishment for the betrayal of his people.*

It is a great sacrifice he offers, Iepa sent. *To save the soul of Femke Svennson in such a way surely will erase his original sentence.*

We will care for him, Charlotte sent, nodding to me, fear flickering briefly over her face. *And when Leader Svennson is once again whole and recovered from the evil that was done to her, it will be her decision as to his ultimate fate.*

If Danilo dies with Konstantin's soul in him, I sent in a tight aside to Iepa, *will he take the sorcerer with him?*

I don't know, Iepa sent. *Though it's likely.*

Good enough for me, I sent. And hastily qualified my statement. *I don't want him to die.*

I know. Iepa's eyes registered empathy and kindness. *But you had to ask.* She looked back to Danilo who had regained human form. His dark brown eyes met mine a moment, jaw tight under his heavy beard, more determined than ever.

"I'm ready," he said, voice gruff and deep.

"Then guard yourself well against him," Iepa said, gesturing with her right hand, releasing Konstantin's soul. The black cloud dove into Danilo, hitting him physically, rocking the werewolf back. His hands spasmed, releasing Femke who sagged to the ground in a graceful wilt, like a delicate flower slowly dying under the heat of the sun. I rushed to my friend's side even as Danilo fell to his knees and howled.

I dropped my shields then, no longer needing them, cradling Femke in my lap while Charlotte's magic enveloped her brother. We had no idea if Danilo was actually capable of containing Konstantin. Time would tell. But, if he did deteriorate like Femke had, at least he wasn't the leader of the World Paranormal Council. As a prisoner and a criminal, he created the perfect containment for Konstantin.

I ignored the bodies rushing into the cavern, stroking Femke's hair back from her eyes, the thinness of her making her feel light, almost wasted away. I knew it was Oliver beside me from the faint scent of fabric softener, the gentle touch of one big hand on my shoulder comforting as those blue eyes flickered and opened and Femke looked up at me.

She stared at me for a long time, tears tracking down her temples into her hair, lower lip trembling while she drew purposeful, steady breaths. Shaking hands finally rose, grasped for mine and I held hers tight, pulling her up into a sitting position, cradling her against my shoulder for a moment before she firmly pushed against me and swayed under her own power for the first time in months.

"Sydlynn Hayle," she said, voice shaking but firm and carrying. She hesitated, lips moving but pale cheeks bright with pink, as if she barely held herself together. I had no idea what she was going through and equally had no clue how to help her or even how she was even awake, aware, speaking, breathing. When she finally went on, her voice was stronger, if thick with emotion. "You have saved my life when I begged you to end it. Rescued me from the clutches of the evil one who tried to destroy our council and our peace." Honestly, where was she getting the reserves? She never failed to amaze me. But I knew, in that moment, Femke Svennson was the strongest person I'd ever met in my entire life and I would never, ever forget this instant of pride and grief as she nodded to me like nothing untoward had happened. "For your tireless efforts on my behalf, I grant you the deepest thanks my soul can express."

TWENTY-ONE

And that, as they say, was that. She was taken from me then, by Enforcers and the Order, carried away to be cared for and, I hoped, healed the rest of the way. I sank back a moment into Oliver's arms, not caring there were a multitude of people milling around like they couldn't believe it was over this fast. Let them see my moment of weakness, if it could be called that. Let them judge me if they chose.

Damn, I was tired.

You did it. Oliver's mind embraced mine as much as his body did. His power formed a cocoon around us, a protective barrier I welcomed and was grateful for. *You saved her, Syd.*

No, Iepa did. I rested my cheek against his chest, head tucked under his chin while his big hand hooked over my thigh and pulled me into his lap.

She finished the job, he sent. *But you made it happen.*

I shrugged then, sighed. *Danilo?*

Charlotte took him. Oliver's head moved while my eyes drifted closed. The cocoon he'd made was so quiet, so warm and lovely. I could sit here forever. *We'll check on him later.*

Yes. I really had to get up, to talk to Mom and Gram and Iepa. To figure out what to do with Quaid while Femke recovered. But the dream was with me, flashes of drachback battle and flaming swords prodding me.

He saw, he must have, because Oliver tensed. *Mind telling me what you're thinking?*

The end isn't over, it's still coming. That didn't make much sense, fair enough. Instead of trying to find words, I showed him the dream in full, terrifying technicolor.

Oliver didn't say anything after I was done, though the warmth of his protection didn't waver despite the fact I could feel his tension rising.

I won't let you die. Such conviction, such passion. It burned like a flame between us, a bonfire fueled by his heart.

You won't have a choice. He really did make a great pillow.

If you go, he sent, *I'm coming with you.* I'd heard that before, but from a demon cat, not a man in love. I looked up again, began to shake my head in protest, but he silenced me with his lips settling over mine. I let him kiss me, soft, sweet, without pressure or any kind of demand behind that kiss. When he finished, his forehead touched mine. *I'd rather die*, he sent, *than not be with you.*

He had no idea what he was saying. What a childish pronouncement to make. And yet, as I absorbed not only his words but how he felt, I realized he meant it. He actually meant it, the big idiot. Tears burned as he went on. *I've never been allowed to feel this way*, he sent. *My people…* his mental voice choked off. *You know about my people, our training, our control by Dark Brother.* I nodded and let him go on. *It's like a drowning man finding a gulp of air, Syd. Air I didn't know I needed until I had it inside me.* He frowned a little, grimaced. *This sounds ridiculous and entirely trite, but when you sent me away the past few weeks, I pined for you. Literally.*

I didn't know what was more amazing. The fact he was so open and honest with how he felt or that he was willing to tell me about it. I kissed him back, hugged him.

I'm sorry.

I know. He nuzzled my ear. *I understand. And I don't. How could I? You gave up everything so many times. Then to have to release your son… I have no idea how you did it.*

We weren't going there. Thankfully, he went on before I could turn into a bawling wreck.

This dream of yours, he sent. *It can't come true, Syd.*

That's not up to us. I'd learned enough from my dealings with fate to know I was right.

But Max. Hope made its way into his mental tone. *Without Max the vision can't come to pass.*

There was that. I'd not allowed myself to go too far into such introspection, not yet.

Fate has a way of making things work out the way it wants, I sent, knowing how fatalistic that sounded.

You accused me of having a death wish once, he sent. *Have I infected you?*

I laughed, felt lightness replace the weary feeling that had taken me over the last few minutes. I pushed gently against his magic and felt his protection retreat with some sorrow on his part, turning to look up at him while he stood, helping me to my feet. The world emerged around us, sound of voices murmuring, scent of mildew and damp, earthy air filling my lungs. Maybe it was an odd reaction, this lifting of weight and darkness, but instead I felt more at peace right at that instant than I had in a long time.

Let's blame you, I sent, hugging him on impulse. His tall body felt heated, powerful, hard like a column of metal that melted against me like we fit together. Something stirred, a memory I should recall but it was gone again and I let it go without a fight. *It'll give you something to beat yourself up over at least.*

Oliver chuckled in my head. *No fair,* he sent. *How did you know I do that?*

Takes one, I sent.

I stepped back, smiled up into his eyes, even as someone cleared their throat and brought me back to reality. That was okay. I was ready for it now.

Or, so I thought. Until I realized it was Mia Dumont staring me in the face, her icy eyes beneath a panel of perfect black bangs glaring like I'd kicked her puppy.

"Now you've gone and done it," she said.

TWENTY-TWO

She was about a half a heartbeat from feeling my foot in the crack of her ass.

"You're not my Fate," I said through clenched teeth, forgetting on purpose I actually liked Mia in the moment I needed to get my mojo back. "I don't have to listen to you."

She actually seemed surprised. "I don't know what that means."

Right. One Universe, not two. Two Fates, though, where maybe there was only supposed to be one? Gabriel was juggling more than I understood, I guess.

"There have always been two Fates, Syd," Mia said, quashing my worry over my son, at least in part. "Two sides of the story. You must know that. I'm not yours, and neither is Zoe."

Whatever. I was far too over it to worry about

sophistry at this point. Let the mess inside my head sort itself out. I was done worrying if anyone thought I'd lost it. "So tell me something useful already," I said, "rather than accusing me of making a bigger disaster than the Universe is presently heading toward."

Mia's frown didn't make her any less beautiful, but it did serve to remind me of the girl I used to know. "Who," she said, jabbing a finger at Iepa who stood to one side with my mother holding her arm gently in one hand, "is that? And why is she messing with my timeline foretelling?"

"That," I snarled back, "is a maji. And she and her people are a bigger pain in the butt than you will ever possibly imagine. Until and unless that is you remember everything that happened before my son became Creator." Oh, how I loved the confusion on her face. Shouldn't have. Probably should have been upset and angry and other irritated emotions. Instead, I kissed her cheek and grinned. "For the first time ever," I said, "I know something you don't. Awesome."

She shook her head, glossy back hair swinging. "Don't be so cocky," she said, sounding genuinely worried. "Somethings terribly wrong, Syd."

"You don't say." I crossed my arms over my chest, the urge to giggle hysterically so powerful I clamped my magic firmly around it and pinned it inside my chest so it wouldn't escape. I'd adapted to the disorientation and discomfort, embraced it now as confirmation I was heading in the right direction. "Tell me all about it."

She seemed totally thrown by my attitude. "This is serious." Mia glanced up, met Oliver's eyes. "Talk to her, would you?"

He shrugged and I was amused to find him grinning, too. "Not my job," he said. "I'm just the love interest."

Snort.

Mia's irritation flashed as she returned her scowl to me. "Okay fine," she said. "Be a smart ass. But be ready."

She didn't have to tell me something was coming. But maybe she had info I needed after all. That sobered me a little. Enough to nod and focus.

"Tell me," I said

She tossed her hands in the air instead of answering, huffing a sigh. "I have no details at this point," she said. "All I know is as soon as that person," she shuddered faintly, "appeared in this timeline, everything went to hell. So be ready." Even she seemed frustrated by her message. Mia sighed then, sagged. "Syd," she said, voice barely above a whisper, "you've done so much. Have had so much asked of you. And this last sacrifice…" She seemed stricken by her visions, met my eyes again and I nodded to her, patted her hand.

"I know what's to come," I said, so kindly she flinched. "I've seen it."

Mia swallowed as she hugged herself. "If there was

anything we could do—"

"There is." I pinned her with power and with my gaze. *Watch over my family. And give them fair warning when I'm gone. No more games, not with them. I'll pay this price. But only if you promise to keep them safe.*

I'll do my best, she sent. *I'm Fate, Syd. You act like you think I have a choice in all this.*

That was the rub, wasn't it? All my anger and frustration toward her and Zoe washed away in that moment. Because I knew, didn't I? How hard it had to be. To be them. They didn't keep things from me out of spite or to be hurtful or irritating. They did it because, like me, they had no choice.

Just once, I sent, softly to cut the harshness of the words so she'd know I wasn't angry, *it would be nice to just talk and not have an agenda.*

If we can possibly make that happen, she sent, *I'd love it.*

We stared at each other for a long instant, and in the end I hugged her, my friend, grateful to have Mia back in my life again. Even if she wasn't exactly my Mia.

I wasn't looking forward to forever, you know, I sent to her, private and tight so only she'd hear. *So this is a good thing.*

Oh, Syd, she sobbed once in my head before pulling away. I let her go, watched her hesitate before waving and vanishing into thin air, replaced quickly by my advancing mother.

I have to find a way to bring Max back. I didn't mean to

direct that at the people sharing my headspace, but they took it as such, even as Mom came to a halt next to me and hugged me.

"Syd," she whispered in my ear while my demon chuffed.

Maybe it wasn't Max after all? Even she sounded like she didn't believe it.

"Mom." I hugged her back.

It was him, Shaylee sent, firm and convinced. *And yet, he felt different, didn't he?*

Mom pushed her hair back from her shoulders, a habit she'd picked up along the way, heavy waves and curls cascading down her back. "You took a huge risk." There was laughter in her voice, but not the good kind. The "holy crap what were you thinking and you're lucky it worked out" kind.

Harsher around the edges, my vampire sent. *And his body was altered.*

I nodded to her, disoriented by the mix of conversation in two totally different veins. "I know," I said. "But I was tired of losing. And Femke was out of time."

Battle drach, my demon sent.

Would you three just hang on a second? I came across huffier than I planned.

Well, excuse us, Shaylee sniffed.

Sigh.

"Will she be all right?" Mom glanced back over her shoulder, diplomat's smile on her face for Iepa who stood waiting, hands folded in front of her, faint smile of her own in place on her full lips. "Your friend explained a little of what she did, but…" Mom shrugged, laughed for real this time, that throaty sound I loved so much. "I honestly barely understood a fraction of it."

Maybe it has to do with the ribbon soul Syd wears. Clearly my demon didn't take the shut up hint.

"Iepa has her talents," I said, nodding to the maji. *Thank you.*

It was my pleasure and, to be honest, it felt good to act, Syd. For once.

She could preach that to the choir of Sydliness.

Perhaps, my vampire sent. *At least, it's possible Max's alternate soul could be of help.*

If you three are done, I sent, *I'd like to get out of here.*

By all means, my vampire sent. *We've been ready for some time now.*

Oh no, she did *not*.

The three of them giggled then. Bratskis.

I left the cavern with a soft touch to Gram's mind we'd be home soon. Iepa followed me quietly, Oliver on my other side, as the three of us crossed the veil into Irish territory.

They'll be coming for me. I'd forgotten about Quaid and his returned residence in Wilding Springs.

Not until Femke is better, I sent, feeling him clearly, so clearly I could see him hugging Payten, their twin girls in their bassinet. And Ethie hovering, staring at them with an expression I found hard to read. Seeing her, knowing she was in Wilding Springs and had made no effort to see me, had blocked herself from me while I was there, made my heart hurt. Then again, I hadn't exactly gone after her, had I? Better this way. *They have bigger things to worry about now that they know what really happened to her.*

I hoped.

His mental state told me there was a fight brewing, at least on his end. I cut him off and let him stew. I'd saved him from dying, the ungrateful bastard, and delivered him into the loving arms of his new wife and babies. And my troubled daughter. So he could just bloody well bite me already.

Piers waited for us at the entrance to the main corridor where Danilo had been kept previously. The Enforcers lining the hall seemed nervous, ready to take me on. Only Shonya Opal's presence—that and a handful of her armored people—seemed to keep the peace. I grinned and waved at the prison guards, knowing it would piss them off and push them to act.

Let them try.

Considering the last time you were here you took Quaid away, the Sorcerer League leader sent, one arm hooking through mine as he waved his own salute at the guards with a jauntiness that was pure Piers Southway, *and the time before that you stole Danilo out from under them and there wasn't a thing they could do to stop you, it stands to reason they are a tad jumpy. And pissy, too.*

I winked at him. *You don't say?*

His long, silvery blond hair swung forward as he ducked his head, hiding a smirk, the silken strands of it sliding over the thigh of my jeans, clinging in shining, static strings.

I've missed you, my darling Syd. His gray eyes glittered. *So much.*

I touched his cheek, my only response. Because, honestly, there was nothing to say.

Danilo's door stood open, Charlotte waiting inside, arms firmly clasped across her chest, glaring blue eyes meeting mine. While I'd known she wasn't happy about Danilo's suggestion, I had no idea she'd be this upset. And she was upset. More so than I'd ever seen my werefriend.

Well, he was a grown wolf, wasn't he? And it was Danilo's decision. One that saved Femke. Sure, Syd. Keep telling yourself that. Maybe you'll feel better when he cracks down the middle right around the time he loses his soul and his mind.

But Danilo's reaction was totally different than I expected. I met his eyes and saw the peace there, the quiet behind his dark gaze. So far from the troubled, tortured werewolf of late. And, to be honest, from the wereking I'd known. Even when married to his beloved Yana, when he had the throne of the werenation beneath him, Danilo had always seemed restless if not stressed out. This Danilo Moreau felt more like his sister normally did.

Iepa stepped forward, head tilted to one side, smiling faintly still. "You are well?"

He nodded to her. "So far, so good, as they say." Danilo's fingertips tapped on the table, stilling again as he noticed their movement. "It will take some getting used to," he said, a faint strain appearing around his eyes, "but I'm prepared for whatever comes."

He certainly did seem a far cry from the way Femke came home to us. Maybe he did have an advantage, as he'd claimed. Or, maybe his descent would simply be slower. Was it wrong for me to be grateful he took the burden from my friend onto his own shoulders? Yes. Yes it was. And yet, I was grateful, damn it.

"This burden," he said in his deep, steady voice, "I will carry with courage and honor, as penance for the ill I've done my people, all the days of my life."

Charlotte made a noise, a soft sound I almost doubted I'd heard, her lower lip thrusting forward just for a second before she stilled again. And, when the air behind her parted and she spun to go, I wasn't surprised she refused to meet my eyes.

TWENTY-THREE

I'm flying and I'm grateful for it. I know this journey, have waited for the end for so long. The armor I wear is heavy on my shoulders but I barely feel it, welcome its presence. It saves me from a hit to the chest while my mount wheels and dives. The pressure of building power pushes against me, burning through the metal and scorching my skin, bruising my damaged body, crushing my chest so tight I have to fight for breath. I force my lungs to inflate out of sheer spite, scream a soundless yell of defiance, voice already parched and cracking—

There were moments when I surfaced from the dream I felt at peace, but not tonight. Instead, I found myself pulling on a robe over my pajama bottoms and t-shirt and stumbling downstairs to the back door, past the room where Payten delivered her babies, where Iepa was saved and out into the icy evening of middle autumn. The weather had turned, shifting toward frost in a rare low pressure system that threatened of snow. I ignored the temperature that did nothing to harm me and stood in the center of the yard, hugging myself and watching my breath rise in puffs of white mist toward the distant sky.

I knew he'd followed me, felt him ease his way outside. But Oliver made no attempt to join me, simply settling himself on the bench by the door to wait. It would have once been Sassafras to fill that role, to talk me down from the ledge or out of the blues. My darling demon cat turned boy again was gone to the Stronghold with Jiao to check on Max. And honestly I was glad.

There was something so comforting about Oliver's presence I would have despaired if he'd gone away again.

When I finally turned, sighing into the quiet night while in the distance someone's restless dog barked its unhappy cry, I smiled at the Order soldier who watched me with a mix of worry and protectiveness that made me want to laugh and hold him. And maybe cry a little before kissing him.

"You can't protect me, you know." I crossed to him, ran one hand through his dark blond hair. Oliver shrugged, biceps bulging as he folded his arms over his chest, sticking his legs out in front of him.

"Try and stop me."

I sank into his lap, surprising myself, surprising him. He immediately made room, sitting up, arms encircling me while I huddled in his embrace and swung my feet as I lay sideways on him, heels thumping softly into his legs.

"I could pick another fight with you," I whispered. "Chase you off."

"I know your ways now," he said with far more cheer than he should have had. "You're never getting rid of me again."

"Promise?" It hurt to ask, my chest squeezing against the ache and only then did I understand. That I never believed I'd find someone. That even with Quaid I knew someday he'd die and leave me alone. That Liam and I had so little time to even consider what our future might hold. And that here, in this man, this Order soldier, I had the chance to find a love that could last as many lifetimes as I lived.

Except my time was running out. I sat up, tried to pull away as I realized my mistake. This was right, better. I was supposed to be alone, clearly. Quaid and I were necessary to make Ethie. And Liam... well. Gabriel was the most necessary thing of all. But if fate had taught me nothing, I wasn't meant for happily ever after, was I?

Oliver refused to let me go. Did he know what I was thinking, feeling? I have no idea. But he must have felt the shift in me because he tugged me, gently but firmly, back down into his arms and kissed me softly on the temple.

"Do not run from me," he said. "I'll just follow you.

Be all creepy and stalkerish and stuff." He stroked my hair. "Adore you from a distance. Fight off all comers before you even realize you're in danger. And worship you for the rest of my days."

I sniffed in some tears that had no right to rise. "Stop it," I said.

"Never." Lips on my temple, hands in my hair. "I love you, Syd."

He had to do that, didn't he? Shatter any kind of resistance I had to him, to his wiles and his warmth and the way his body made me tingle.

I didn't fight him, decided I didn't want to, when Oliver stood at last with me in his arms and carried me into the house.

We didn't sleep for a very long time.

TWENTY-FOUR

I stood in Femke's office not sure if I should be proud or furious to find her back at her desk. Less than twenty-four hours had passed since I'd kidnapped her. Certainly not long enough for her to have even processed what happened let alone recovered enough to return to work. And yet, here she was, smiling at me with a strained, tight expression that told me she knew I wasn't going to be happy with her but she had a job to do.

Okay then. That at least I understood.

Mom had joined me, standing quietly and a little less judging at my side, though I could feel her quiver of denial as our hands brushed against each other. I had intended to come to Hong Kong this afternoon, to give the WPC leader at least a day to catch her breath after freeing her from Konstantin, but she beat me to it.

Her summons felt like her old self, at least. And the

woman I observed, who crossed from her desk to my side to embrace me, was as much Femke as ever. Though she didn't carry any outward signs of her struggle, when her lips touched my cheek I felt them tremble, as much as her hands did as they clasped mine. If I didn't know her as well as I did, I would have missed the fact her whole powerful witch and unbent leader act was exactly that.

Veneers. We were good at faking it.

Please don't tell me to go lie down, she sent while she gestured for Mom and me to sit. *I need to be here, Syd.*

Your call, I sent back. *But if you collapse into a heap and lose your crap, that won't do much for appearances, Femke.*

She laughed with a hysterical edge in the depths of my mind. *I'll hold together*, she sent. *Long enough.*

Whatever that meant.

I yawned then, not meaning to, the weariness I felt catching me off guard. I hadn't exactly gotten any sleep last night. I'd expended a ton of energy on Iepa, then Femke, only to output even more thanks to Oliver.

Yeah, blame him, my demon sorted.

I blushed, couldn't help it, while Shaylee giggled in the back of my mind. Thinking about the Order soldier and our few hours of fun wasn't the headspace I needed to be in right now.

Who says? My vampire's wistful happiness wasn't lost on me.

You, too? I'd thought you more practical than those brats.

She sighed with contentment. *Even I have my hungers.*

Oh dear.

I rubbed at my red cheeks while Mom raised an eyebrow at me. Just made me blush brighter. At least Femke didn't notice, or didn't seem to, settling on the edge of her desk with her long legs crossed at the ankles, cream pencil skirt to her knees. Her pale pink silk shell and perfectly applied makeup and styled hair was all Femke. There was no doubt in my mind she was back. And yet, I could feel the shift in her, the weariness. We'd succeeded, yes, but I worried we'd been too late.

She'd been free less than a day and I was writing her off? Shame on me.

"Forgive me for calling you here so early." It might have been afternoon in Hong Kong but we were half a day from that at home.

"No forgiveness necessary," Mom said at her most demure. "We're delighted you're feeling better." MomDiplomoSpeak. Had to love it.

Femke's soft smile and nod of her head told me she was as deep in her politico as my mother. "Thank you, Miriam," she said, blue eyes meeting mine, blinking and moist. "I am."

Silence fell over us, only the faint rustle of cloth from one of the guarding Enforcers stirring the air. Femke finally cleared her throat with a grateful embrace inside my magic for allowing her a moment to catch herself from weeping before she spoke again.

"There are many things to be done in the next several hours," she said, slightly brusque but mostly accepting, calm. Why did I get the feeling I wasn't going to be happy with the rest of what she had to say? "The sorcerer Konstantin's control has created a fair amount of havoc that will take me some time to reverse, though I know now that job belongs to someone else."

She said *what*? I spluttered, half rose even as Femke's power, linked through the WPC magic, opened to every witch and paranormal on our plane.

"For those that are unaware, I have, until recently, been under soul possession by the Black Soul sorcerer, Konstantin." I felt their shock and fear through the link, wanted to shut Femke the hell up even as she went on, determination on her beautiful face. "Thanks to the hard work and intervention of Sydlynn Hayle, I am free of that control." Relief, curiosity, anxiety. "Thanks to her refusal to back down, we are again safe. She has our eternal gratitude as a council and a plane." While the wash of thanks was gratifying, I didn't want it. Never asked for it. "Now that I'm free, I understand clearly where I failed this Council and you, my people." Oh no, she did *not*. "I have served to the best of my ability, but that ability has put you in harm's way."

Don't you dare, I shot at her. *Don't blame yourself. It could have happened to anyone.*

I've made my mind up, Syd, she sent, quiet and serene. *You can't stop me.*

You didn't want this job in the first place. I really had to accuse her of quitting now?

Femke just smiled at me in all gentleness. *I love you,* she sent. *My best friend, my sister. Let me rest.*

That cut everything short, didn't it? I nodded, sat back, looked away. And let her have what she needed, because I couldn't have it myself. And that was the real reason I was angry, wasn't it? She got to be free. And I got to die.

Awesome.

My people, Femke sent out across the network, no longer speaking aloud for our benefit, *I have served you to the best of my ability. But my time is done. I am stepping down officially as WPC leader and ask that you honor my decision without argument or any attempt to convince me otherwise.* Crickets answered, total silence. The assholes. That just made me angrier. She'd almost lost her soul for them and not one of them spoke up.

We'd see about that.

You are the best thing that happened to this council, I sent. *And your steady strength and brilliant mind will be missed. We are lesser for losing you.*

Murmurs of agreement down the line. Jerkfaces.

I am aware we cannot be without a leader while a new one is elected, she sent. *But it will take some time to find the right person for the job.* Mom tensed next to me. I think we both knew what was coming. *I would ask the esteemed North American Council Leader, Miriam Hayle, to fill in my place on an interim basis while a new permanent leader is debated.*

I should kick your ass, child, Mom sent on a tight beam I caught the edge of only because I was sitting beside her.

I'm sorry, Miriam, Femke sent. *But I just can't carry this now. And you've sat in this chair before. I trust no one else to do what's right.*

Mom relented immediately. *I'm honored by the appointment,* she sent plane wide, not a trace of the weariness showing on her face ending up in the message. *Nominations for the new leader will begin immediately.*

TWENTY-FIVE

I left Mom to her new old job—temporary, my ass—knowing she had a ton of things to do that had absolutely nothing to do with me. And while I knew, now Femke was whole again and the WPC in safe hands, I was free to focus on my own impending doom, I wasn't satisfied with this particular ending.

I caught up with Femke in her quarters, packing. It was pretty obvious from the organized piles of her belongings she'd known from the moment she regained control of herself this was her plan. She looked up when I peeking in her door after knocking and being welcomed, waving me inside while her magic sorted a pile of neatly folded blouses into a large, black suitcase.

As the familiar silk settled into place, her face crumpled at last. Both of her hands rose, covered her gaping mouth and eyes squeezed shut, her narrow shoulders shaking as she bowed her head and wept. I went to her immediately, not knowing what to do or say, only to have her drop her hands and grasp me tightly to her, body taller and leaner than mine clinging with physical strength and magic.

Syd. Her mental voice wailed. *Oh my elements. Syd.*

I cried on her shoulder, hugging her back, shaking with her as she emptied her grief on me. And let her, welcomed the punishment of it though I was sure that wasn't her intent. I felt honored when I was able to process she felt comfortable with me and me alone to let all of her hurt and terror out at last. Knowing I was, in part, responsible for the state she found herself in wasn't helping me any and taking on the brunt of her agony felt like penance.

Femke finally leaned back, drawing several shaking breaths, her hands wiping at the wetness on her cheeks, pushing her blonde hair back from her narrow face. She sank into a pristine white chair, the leather sighing under her as she did. I sat next to her, hands folded in my lap, feeling ineffectual and lost while she pulled herself together.

"I don't want to talk about it," she whispered. "Not yet. Maybe one day. For now..." she stared out the window, the last of her tears drying on her pale cheeks. "For now, thank you. Though, I would have been grateful to die."

"I couldn't," I choked. "I just couldn't let you go."

She spun toward me, grasped my hands. "I'm not blaming you," she said. "I would have done the very same thing, so stop that at once."

I nodded, looked away, stared at the fluffy white carpet under my scuffed sneakers.

"I just need to get away from this place." She inhaled, voice catching. "I thought I was strong enough, Syd. I was wrong."

Denial almost smothered me. "You survived," I said. "Most wouldn't have. You held on, Femke. No one could ask for more than that."

She shrugged, sat back, seeming to relax. "If survival is success," she said, "our bar is too low."

"And yet," I said, meeting her eyes again, "I'm grateful for it."

Femke smiled at me, fresh and young looking again, reminding me of the optimistic and outgoing woman I'd first met so long ago.

"Don't hate me for running away when you can't." She must have known what I'd been thinking, involuntary or not. "You're not done, are you?"

I didn't have to answer. Just stared back at her. Because if I opened my mouth I'd tell her I was going to die. And she didn't need that, not now. Not when I wouldn't allow her that fate.

"Where will you go?" I cleared my throat and tried to

feel good for her. To do what was the right thing for my friend.

Her smile widened a little. "Home to Sweden and my family," she said.

Why did it seem so strange to find out she had a family? But of course she did, a coven, likely relatives who loved her. I felt suddenly on the outside of her real life, of everyone and everything with the acknowledgement I only thought I knew those I cared about. But I hadn't even taken the time to ask her, in the good times, such a basic question.

Femke leaned close, touched my cheek. "I meant what I said," she whispered. "Sister, best friend. Family, more than my own blood has been. Even if we've only been so thanks to our power, we have come through so much together I can't imagine my life without you."

More tears. I was used to them by now. Certainly wouldn't be the last ones I shed before the end.

There wasn't much more to say aside from the platitudes I knew were coming. Stay in touch seemed such a useless sentiment, something I knew we might do once, maybe twice—if I had that long—before we fell out of each other's lives forever. I left her to finish packing, pale but bright again, and wished Femke well in my heart.

I returned to Mom, not sure how I was feeling, to find her firmly ensconced behind her new desk. I went immediately to the tall, handsome man who sat next to her taking notes with a magic pen and hugged my dad while he kissed my forehead, his writing utensil still scratching away without his help.

"Cupcake," he murmured. "You're okay?"

I nodded and shrugged. "Just said goodbye to Femke." It felt so sudden, so final. Things weren't supposed to happen this way. I was going to heal her, abolish Konstantin and save her. And then she'd be back and we'd be business as usual.

I should have known better than to rely on my expectations.

"Your mother has asked Karyn Barrett to take over as NAWC Leader in the interim," Dad said.

Bless him for changing the subject. "Perfect choice."

Mom's blank expression refocused as she ended her distant conversation and nodded to me. "The only one, really," she said. "I'm thinking at this point we'll make it permanent, no matter how the WPC leadership turns out."

"You want to retire?" I hardly blamed her. She'd done so once before and had been sucked back into power thanks to Erica's betrayal.

Mom made a face, nose wrinkling, before she shrugged with a smile. "I know better than to try to dodge my responsibilities. If I end up in this seat for a while, I want someone I can trust back home taking care of things."

"Will anyone try to contest her?" Mom's changes to the council meant all covens had equal say. Would that muddy up succession?

"They'd better not." Dad laughed and winked at Mom. "Miriam's made it very clear she wants Karyn in that seat. *Very* clear."

Mom blinked, all innocence. "Just a suggestion, Harry."

I snorted. "Sure, Mom. Millions would buy that."

Mom laughed then, sat back in her seat, no longer looking tired but invigorated and I knew then this was the right thing after all. I could stop worrying at last. Turn things over to her and do what I had to do.

"Speaking of responsibility," I said, "I guess I should go." I hesitated, thought about the dream. I had no idea how much time there was between this moment and my end, though from the steady worsening of the wrongness growing inside me time had to be short. Mom and Dad needed to know something was coming. I'd warned them, yes. But they didn't know details. Should I unload it on them now? Or wait knowing it would likely be too late by then?

"Keep us posted." Mom was already gone again, face blanking as she carried on her new job. Dad's curiosity lingered, but I knew she needed him more than I did. I told myself there would be time later, no matter my paranoia. I hoped. For now, let them feel like they had everything under control.

Gave me a bit of peace of mind, too.

I kissed his cheek and left, stepping into the veil and hovering in the dimness, gaze travelling out over the endless lines of barriers between planes while I tried to figure out what to do next.

The maji have to be our next objective, my vampire sent.

Damned maji, my demon sent. *We should just burst their damned bubble and let them implode on their damned selves.*

You know, Shaylee sent, thoughtful, *that might not be a bad idea.*

Burst the bubble. I tensed, thought about it. *Is that even possible?*

I was kidding, my demon sent. *But let's think about this a second.*

You're talking about rupturing the edges of a Universe, my vampire sent.

So? My demon chuffed at her.

I didn't say it was a bad idea, my vampire sent, cool and calm. *Just that it's a huge thing to consider.*

What would bursting it do? I had no idea.

I think that's a question for Iepa, my vampire sent.

Or the drach? Shaylee hesitated. *We need to find out what to do about Max, Syd. He's still in the visions.*

True enough, my demon sent. *But how? He's quit on us.*

Perhaps not quite yet. My vampire fell silent a moment then sighed. *First Max*, she sent, *then Iepa.*

And then? I reached for the veil, heading for the Stronghold. I knew she wouldn't have an answer for me, it was just nice to have them sort things out and follow orders for once.

And then, Sydlynn Hayle, she sent with quiet intensity, *we find out what we're made of.*

TWENTY-SIX

I greeted the Stronghold as I stepped through into the undercavern.

Light One, he sent, the deep, rumbling of his mental voice crushed rock. *I am pleased to see you, as always.*

You, too. I hesitated, stared at the statue of the drach lord I'd come to see, hated how much it hurt he'd given up on me the way he had. And yet, could I blame him, ultimately? He'd paid such a massive price for our last victory. He had to have believed it was over to take such a step as this. Still.

Still.

The drach lord sleeps. The Stronghold sounded sad.

He's not dead? Damn you, hope. Take a hike. I didn't need it churning me up inside right now.

Ah, the massive pile of rock that was the building I stood beneath sighed. *What I call sleep you might interpret as death?* He seemed confused. *Mortal ways are so different from mine.*

I crossed slowly to Max, stared up at the blank grayness of his solidified form. *Is he in there yet?*

He lingers, the Stronghold sent. *But his time grows short.*

I stroked the black ribbon on my wrist. *Can you help him?*

The soul that was Max from the other Universe shivered before falling still. So no, obviously. This had been a waste of time. I needed to come, though, to see Max on my own, without others hovering. On impulse, heart aching, I clambered up and into his lap, resting my head on his cold, hard shoulder.

I miss you. I sent that as far within as I could, knowing it didn't matter, that he was lost to me but wanting him to know. Especially after my outburst the last time I was here. *I don't know if I can do this without you.*

And then, the floodgates opening, I told him everything. About the dreams, Femke, Oliver. My fear of forever and the near relief I felt that it might be over before too long. Honestly, I'd never had a craving to end my life. But this felt like the only solution, like fate had caught up with me at last. *I need you,* I sent, desperate and small. *Now more than ever. We're supposed to go out together, in a blaze of glory or some other cliché.* No whisper of response, nothing that told me he'd heard. Didn't matter. I wiped at my running nose, at the tears that wet his stone shoulder, sighed out what remained of my stress until I sagged there, empty and spent and so, so weary.

I guess I'll just carry on then, I sent to him. Patted his knee and slid down. *Be well on the other side, my friend. You've earned your rest.*

I stood there a moment, looking up at him. And felt the veil part, the presence of Oliver, his hands on my shoulders.

"The dream, the vision," he said. "Maybe Max had it, too. And this is his solution, to keep you safe."

I hadn't thought of that. That would be like Max in some ways, and nothing like him in others. I turned and reached up on my tiptoes, kissing Oliver softly on the mouth before shrugging and offering a small smile.

"If I've learned anything," I said, "fate will find a way, regardless of what I want."

Oliver embraced me, kissing me again. *I won't let you go.*

When the time comes, I sent, *you won't have a choice.*

Insistent, those lips of his, the need in him, his heart wide open to me. I let him have my own in return, allowing this connection despite knowing how much it would hurt him when I had to go. Because I'd be going. I'd never felt so sure of anything in my entire life.

When we parted, I was surprised to find we weren't alone and felt a tiny twinge of guilt I squashed instantly. Quaid observed us with a hearty frown. That helped, his jealousy. He didn't get to judge me.

Oliver grinned, arm draped over my shoulder as he nodded to my ex-husband. "Still free and clear, I see."

Quaid's lips quirked, anger flaring visibly a moment before he focused on me. "Miriam pardoned me," he said.

"I'm glad." I leaned on Oliver, knowing it wasn't fair to use him against Quaid but so over his whole childish protective possessiveness. "Payten and the babies need you. And Ethie."

He flinched slightly, my purposeful jab hitting home. Just seemed to make him more irritated. "I should be in prison."

Oh. My. Swearword. I smacked him with magic. He jerked back, shocked.

"That," I said, "is the last time you get to say that out loud."

Quaid shrugged. "Payten's a Hayle, now. The girls." There was a question in his voice. He seemed uncomfortable, glancing with the barest of attention in Oliver's direction. But I wasn't giving him an out. He had to face this like an adult.

"Gram admitted them into the coven," I said. "I'm sure she'll recreate your bond if you're willing."

He didn't say anything but I could feel the hum of relief running under his magic. What, he thought I'd fight it?

"I'm not an Enforcer anymore," he said, looking away, hands in his pockets, powerful body tense but at rest. What an odd conversation.

You realize, Oliver sent, *there's likely things between the two of you that you don't remember.*

Sorry? I glanced up at him.

Two Universes, he sent, sounding empathetic toward Quaid. *In mine, Ameline killed you, remember? So who knows what the combination has done to his memories of your time together.*

Okay, so I hadn't actually considered that fact. It definitely softened me toward my ex-husband and sent me forward to hug him. Quaid reacted with tension before hugging me back.

I'm sorry, I sent.

I'm not. He seemed more content now I'd let him in. *I made mistakes, so many, Syd. But you were right. I just couldn't handle being in your shadow.*

So, our history was far more like I remembered than happened on Oliver's side.

Quaid let me go, frown mostly vanished, smirk returned as he addressed the Order soldier. "I hope you know what you're getting yourself into," he said. "She's a handful."

"I love her," Oliver said, simple and direct. "She's my partner. She's perfect."

Quaid's mouth opened, a flare of anger returning

before he closed it again, shrugged. "You're a better man than me, then," he said.

Wow. Just wow.

Syd...lynn.

All thoughts of Oliver and Quaid, of tracking down Iepa vanished in a flash of fear. I knew that mind, latched onto her touch, shocked at how weak Moa felt. The vampire Empress's magic was so powerful, usually. But even as I reached for her, I felt her slipping.

The veil parted at the command of my vampire and sent me lurching through into Moa's bedchamber in Nepal, Oliver and Quaid hurrying after me as if nothing had happened between the three of us. For now, it didn't matter. Not when I found the Empress collapsed on the stone floor, her withered body seemingly lifeless, three vampires scattered around her like limp dolls tossed aside. I fell to my knees beside her, my hands grasping her face, feeling the faintest flutter of her as her soul and power continued to drain from her.

Just like Iepa's had. By whom? I tried to dive after the exodus but her black eyes opened, the dark, shining buttons commanding me with the last of her strength to stay, to be with her. And, in that instant, she cracked open her soul and thrust upon me the fragment of the vampire essence she'd managed to hide from whoever attacked her.

I gasped as it returned, my vampire trying to give it

back, but Moa's eyes flickered, the spark within her going out as she exhaled a slow, rattling breath. Even as I held her, the ancient form that was her physical body sighed and shuddered, turning to dust in my hands. I stared in shock, the powdered remains sifting through my grasping fingers while my vampire keened softly in the back of my mind.

My daughter, she whispered. *Who has done this to you?*

Someone giggled. My head snapped up, gaze locking on Batsheva Moromond. She huddled, pale and trembling, beside Moa's bed, cowering with the heavy curtains pulled around her. How had she survived? Because it was clear the other vampires in the room were dead like their Empress.

"Who?" I threw the question at her, hit her with it. Batsheva flinched and giggled again, hysterical.

"You know who." Singsong, those three words.

And I did. My vampire howled her grief as we all felt her, the former Fate, tied to Batsheva. That, through her, Bellanca had killed the oldest living vampire.

The former Fate's presence fled before I could chase her, like I had a choice. My vampire drove me to my feet, lunged for Batsheva. She shrieked her fear, trying to backpedal away, to escape me, fangs appearing, skin whitening as she called on spirit magic in a desperate attempt to buy herself space to flee. But there was no escape this time. Never again.

It wasn't lost on me this was my fault. I'd let Batsheva live only a short time ago, as I had too many times before. Should have been more curious as to why she remembered what she should have forgotten. And realized she remained connected to someone who had the power to sustain her memories before the Universes came together.

My vampire didn't seem to care about any of that. Rage like I'd never felt from her, icy hot and devouring, poured through her and into me. "I should have done this long ago." She snarled her words through my mouth. And tore open the veil.

The glare from the other side of the slice burned my eyes, heated even my insensitive skin as four suns beat down over a barren, dusty landscape. With determined intent, my hands her tools, my vampire latched onto Batsheva's quivering body and threw her bodily through the gash. My old enemy skidded on her hands and knees in the sand of the blasted plain, puffs of dust rising around her red velvet dress. She screamed as the heat hit her, but didn't burn up.

She won't, my vampire sent, grim and furious. *Not right away. White sorcery has seen to that.* Batsheva began crawling toward the gap, body shaking, mouth gaping wide as she wailed her denial. Faint tendrils of smoke began to rise from her exposed skin, darkening patches turning red almost immediately. *She will die, eventually. Alone. After suffering a long, long time.*

I didn't get to argue. My vampire's power sealed the slash in the veil in one abrupt motion, cutting off Batsheva's cry and leaving the room silent as death.

So be it, my demon whispered, shaken but clearly in agreement.

Now, Shaylee sent, grim and furious, *we go tear Bellanca into tiny pieces and feed her to demon.*

Yum, my demon sent.

"Syd." Oliver's grim tone turned me around. He and Quaid watched me, my ex-husband with a faint green tint to his skin but a satisfied look on his face. We had, after all, just banished his adoptive mother to a fate worse than death. Since he hated her about as much as I did, I knew he wouldn't protest. But his unease just made me sad. Was I really that cold hearted I felt Batsheva deserved such a fate?

Oliver, on the other hand, just looked worried. About me, probably. "Bellanca?"

I nodded. "Nice guess." I reached for her, trying to find her. She must have fled back into the bubble protecting the maji. But I'd be ready for her the next time she came into my Universe.

So ready.

Oliver shook his head, confusion mingling with his concern. "Why?"

"Why what?" My hands shook, an aftereffect of the

last few minutes. Dear elements, was it only a few minutes?

"Why attack Moa?" He looked down at the faint outline of her form, the dust disintegrating further. Time finally had its way with the vampire Empress. "What end does her death serve?"

Excellent question, my vampire sent. She sounded calm again, level. She never failed to amaze me at her ability to recover. *One we should find an answer for?*

Why? I sounded like a repeating meme. But she was right. There had to be a reason.

We didn't get to talk it out, at least not right then. Because Shaylee suddenly screamed inside my head, her power reaching out in a whip crack of terror.

MOTHER!

TWENTY-SEVEN

I knew as I dove with Shaylee in control back through the veil her mother was under attack. It felt exactly the same as the power draw on Moa had, Bellanca's transfer of interest so fast it made my head spin. She was clearly making her move and had no intentions of letting me stop her.

Despite following me my whole life as Fate, she had no idea who she was dealing with.

We tore through the veil into the magical clearing where Aoilainn held court. The green lawn flooded with Sidhe fighting maji as more of the second race poured into the opening of the white tent where the Sidhe queen and her following stood their ground. Aoilainn and her consort, Padraic, King Ohdran and Queen Niamh of the Unseelie battled their attackers, the ground beneath them rumbling with their fury.

This was the first time I understood the ineffectual nature of Sidhe power. Yes, they were connected to the earth and had control of that element. But the bulk of their ability lay in glamour and misdirection, not in direct response. As I allowed Shaylee to push me through the crowd of fighting Seelie, Unseelie and maji and toward the pavilion, I knew my alter ego's people didn't stand a chance.

Not unless I could put an end to this here and now.

Aoilainn's grasping magic broke loose as something—a dark and devouring power—sucked her almost dry in a huge heave of intake. Bellanca spun with a snarl in my direction where she hunched on the steps to the pavilion, her fury at my arrival holding no surprise. So she expected the Sidhe queen to call on her daughter in her moment of need.

Be cautious. Oliver's warning wasn't protective but honest. *She has a plan, Syd. And I worry it involves you.*

We'd just see about that.

But it wasn't up to me right then. Not when the three souls living inside me, sharing my space, bonded together without my assistance and slammed their combined magic into the former Fate's chest. She staggered from the blow, shocked now, almost fearful as she backed away from the gasping Aoilainn. Shaylee's mother pressed a shaking hand to her bone thin chest, the true visage of the Sidhe showing now she had no glamor to hide her. I'd seen the sharp pointed ears and long, thin face before, the preternaturally glowing eyes, the transparent skin. That didn't bother me, not even a little. What troubled me was the terror on the queen's face.

I'd never seen her afraid of anything before.

"How did you do that?" Bellanca's people fled behind me as Oliver's white sorcery, the mighty power of the Order, cut them off from their easy prey and sent them scurrying like the rats they were. But Bellanca didn't leave. She stood there and stared at me like she'd never seen me before and had no idea where I'd come from.

"There's more," I said, false cheer bubbling. "Care to find out?"

It could have ended then and there, should have. Except for the courage and foolish honor of the Unseelie King. Ohdran, his power returning, spun on Bellanca and lashed at her with earth magic. That caught her attention, but only as an irritation. She swatted at him, knocking him to his knees, one hand falling on his shoulder as Niamh cried out and dove for him.

Too late. Bellanca waved one hand, blackness engulfing them while I tried to stop her. Tried but failed because I had no idea—none—what she'd just done.

Stay out of my way, she sent, the darkness engulfing her and carrying her away, taking the remaining attacking maji with her.

Not a chance. I panted, glaring, fight over as quickly as it had begun while the Unseelie queen shrieked her fury at the sky.

Oliver rushed to my side, hand on my elbow a little tighter than he likely intended. But his gray eyes were alight and from the excited feeling of him, he had good news. I could use some right about now.

I know how she's doing it. He practically chortled in my mind. And showed me.

Sorcery. Not the white stuff we'd become accustomed to, but the deep, black flowering of power I'd discovered inside myself all those years ago, the power that thwarted and aided me more times than I could recall. Oliver wasn't done, pushing me deeper inside the power. And to the answer.

"She's splitting it." Sorcery. She was using Max's mistake as a tool. He'd once split the first power into its base elements by accident and forced Creator to make a new Universe where Her Dark Brother, formed of the split, ruled. Bellanca had figured out how the drach lord did it. Only she was harnessing that power to her own ends.

"More than that," Oliver said. "Every time she does it she reinforces the break between the two new Universes—ours and the one she made to separate the maji from us."

"She's building a bomb," I whispered.

He nodded, elation at understanding gone. "If she keeps this up," he said, "if she tries to reconnect the two at any point…"

"We're all dead." She had to know. Didn't she?

"But why is she attacking other races?" That didn't make sense. I watched Aoilainn recover, regaining her stunning beauty and, to my shock, watched her cross to Niamh and begin to comfort her fellow queen. The Sidhe quickly restored their glamor, any hint of a battle disappearing with the vanished maji. Appearances, at a time like this? If that made Aoilainn feel better, fine. Her realm, her rules. But I would have thought she'd have more important things to think about.

Then, sadly, Shaylee sent, *you've overestimated my mother.*

Oliver clearly heard her words, but forged on with his own conversation anyway. "Bellanca is attacking to take their power," he said. "The more she has, the easier it is for her to cross over?" He shook his head. "I still don't have it entirely, but I'm sure of one thing. If she's allowed to finish what she's starting, she and the maji might think they are building a new Universe in their own image, but they will only end up destroying everything."

Over my dead body. Yeah. There was that.

And then, my heart stopped. "That means—" Faces flashed in my head, people I loved. So many, too many. Piers, as master of the Sorcerers League. Charlotte, queen of the werenation. Gram, Hayle coven leader—

Scotland and the castle first, my only choice when Piers failed to answer my call. I staggered into his personal quarters, leaping forward to crush the woman who hovered over his still and silent form.

Eva Southway shrank from me, weeping as she wrung her hands in my face. Not the reaction I was expecting, to be honest. She fell into my arms, shaking and sobbing while Oliver crouched next to Piers who sprawled on his bed, pale but breathing.

"He'll be okay," my Order (boy)friend said. "We got here just in time."

I should have been throttling Eva or crushing her heart or at least calling for Mom to arrest her. Instead, I held her while she choked out the last of her anxiety riddled grief before meeting my gaze with hers.

"Syd," she said in her British accent, all arrogance and madness gone. "It wasn't me."

Who attacked Piers? I shrugged. But she wasn't done.

"All this time." She whispered those words like a curse, sagging into me again, mouth gaping as she fought to breathe past her sobbing. When she straightened again, her eyes bulged with loathing and regret. "All this time."

Dear elements. "Eva," I said. "Who's been controlling you?"

The door burst open and Piers's sister, Clover, rushed inside. I watched as something snapped inside Eva, jerked her free of her own will and spun her on the terrified young woman whose only thought was her fallen brother.

I'd been slow lately, missed a lot. Failed many. And today was no exception. I didn't understand just how far Bellanca would go. Because it was Bellanca, there was no mistake. I could feel her, traces of her everywhere in Eva. As clear to me as the now near constant discomfort I was forced to shunt aside and live with. Perhaps it had been Liander Belaisle who stole Eva's free will in the first place. But the previous Light Fate, she was the present owner of Eva's soul.

With a snarl of pure hate, the former Steam Union leader under the geas of an old and bitter maji lashed out at Clover Southway and struck her heavily with black power, slamming her into the stone wall with crushing force. I smothered Eva's magic, too late—always too late—even as Clover went limp and slid to the ground with blood gushing from her open mouth and nose.

I will never hear such denial in a single scream as I did then. The piercing, deafening loss that emerged from Eva tore a giant hole in my own heart. She staggered from me. I felt her pull free of Bellanca, grief so powerful it cut the cord of control with a violence that had to hurt the former Fate on the other end when it recoiled back to her. I had that small comfort as Eva fell to her knees beside her daughter. I could see there was no hope, that Clover was dead, likely on impact. There was nothing I could do, not even when Piers's eyes opened, fluttering first before he woke with a start, upright an instant later.

And stared, open mouthed and shocked at his mother rocking, rocking, the dead body of his sister.

I didn't get to grieve for him. Because, in that instant, nothing mattered but the woman reaching across the miles to me, her own life draining away so fast I barely had time to draw breath.

Syd!

MOM.

TWENTY-EIGHT

Too late. Too late.

Too. Damned. Late.

I knew it as I tore at the veil. I knew it while a shriek so powerful I would never contain it built in my chest. I knew it even as I slipped and slid my way out the gap, across the floor, landing on my knees at her side.

Too late. Oh, Mom, how could I be too late? For you of all people.

Fate, so cruel. So heartless.

Miriam Hayle was dead.

No. This couldn't be right. I had to be mistaken. My mother, my beautiful, amazing, incredible, talented, powerful mother...

I grasped her to me, clinging to her, power diving inside her, searching for her, begging her to come back.

Echoing empty nothing answered.

Nothing.

The room flooded with people, Dad crashing to the floor next to me, but I held him off with a snarl of fury, forcing him to hug both of us, tears pouring down his face.

No. No. No.

I was supposed to die. NOT MY MOTHER.

It had to be there somewhere. Out there. Her soul. And I was going to find it. Because, even if it meant my life right here and now, this I would never, ever accept. I was forced to watch my true love die. To let my son go. To choose to give my own life to save the Universe. But I would not let Fate take my mother. Especially not a false Fate who I would tear into tiny pieces and grind into nothing before I used every last scrap of my power to erase her from memory—

MOM. I dove in again, searching. Her echo I could find, I was sure of that. But her soul was another story, wasn't it? Further and further I went, deeper and past any point of return. Until I fell, head first, into the void and understood at last just what it was.

What the void between the veil and the Universe really was.

And screamed for her with everything I had.

Nothing. It couldn't be nothing. She had to be there, she had to be.

Girl. Gram was there, hands grasping mine, Dad's power feeding us. Then Oliver and Quaid and, in layers, the souls of the room. All pouring power into me, into that cry for Mom to come back to us.

I don't know how it happened, who reached out first beyond our group, beyond Hong Kong. But I felt them come through the alter egos within me. First the Sidhe, led by Aoilainn of all Seelie, then the Order patched into Oliver through his mother. Sunny and Sebastian, Frank and all the vampires turned Order themselves, flooding me with as much magic as I could take. I grew vast, gigantic, while the demons leaped to action, Meira and the pulse of Ahbi Sanghamitra in the Node of Demonicon while my sister wept and begged our mother to come back.

Come back. Please, Mom. Please, just come back to me.

Sassafras and the drach, Jiao and her *lóng* family, all that remained of the drachmor. Mabel's first race power tied into the Stronghold itself. Calling, weeping, pleading for Mom.

The touch of Mia and Zoe. Of Trill Zornov.

And then, the heart of one I loved more than life. Gabriel.

Mom, he whispered. *All you need is this.*

He showed me and I caught it, the thread of white sorcery that held my mother to me. I yanked on it, as hard as I could, supported and fed by every paranormal power on our plane and beyond as the races of magic combined together to save Miriam Hayle.

Not even death, Gabriel smiled in my mind. *You knew it when you shared it with her originally.*

I did, I remembered. Not even death could break that connection.

Mom inhaled, slow and quiet, as if waking from sleep, not this incredible feat of coming back to life, to me. To us. The room erupted into massive cheers, the entire Universe celebrating, it seemed, after a long, hurt moment of worry this wasn't real, as if Mom blinking and smiling up at me was a dream.

"Syd," she said. "Hello, sweetheart."

I hugged her tight, rocked her as I'd seen Eva rock Clover, though my ending was happier than I ever believed it could be.

Bellanca, Mom sent, sounding slightly confused. *I only remember she appeared and then everything went dark.*

She didn't have to tell me who was behind this, but the confirmation was good to have. I didn't have time to sit here on the floor and hug my mother, but I couldn't bring myself to let her go just yet, especially when Meira appeared in a flare of amber fire and leaped on us, Sass wiggling his silver Persian body between us, Dad hugging me and Mom and Meems and Gram who forced herself into the bubble of Hayle joy no one dared interfere with in that moment.

Just let them try.

I finally sighed, sniffing as Piers gently, sadly, prodded my mind.

I'm sorry, I sent.

So am I, he sent. *I'm just grateful we could save Miriam.* He helped, of course he did. Even in the face of losing his own sister. I didn't get to say more. *Mother wants to talk to you.*

And I wanted to talk to her. I released my family, shaking and exhausted from the emotional strain but feeling more connected and even more powerful than ever. From the grins and tears and group hugging going on between the Sidhe, witches, Enforcers and various others crowding the office, I wasn't the only one.

We accomplished the impossible. We saved Mom from death itself. Let's just see if Bellanca could top that.

Mom hugged me fiercely before leaning away with an odd look on her face. *Syd*, she sent privately. *One question before you go.*

I nodded.

Who is Gabriel and why did he tell me he loved me?

I couldn't answer. Shook my head at her, kissed her cheek. And left with my heart aching in my chest.

TWENTY-NINE

I wasn't in a very good state of mind when I returned to Scotland, Oliver beside me. Maybe I should have been feeling better than I was. After all, we as a collective had prevented the loss of one of my absolute favorite people in the entirety of creation.

And yet, there was still this crapshow to face, wasn't there? Still Bellanca and the damned maji to deal with. Still my own end to ponder and anticipate.

How would my mother feel if she knew it would be her turn to argue with death soon?

That's where my head was, then, when I stepped through the veil and into a small stone room in what felt like the heart and possibly bowels of the castle in Scotland. No windows, a single door. Wait, yes, I knew this place. I grimaced at Piers who simply nodded as I realized this was the room where Liander Belaisle trapped the ribbon souls of the drach.

I just loved it when things came full circle.

Eva hunched in a chair, shoulders bowed, face in her hands while her son glared at her with what looked like an equal measure of evil amusement and hurt no one would ever find a way to heal. I went to him first, squeezing Demetrius's hand on the way by. My grandfather for all intents and purposes squeezed back and let me go.

But Piers stepped away from me when I drew close. I knew better than to push him, to push this. And spun, standing at his side, to face his weeping mother.

"Eva." My tone was softer than I expected. The empathy in it surprised me, though the fact my vampire cleared her throat in my mind told me I wasn't completely in charge of this conversation.

Softly, she sent. *You'll get more from her with kindness at this point.*

Kindness she didn't deserve? And yet, if Eva was to be believed it was likely, similarly to Femke, she'd been under control of others and not able to stop what happened.

On the other hand, I was pretty sure Piers's mother had a bit of an ego issue in the first place that led her to this end. Rather than being kidnapped and forced into it, more likely she'd chosen it, if subtly, from day one.

Still, no one deserved to be used as she had, to be the cause of her own child's death. I thought of Gabriel and the choice I was forced to make and crumbled a little inside. Not the same. But, damn it, I was a mother. I got it.

I did.

Eva didn't try to excuse what happened. She looked up, met my eyes with her own pale ones and grimaced.

"You have to stop her." Her voice shook, her hands, too. She gripped her knees like it was the only thing keeping her together. "Bellanca."

"What have you done, Mother?" Piers's tone was so cold and purposely hurtful I hissed at him before putting myself between the Sorcerer League leader and his mom.

"Eva," I said, crouching in front of her. "Tell me what she's doing."

Oliver's tall body leaned closer, face tight in a frown as she spoke.

"She's gathering power," Eva said. I resisted the urge to mutter "duh" as she went on. "From the strongest of every race. Or as near to it as she can reach."

A moment of panic hit me when I realized there could be people out there right now falling to her and I was here, talking, listening. I'm certain every single person I cared about immediately felt it when I grasped their connective threads and tugged to be sure they were okay as Oliver spoke.

"Why?" Oliver's soft interjection didn't seem to trouble Eva. She remained focused on me.

"She needs it to access this Universe when the time comes." She what? "To weaken the edge of the veil and split it so her new Universe can connect."

"That will destroy us all," Oliver said without judgment, sadly, even.

Eva sobbed once, rocking forward. "I think she knows that." What was she up to? "But that's what she told Zeon, the plan. She's been feeding him lies all along." Eva gulped some air, hugged herself now. "The dark maji are starting to question, Trinol and his people not believing her any longer. Partly because Thanos has been challenging his sister."

Trouble in former Fate paradise. And nothing Iepa hadn't already told me. "But she wants that, too." The blood of the maji would be on my hands…

"Zeon wants your son removed as Creator," Eva said, barely a whisper. "The old Creator's betrayal will be repaid in the end of this Universe as he and the maji create their own, new truth."

"But that won't happen," I said.

"I believe Bellanca is purposely playing both sides against each other." Eva choked on that. "Liander does, too."

Belaisle was with Bellanca? Damn it, when would I be rid of the old Brotherhood leader?

"Is he trying to stop her?" Maybe he'd be helpful for once.

Eva looked away. "No," she said. "He's still under the belief that if Bellanca succeeds, it will bring back his Master."

Oliver gasped but shook his head at me in apology. *Dark Brother is gone*, he sent. *Isn't he?*

I had no idea. But there was someone—two someones—I could call on to ask. And they'd damned well better be in a talking mood.

But when Zoe Helios and Mia Dumont appeared, I knew I was out of luck. The fact they came at my call was telling despite their downcast faces and clear confusion.

"We've got nothing." Mia's frustration matched mine. Right. Because catching any kind of break had to be written out of the rule book by now.

"All we can see," Zoe said, "is the end. Over and over." Her face twisted slightly, tears in her eyes while her Fate sister comforted her with a hand on her arm.

"You know the end we mean." Mia's blue eyes held sadness and regret.

I nodded. "That doesn't matter right now," I said, a bit brusque. I really wasn't in the mood for compassion from the Fates. We all knew choices were slim pickings at this stage in the game. "Time to reconnoiter, though." I glanced at Piers. "Who's left to attack?"

"The Order," Oliver answered for him. "And the drach."

"What about the werewolves?" Demetrius finally

spoke, cocking his head to one side. "Charlotte is fine, by the way."

We hadn't spoken since Danilo took over Konstantin's soul. I'd have to find time to mend fences with her before this was over. Since it would be the last chance I had to make amends for turning her brother into a receptacle of evil. I reached for Sebastian while I felt Oliver's power connect with his mother.

We're fine, the former DeWinter Blood Clan leader sent. *Grateful for the return of Miriam.*

Thanks for that, I sent. *Just stay alert. It's possible she'll come for you next.*

Oliver shook his head to me when I refocused on the room and its inhabitants.

"Nothing," he said. "Maybe she's done."

"I'll believe that when she's dead and burned to ashes under my feet," I said.

THIRTY

I sat in Mom's new office, the setting sun casting long shadows over the interior of the space, glass glowing in that almost supernatural way it had when the sun hit it just right. I stared into the red horizon, knowing it foretold a good day tomorrow, that color. And wondering if I'd get to see it.

Morbid much?

Mom circled to my side, sitting in one of the white leather seats, handing me a cup of coffee while she sighed and leaned back. She'd been dead just a few hours ago. Dead, gone, soul missing, just a shell of a corpse left behind. And here she was breathing, cheeks glowing softly in the light of the sunset, as beautiful and powerful as ever.

Were those new lines around her eyes, though? More threads of white in her lustrous black hair? Had dying made any impact on her or was I the only one who felt a tightening choke hold of terror at the thought of her lying there on the floor, lost to me?

Mom leaned in, touched my cheek with her fingertips. She must have known I was in a terrible frame of mind because she smiled in that kind way she had, the Mom way that made me feel better when I had no right to. "Stop," she said.

I nodded, cleared my throat, sat up a little straighter. "Right," I said. "Just stop thinking about the fact I almost lost you. Okay then."

She chuckled, ran one hand through her full curls, face calm and relaxed as she took her turn gazing into the setting sun. "I don't feel any different," she said. "I barely remember it."

Probably for the best. Now, how did I tell her it was going to be my turn soon?

"I love you." I choked on the words, knowing this was the only goodbye I was going to get. The discomfort within was so constant now, so real I couldn't ignore it or the obvious message behind it. My time was close, so close. And there was no way I was going to dump what was coming on my mother. She'd argue and stress and fight, only to end up in the same place with me gone and her left to pick up the pieces. Maybe that wasn't fair of me, but I wanted my last memories with her to be like this. Quiet, peaceful. As painful as it was, this was right.

Mom's eyes moistened, her smile growing. "Sweetheart," she said, her own voice thick. "I'm the luckiest mother in the entirety of the Universe."

I leaned in, kissed her in the same spot on her own cheek where she'd touched mine. Sat back with my chest crushing me under the weight of my sorrow and stood abruptly, so much so she started before joining me.

"Syd," she said, coffee set aside, mine already discarded untasted. "Something else is going on."

I shrugged, hugged her. Couldn't speak. And left her there, the veil engulfing me when I plunged like the coward I was into the dimness of its embrace and left her behind.

Fate pressed in on me, the nearness of my ending like a living thing that whispered in my ear.

Better say our other goodbyes, then, my demon sent, all strong and blustering.

I wasn't the only one to see past her act. Shaylee embraced all of us before sighing herself, much as Mom had. *It's been wonderful*, she sent.

We're not done yet, my vampire chided them gently. But she didn't argue with me when I reached for Demonicon and crossed to Meira's office.

Hugs, tears, whispers of support and love passed between me and my sister. I didn't linger though she wanted me to. I had others to see, to embrace. Uncle Frank and Sunny, Sebastian himself. Piers Southway, though he barely noticed I was there, I think.

So many souls, all those hugs and kisses and expressions of caring. Rather than adding to my burden, they lightened it, until I stepped out onto the grass outside the werepalace and paused.

She might not see us. Shaylee sounded nervous.

She will, my vampire sent.

Damned right she will, my demon snarled before falling still.

The doors parted in front of me, both guards nodding as the werewolves who watched over the entry stepped aside to let me in. One last time I observed the beauty of the foyer, the gold and ivory perfection. I felt her in the quarters above, her coldness, and almost didn't proceed. But I had to see her, had to have the chance to at least hug her one last time.

Sage met me at their door, embracing me hard. The Prince Consort kissed my cheek before guiding me into the sitting room with one hand on my lower back, a sad smile on his face.

She doesn't blame you, he sent. *But she's struggling with this, Syd. You know Charlotte.*

I did, indeed. And went right to her where she stood, stiff and formal, next to the fireplace. I didn't give her a chance to argue, latching onto her and pouring love into her power as I held her more for my need than to comfort her. Charlotte held still for barely a moment before crumbling into me and holding me just as tight.

Our people have failed for the last time, she sent to me, fierce, proud.

Charlotte, I sent. *I love you.*

She pushed me back, stared into my eyes, her own blame and grief forgotten. "What?"

I shook my head. "No matter what," I said. "Okay?"

She tilted her head, frown creasing her perfect brow. "What aren't you telling me?" She needed something to latch onto. I did know Charlotte, didn't I? And laughed as I stepped away.

"The werenation," I said, "has never had a better chance than it does now."

I left without another word, feeling her gaze on me, her worry. I had to flee, quickly. Of anyone, she would figure it out if I didn't go before she could start prodding deeper.

Her, and one other. But he already had a good idea of what was coming. How was I going to break it to Sassafras where I went he couldn't follow?

More to do, though I left the hardest for last. Ethie slept peacefully under her covers, her dark hair spread over her pillow in perfect, shining curls. I wept then, for the first time, openly but silently so she wouldn't wake. I didn't want her to see me like this, to know what was coming. She had Quaid, now a full member of the coven again. And her new mother and sisters. She didn't need me.

As for the other way around, well. After losing Gabriel I wasn't sure I'd be able to say goodbye to my daughter, too.

Ethie's eyes fluttered, long lashes touching her round cheeks. She caught me there, wiping my face in a desperate attempt to hide my tears from her. We'd had a rough go lately, and I hardly blamed her for being so angry with me, so hurt. And yet, she didn't remember anything that went before, did she? Her brother, me leaving her behind.

The flat stare she gave me as she rolled over told me no matter what Universe survived in the end, my daughter wasn't about to cut me any slack. That hurt more than I would ever tell her.

Instead of fighting it, rather than mourn the loss of our relationship, I exhaled softly into the dark of her room and spoke. "Just do your best," I whispered. "It's enough, Ethie. More than enough." She looked away from me, little arms hugging her pillow, jaw jutting out as I went on. An immobile wall of Hayleness. "I love you, no matter what you might think. And I always will."

She refused to relent and I wasn't in a state to make her. Instead, I left her there, glaring at the wall while I closed the door softly behind me and did my best not to crumble to the floor and sob over her hate. It was my fault, after all. I'd put her second, third, last. Thanks to fate and the Universe and all that mess, I had to.

I turned, found her namesake watching me with pursed lips and a frown so deep I knew Gram had to suspect something was coming. She didn't approach, just stood there in the semi-dark of the hall, the light behind her casting a halo around her hair, her stiff shoulders.

"You're leaving," she said, voice low and hurt.

"I have to." I hitched a breath.

"When?" She cleared her throat.

"Soon." I shrugged. "I don't know, but it feels like soon."

She nodded, stiff and abrupt. "When are you coming back?"

I didn't answer.

And, in her own silence, I knew she understood.

No hugs, not from her. I couldn't bear it.

Instead, I parted the veil and called out to the one person I needed now. A moment later I stepped out into the cavern, grateful to find her waiting there. Iepa wasn't alone, though, Oliver and Sass and Jiao silently observing as I crossed to the maji and nodded.

"They insisted," she said. Shrugged.

It didn't matter. They couldn't stop what was coming. Not now that the discomfort grew so large and rumbling in my chest I could feel it pressing outward against my ribs.

"It's time," I said, wondering at the calm in my voice

when my entire being vibrated with wrongness. "Isn't it?"

But it wasn't Iepa who answered, who stepped from the shadows, tears on her cheeks and a look of endless hurt on her face. Trill bowed her head to me and offered her hands.

"It is," she said, waving off the others as she drew me to her. "I'm so sorry," she whispered. "This you must do alone."

Oliver protested immediately, with power and his voice, but it was too late. I'd already known it would be. Last night was our goodbye.

As for Sassafras, he called my name as I left him at last, in a mournful howl that sounded more cat than human.

THIRTY-ONE

The veil embraced me, love and kindness in its own knowing. But its tender greeting didn't last, overshadowed by the roar of an approaching storm. Before I could shake my shock—a storm in the veil?—the sound of pounding hooves in the rushing wind triggered memory so instantly I gasped a breath and spun to watch the Wild Hunt swoop toward me.

Gwynn ap Nudd drew his galloping stallion to a halt, the swirling black clouds that hid the rest of the Wild billowing behind him in a giant wall of pending destruction.

"Gwynn!" It was Shaylee who called out to him, the Sidhe princess within whose voice ached with longing at the sight of him. We hadn't seen him since we'd released the Wild Hunt back into the realm, though it was less than a year ago now since his return home. What was the Wild Hunt doing here?

Violent, uncontrolled magic sizzled around me, tossed Trill's hair while she remained silent, grim, observant but seemingly outside this conversation.

"My love." The Wild Hunt leader's deep voice sounded even more so, vibrating with the power of the storm he fronted, with the multitude of voices of his hunters. Two giant hounds, black as a starless night with eyes licking red flame came to a halt beside him, tongues lolling outward. The rest of their pack howled from within the cloud bank as I raised one hand to Galleytrot and the dog that was formerly Erica Plower.

"You were meant to rest." That from me directly, Shaylee too shaken by the sight of him to comment.

"Were that the case," Gwynn boomed, thunder in his tone. "But the Wild Hunt will not rest until our task is done."

It made sense, I guess. "The end is coming," I said. I suppose in this chain of events the combining of the Universes meant Gwynn and his people never went home.

But no, he seemed to understand my confusion. "At last, yes," he said. "Though we were freed, Sydlynn Hayle, I always knew it would be our calling one day to leave the realm and fulfill the role we'd been assigned so many years ago. While we might have been allowed respite, the doom of the Wild Hunt remains. As does the doom of the Universe."

That was it, then. He hadn't risen when I'd fought Belaisle on the Stronghold plane. Nor when Gabriel, as a baby, first opened a Gateway to the Dark Universe. Neither did Gwynn and the Wild ride when the two Universes were dying, crumbling into the void to be made again by my son as the new Creator.

The fact that the Wild Hunt rode now, after everything that came before? Terrified me.

"I'll die in vain, then," I said to Trill, surprised at my own calm.

She shook her head, looking angry. "Don't do that," she said. "Gwynn, get lost for now, would you? The ozone is giving me a headache."

He laughed, but there was no humor in his voice, just the booming echo of a massing storm. "Would that I could undo what is to come," he said. "But my task is set. As is yours." Gwynn's horse rose onto his back legs before he spun the stallion, gleaming gold despite the dimness of the veil, and saluted. "I will see you at the end, Sydlynn Hayle."

I watched Gwynn ride away, Galleytrot and Danae going with him, the massive black clouds blotting out everything for a time until they disappeared into the veil itself. I shivered then, hugging myself, still staring after them.

"Okay," I said to Trill at last. "I get it. And I'm ready to go. But I can't, can I?" I turned to her then, frustration finally winning. "I need Max." The ribbon on my wrist flexed in its own unhappiness. "And he's dead."

Trill hesitated before turning her back on me with a hurt look on her face. "I can't help you," she said in a wail before disappearing into the veil.

Alone then, and lost. Not in time and space, but in what to do next. I drifted there for a while, knowing the longer I stayed the more likely it was I'd run into someone who might try to convince me to come home. Or stop fighting. Or quit. Because I'll tell you something, being alone in that moment, knowing what I faced, made me feel the smallest and most vulnerable I'd felt in my entire life.

Indecision held me in place, the strain of not knowing what to do, where to go, driving doubt into my heart and soul. Even the girls were silent, the drach soul I wore. None of us seemed willing to choose, to make a decision. For fear it might be the wrong one? Or the right one. Was I really ready to die?

I thought of Max. And knew what came next, after all.

He sat where he had the last time I'd come, perched on Creator's throne, his massive body solid stone, the Stronghold himself silent as if knowing I needed quiet. I approached Max, touched his knee, stared up into his blank face and willed him to wake.

His wings. My demon choked. *It can't be him.*

It feels like him, Shaylee sent, fretting. *In the dream.*

The vision, you mean, my vampire sent. *And yes, I agree. So, not the other Max then, either?*

I don't know how it could be, I sent to them, stroking the black ribbon as he sighed against my suddenly cold skin. Once again I looked up. *We can't do this without him. But he's gone.*

Does that mean the end won't come? Shaylee sounded a little hopeful, but my demon snorted at her while the wrongness built and built within all of us.

If that was true, she sent, *your old flame wouldn't have shown up with a few hundred of his deadliest friends.*

I sat on the floor of the cavern and leaned against Max's leg, the darkness in his shadow calming me, quieting my heart.

"I'm afraid," I whispered to him. "But you're the only one I'll admit it to." I rubbed my arms, rested my temple against the stone of his knee. "I wouldn't be. If you were with me."

Silence. Stillness. I don't know why I was expecting anything else.

Until darkness passed over me and I looked up. To find Bellanca watching me.

THIRTY-TWO

She wasn't alone. It took me a bit to process the lumps of forms that crowded around her feet, the unconscious people she'd brought with her from who knew where. All while struggling to stand, to act, to fight her. Anything, something.

Nothing.

"Are you done?" Bellanca's disdain wasn't lost on me, but I'd pay her back. Just as soon as the power she used to pin me down gave way to the flare of my temper. I'd faced strong foes before, seemingly endless sources of magic. Hell, I'd faced off with Dark Brother Himself, been stripped to the bone and lived to tell about it.

With Creator's help, mind you. Details.

No way was I relenting completely. But she could think so, if that gave me the edge I needed. The girls tensed inside me, their own powers sniffing for an opening as I pulled back and conserved my strength against the moment I could crush Bellanca's throat under my heel and grind.

"Better," she said, turning away from me like I didn't matter. "It took me a bit to track you down," she said, bending to grasp one of the unconscious people at her feet by the upper arm. He rose in a fluid motion, clearly not in control of himself or even aware of what she was doing. A demon, still in demon form. How was he here in the Stronghold? From his features he was family, one of the many third or fourth plane demons, I could only imagine, who made up Meira's court. At least Bellanca hadn't gone after my sister. Though, I would have liked to see her try.

My demon snorted as the former Fate went on, dropping him in favor of another body, this one more than familiar. The charred corpse wore an elaborate red gown, her long, blonde hair singed and curled black on the edges hung from a tangled ball where her fancy hairstyle unraveled into a knot.

"You have something of mine." Bellanca inhaled sharply and the vampire that had been Batsheva Moromond shriveled further, a crisp mummy that toppled to one side. Bellanca's eyes flared, youthful face aged past middle years now. She'd let herself go since I saw her last.

"If you're referring to the part of my vampire essence

that was Moa," I said, keeping my voice low and bored, "come and get it."

Bellanca shrugged, her white gown torn at the hem barely covering her dirty feet. She'd clearly lost what last little bits and pieces of her mind she'd clung to. And yet, that made her more dangerous, didn't it? Destruction for the sake of it didn't seem so unlikely just then.

"I replaced it," she said, humming softly as she bent again, this time pulling up the form of Ohdran. My heart twitched then, begged me to act even as Shaylee turned away. The demon was family, sure, but I didn't know him personally, so that was easy. And Batsheva was already dead to me when Bellanca found her, burned and hopefully still suffering. But the Unseelie King? Ohdran was my friend, damn it.

Damn it.

"So tasty." Bellanca let him drop before gesturing, her final captive rising like a puppet with his strings cut, jerking his way toward her. I almost laughed. So close to it I actually swallowed wrong and choked myself instead. The best part was, Liander Belaisle was awake and aware, his pale yellow eyes glaring hate at both of us. The only part of him, it seemed, able to move independently as she jerked him with flicks of her fingers to her side. "Want a bite?"

"Not hungry," I said, smiling at Belaisle. "Besides, he'd give me heartburn."

Bellanca laughed, the echo of the girl she'd been—ancient beyond days but still a girl in appearance to me—when we'd first met. "You're right," she said. "But I'll have to risk it."

"You seem to be missing a few sources," I said. "The werewolves?"

She turned up her nose, sneering. "Constructs," she said. "Disgusting things."

I'd be sure to let Charlotte know how Bellanca felt about werewolves. Who was I kidding? I'd have to exact revenge for that little slight myself. "And the witches." I tsked. "Sorry about Mom, but she's pretty important to me. Couldn't let you have her."

Bellanca snarled that time. "I don't need her," she said, letting Belaisle fall, a new form rising to sigh against her, head lolling back. Not like she had to show me who it was. I'd know Sashenka Hensley anywhere. A brief pang of regret hit me at her loss. "This little coven leader will do just fine."

Shenka had her own coven? News to me. I could have tried to save her, maybe. If the end wasn't so near.

"What of the Order?" I didn't feel them inside her yet. "Or the drach?"

"I have the maji already." Bellanca let me feel Iepa's stolen power. "The Order, well. They and the drachmor would be nice, but I know my limits." In other words, she didn't dare. And didn't need them, either. That sucked.

The one advantage I might have had died with the hope she'd run off the deep end into those she couldn't take down.

"So what, then?" I stood, using Max to guide me to my feet, his legs against my back. My support, even now. "I'm last then?"

She laughed, clutching her sides in hysteria like I'd cracked the biggest joke in the Universe. Then fell still instantly, a faucet shutting off. Creep factor to the power of ten billion.

"No," she said. "Not you. I'm here for him." She pointed then. At me. No, not so. Over my shoulder, wasn't it?

She was pointing at Max.

My turn to laugh, to shake my head, tears burning. "You're a bit late for that," I said. And sighed at last, sagging. "Why, Bellanca? You're going to destroy everything. Out of spite?"

She spit at me, body trembling. "Of course," she hissed. "That fool Zeon thinks he's so righteous, so pure. But he's as tainted as everyone else, as tainted as you." She shook her hands in front of her, as if shedding something she could never let loose. "You don't understand how disgusting you all are. All of you, every single one." Spittle flew from her lips, her eyes bulging as she let her insanity out. "We were all that stood against your filth and the perfection of the Universe. The perfection of fate and the paths all creatures walk. Until She took it away." There it was, the real core of her fury and madness. Not me, nor the Universe itself. Creator. "She abandoned us, didn't She? She gave our place to those who will never understand the purity of our task. And the entire Universe must be purged so it will be clean again." She paused, smiled like I'd get the joke. "Just as we foresaw it should be. My final act as Fate."

"Bellanca." I hadn't noticed he'd appeared, started when Thanos spoke. Her brother's face had twisted into horror and despair, his hands reaching for her. Unlike his sister, the former Dark Fate seemed to have at least partially adjusted to the change in his existence, dressed in a crisp suit and tie, oddly, looking far younger than her. "Please, sister. You must stop."

She hissed at him, crouching with her hands in claws, power striking for him, though he only swayed under that pressure.

I cannot hold her, he sent to me. *She is too far gone and the time is near.* Thanos's apology was in his gaze, in the way his shoulders rose and fell, accepting the end. *I'm sorry.*

There was nothing to say, not when she struck again, but this time not at her brother. I cried out in reaction to the giant wave of magic heading toward me and ducked, cowardly in the instant of attack. I sprawled forward on my face, knowing no one would have survived if that blow had landed, not even me. And felt the ground beneath me shudder when the blast struck the statue I'd used as a support system—alive and turned to stone—for most of my adult life.

I flipped over on my back, tears blinding me a moment while the statue shattered outward, rock whistling past me as it detonated. I barely had time to raise a shield to protect myself, bits of Max pinging off my wards while a giant ball of dust washed back from the exploding stone and buried us in grit.

No. Max. If he wasn't dead before—

Someone roared. Flame burst outward, disintegrating the dust cloud, setting fire to the very rock. A massive shape surged above me, looming in sudden massive threat, a huge eye opening, burning with orange light as a spread of wings beat once, twice, flattening all of us to the ground.

BELLANCA. His voice. His fury.

Max.

Max was alive. And he had wings.

THIRTY-THREE

Bellanca's answering wail cut through even the echoes of Max's vocal rage, bouncing around the stone interior of the cavern in counterpoint. I covered my ears with both hands to block the shriek while she struggled to rise, another down sweep of his massive wings forcing her into the dirt.

"My love!" She managed to raise one hand, to cry out to him but he loomed, a shadow with a blazing gaze, more massive than I'd ever seen him. I shuddered at the sight as he opened his giant mouth and released a blazing gout of liquid fire, blasting her without pause or pity.

I should have known better than to hope that would be the end of her, though Max's show of fury was impressive, I have to say. I wish I'd had the presence of mind to count how long he exhaled, behemoth of a head bearing down over her, the air singed from the heat of his attack. At least I thought to shield myself and those around her, the bodies of the fallen protected from the searing flame.

When at last Max's head drew back, inhale a rush of wind like the world itself drawing breath, Bellanca appeared behind a superheated ward of her own. She meeped terror before flashing into light and vanishing.

Leaving me to face the towering, raging drach who was nothing like the Max I knew.

I was surprised to find Thanos remained, quaking in his own fear. The fact he'd stood against his sister and now refused to retreat spoke volumes to me. With my entire body trembling from the aftershock of Max's return, I crossed on wobbly legs to his sister's victims like none of this was a big deal.

"They're not dead." Thanos's voice shook slightly as he joined me. "Just drained." Weird to have any kind of conversation under the looming shadow of a very angry dragon with a belly full of fire aimed in our general direction. I guess that was just my life though, right?

I bent and checked Belaisle's pulse, grimaced. She didn't even get that right.

Syd, my vampire chided gently. *So bloodthirsty.*

We could kill him now, my demon sent. *No one would know the difference.*

As tempting as that is, I sent, left it hanging while I reached out past Max's massive magic and to his counterpart with as much calm as I could muster. *Mabel*, I sent. *You might want to get down here.*

She appeared an instant after I spoke her name, other drach with her so she was obviously already on her way. Mabel froze at the sight of Max, stared up at him while he glared in return, inhaling and exhaling with giant bellows of lungs and wings that fanned the air into a frenzy with the barest movement.

"You've risen," she said, like she'd expected it. If she did and didn't tell me, I was going to kick her drach ass. But no, from the sudden sorrow on her face she had no idea. "I wish you'd confided in me."

His body shifted, head descending yet again, the diamond of his eyes burning with flame from within. Gone was the smooth, reflective surface of his gray skin, the rainbow hue that graced the flesh of the drach. Instead his hide had hardened into rocklike protrusions, spikes and scales covering him in ragged armor I knew too well.

I'd seen it before.

So, it was you after all, I sent, heart and soul settling, real calm returning despite the returned attention to the wrongness now devouring me.

His giant eye swiveled, the flaring orb taller than me meeting my gaze. *Of course*, his mind boomed in mine as if he'd forgotten how to temper his power to talk to lesser races. *It was always us, in the end, Sydlynn Hayle.*

You let me believe you were dead. Dying, at the very least. Anger rose, my old friend, the ribbon on my wrist twisting in answer to my hurt.

She had to believe me incapacitated, Max roared in my mind, making Shaylee shiver. *And I needed time to regrow my wings.* He exhaled a puff of smoke that choked Thanos and some of the drach before Mabel cleared it away. *I have known my Fate for a very long time. And, in the end, I am glad it is you I ride with.*

So this is it? Of course it was. I let power engulf me, ignored Mabel and her people as they assisted Thanos with the fallen. All of the past fell away as I strode forward and laid one hand on the curve of his nostril, the roughness of his skin unfamiliar though his soul was, in essence, the same.

It is, he sent, softer this time, as if he came back to himself a somewhat. But we couldn't afford that, could we? We both needed to be ruthless to do what had to be done. To end this once and for all. And sacrifice ourselves to see it done. *Are you ready?*

I nodded, dropped my hand. *Tell me this is the last for them, Max. That they'll be safe now.* It was all I needed to know, the final piece that would free me to act.

The maji battle, he sent, *should have happened long ago. In the beginning, when I split the power, when Creator was forced to make two Universes and freed Her Dark Brother to control His own. The maji weren't meant to be. They are on my soul, Syd.* He chuffed softly, sadly, some of his anger leaking out. *They stopped Her introduction of white sorcery by refusing to share. So the fight, the battle of the Light and Dark maji, never happened.*

I don't understand, I sent.

He sighed. *Had the maji been allowed to destroy themselves by having their final battle then, Creator could have repaired what I did.* I had no idea. More guilt for my old friend. *She had to instead protect what She'd done by splitting Her statue. What was meant to be a clean slate evolved into too many new planes and races to count. And so, She couldn't allow what had become to be undone.*

What we're about to do, I sent. *Won't that trigger the end of everything? What She wanted to avoid in the first place?* I couldn't stop thinking about the blood of the maji.

The Universe will be what it is. He shrugged like none of that mattered now. *Our only chance to save what She made is to stop them.*

I take it you have a plan. Because I was fresh out of Universe saving ideas.

I do, he sent. *We must force them to combine their power and destroy the bubble they've created before they can rejoin this Universe.* His giant eye blinked slowly. *If only Bellanca knew her meddling was exactly what Creator designed. That this was the only way things could end and that her desire to destroy us is exactly what was needed to save everyone.*

Everyone but us. How clever, that Creator. The vast and complex organizational skills required made my head want to explode. Well, She was the maker of everything,

246

so I could hardly be expected to keep up.

The maji have to end, Max sent. *Their bloodline eliminated, erased once and for all.* The blood of the maji. Was that what it meant? Had to be. *And, in doing so, the last piece of Creator's plan to repair the Universe will be done.*

And if we fail? There was no failing in this. But I had to ask because I just did.

The bubble will break, he sent. *The maji will spill out into our veil in our Universe and split the white sorcery that was never meant to be split.*

And start this crap all over again? No way.

Not this time, he sent. *The white sorcery that was Creator's true gift will not split, Syd. The maji will instead trigger a chain reaction through every power in the Universe and destroy us all.*

Okay then, I sent. *Thanks for filling me in. I'm ready. Let's get this show on the road.*

Max's chuckle sounded the most like him since he'd woken, full of sorrow and a massive dose of pride with which he embraced me. *I was hoping you'd say that.*

THIRTY-FOUR

I turned to find Mabel watching us with her own sorrow on her face. She had to know what was coming.

"Is there anything I can do?" She looked back and forth between us, no comment on Max's bristling, armored state, nor on my steady resolve.

"Nothing," he said. "But care for our people. That has ever been your destiny."

She bowed her head to him, the song of the drach swelling as his people appeared, filling the dust ridden cavern, their love in their music.

Pretty, my demon sent. *Can we get on with this?* Her irritation I knew well. Just fear hiding behind curmudgeony bad humor. I got it.

Soon enough, my vampire sent.

You three could jump ship, I sent. *Find new hosts.*

Stop telling us what to do, my demon grumbled. *And trying to get rid of us already.*

I have a feeling you're going to need us, Shaylee sent. *Besides, I'm kind of attached to this body. And you.*

Gabriel is gone, I sent. *Everyone else is safe, or as safe as they can be until I do what I have to do. So be it.*

So be it, they all muttered together.

We've given up too much and come too far to stop now. My demon exhaled abruptly. *We need some armor, though. Any thoughts?*

Right. And a sword. Shaylee was all business. *Make them?*

They felt like the Order, my vampire sent.

I'm not talking to Oliver now, I sent, panic rising. *He'll never let us go.*

Agreed, my vampire sent. *We don't need a fight with one we love at this point. We have a bigger battle to focus on.*

Loved one. Oh, Oliver.

Max's head shifted, his voice reaching his people as their song ended. "Thank you," he said, so simply but with such beauty I had to fight tears that rose. "My people, the time we have had together has been precious to me, more so because it is borrowed time." The murmured agreement. "Our new Creator has given me the chance to set right what once I broke apart."

Did you ever think it happened on purpose? That thought rose like a surfacing whale blowing for air. *Think about*

Creator, Max. And Bellanca and Her long game. Do you think She would ever allow anything to happen by true chance?

His eye blinked at me, rapidly. *I had never considered…*

I patted his eye ridge and smiled. *No more guilt or anger or regret. Just the ride, my friend.*

Come. He lowered one wing. My power floated me to his back, where a line of spikes separated, the perfect perch for a crazy girl like me. *We must go before Bellanca is able to act.*

Tell me something. I raised one hand and waved to Mabel who waved back, the entire space filled with dust as Max upstroked once before we flashed out into the veil, suddenly free. *What would have happened if Gabriel had chosen this Universe instead of both?*

He would have still become Creator, Max sent. *Alternatively, if he'd chosen Dark Brother, Liander Belaisle would have taken that role.*

Belaisle? No freaking way. The truth hit me hard, stunning in its truth and simplicity.

Yikes. Demon sighed. *No wonder we weren't allowed to kill the nasty little jerk.*

However, Max sent, winging his way across the veil, gigantic body thrumming with power at each rise and fall of his powerful muscles, *he did not. Combining the two is a slowly devolving disaster.*

But one that was necessary to do what we needed in the end. I might not have understood everything, but I knew a "had no choice" moment when it hit me in the face.

Something like that. Amusement. Awesome. *It bought us time. Made the return of the maji too complicated for Bellanca to unravel. The duality gave us the space we needed for me to recover. As long as the bubble they exist in remains outside our Universe, we are safe.*

And the travel back and forth?

An issue, he sent. *But not enough to hurt us. I hope. At least, that's what I assume.* He sighed then, smoke whipping past me. *Even I don't know everything.*

Snort.

If they are permitted to reattach, he sent, *everything Gabriel has done will shatter. The chain reaction… I don't have to tell you. You already know in your soul. You've seen it.*

The final battle. *Yes,* I sent. *So by pouring our power into their clash, we destroy them?*

Indeed, he sent. *And seal up the last of the mistake I made forever.*

What if we just do nothing, keep them from reattaching some other way? And not die.

Max's shoulders shifted while he tilted to the right, heading for only he knew where. But he was right. My soul understood even as he spoke.

The combined Universes cannot be sustained, he sent. *Eventually one will win out over the other and only one will remain.* He chuckled then. *That's quite the son you have there. He took a huge chance and is even now straining his Creator abilities to the limit to keep things together long enough for the appointed time to come to pass.*

You can feel him? I didn't mean to sound so wistful.

Of course, he sent. *I'm surprised you can't.*

Maybe I just didn't have the heart to go looking.

We must ensure the maji are ended outside the Universe so Gabriel can complete the melding and shed the second Universe. Max's tone darkened, deepened again as his body tensed. *To do that, we must make the ultimate sacrifice.*

I get it, I sent. *I'm ready. I won't fail him or you.*

I never doubted, Max sent while the ribbon on my wrist hugged my skin with warmth and sorrow.

THIRTY-FIVE

I was actually surprised when Max split the veil and landed us on the cold and desolate mountaintop overlooking the familiar plains of Demonicon. I slid free of his back, floating to the ground, missing the warmth of his massive body a moment if only out of the comfort it brought me.

"Don't tell me," I said, "this spot has special significance?" I threw my arms wide, spun in a circle so I didn't have to look over the sheared off edge where I'd first officially met him. "Let me guess, you destroyed some kind of precious something here and Creator needs us to fix that, too."

Max chuckled. *Not quite,* he sent. *I just like it here.*

"So do I." This time I wasn't shocked, turning to find Trill waiting for us, her denim jacket scuffed at the collar, dark hair in a low ponytail. I missed her glasses for some reason, the studious and serious look the dark rims gave her. She hadn't worn them in ages, though, didn't need them anymore, I guess.

The things my mind latched onto when the end was near.

"Thank you both for coming." She paused, paled, choked. Stared with guilt and horror as my eyes flew wide at her words. And then, unable to stop myself, I started to laugh. Max joined me, his deep, echoing chuckle booming out over the mountain while tears of hilarity poured down my face.

I waved off Trill who seemed devastated at first by her wording then grinned sheepishly and finally giggled with me until I was able to draw breath to speak.

"Okay, I needed that." I went to her, hugged her, grateful for the simple pleasure of her return embrace. "Thanks."

Trill's eyes filled with tears but she nodded. "Sorry." She cleared her throat, struggling to speak again.

I gripped her shoulder in one hand. "Is this the part where you tell me who you are in all this?" She shook her head, lips working. "Please, please tell me I'm not going to die with that mystery on my hands."

She flinched, looked away. "I'm sorry," she whispered again.

I sighed and stepped back, shrugged. "Now what?"

Trill gestured and a pile of metal appeared at my feet. I didn't have to reach for it. The silver and gold liquefied instantly, sheathing my toes, climbing my legs, my waist, up over my torso and arms, down to my fingertips. I shuddered at the feeling as the living metal took me over and finally stopped at my neck, solidifying into a shining suit I knew well.

"Order armor," I said.

Trill nodded. "Your great-great-great grandmother would have recognized this metal," she said, fingers sliding over my upper arm, gaze far away. "Or, at least, the basis of it. Auburdeen Hayle had her own run in with it a very long time ago."

Interesting. I flexed my hands inside my gauntlets and shrugged my shoulders to settle the armor. "I'd ask you to tell me the story," I said, "but I don't think we have time."

The sword flickered into being before me, balanced on its tip, the hilt at my waist. Surely it was too big for me to lift, would require magic to heft. But no. The moment my gauntlet touched it the weightless blade came free of the ground and hovered in my hand like it was part of me.

"The time of the maji has come to an end," Trill said. "Those that were never meant to be created must be destroyed if the Universe is to survive."

A part of me flinched. They weren't all bad, after all. I

PATTI LARSEN

liked Trinol, the leader of the dark maji and Iepa was my friend. Trill herself carried maji blood.

"What does that mean for you?" I shouldn't have been thinking about her, I guess. I had my own death to ride to. But I had to ask.

She shook her head. "Don't worry about me," she said. "Though I appreciate the sentiment has always been there, Syd. Knowing you cared has carried me through all of this in a way you will never fully know."

Blink through the tears. Don't let them fall. They might rust your armor.

Freaking supernatural faucet.

"The second race was the real mistake you made, Max," Trill said, turning to him. "The maji exist outside our Universe anyway, the reason they were able to create the bubble in the first place." That was an interesting tidbit. And maybe filled in the last hole in Oliver's explanation for their actions. He didn't recognize their very existence was out of connection with the Universe.

"Does that mean they were able to do things none of us could?" That would make sense.

"And the reason they were compelled in their very makeup to hold themselves apart from the rest of the races," Trill said. "You could no more have elicited their aid than made them real, Syd."

The Universe was hella complicated.

I suddenly wanted to tell Oliver, to fill him in on the

rest of the story. But doing so would alert him to where I was, what I was doing. And open me to crumbling when I needed more than ever to be strong.

"Will they forget me? Us?" I looked up at Max. "When we're gone?"

Trill sobbed once, catching the sound behind her hand. "I don't know," she said. "I think they might."

I nodded, detachment of Gabriel's loss rising suddenly to wash me in gray. So that's what it was really for. Okay then. I'd take it. "That would be for the best," I said.

She wouldn't look at me. I wished I could help her. It seemed she would be the one left behind to suffer and I didn't know how to feel about that.

"I guess, one last question if you won't tell me what your role is," I said. "Why me?"

Trill laughed then, through sparkling tears. "Light One," she said. "Doombringer. The Daughter of the Universe and the Wild Card of Creator. It was only ever you. And Max."

Yup. That was what I thought.

You know, my vampire whispered to me as I turned to leap onto Max's back, *if we had to love again, it would have been him, wouldn't it?*

Oliver. Shaylee sighed over his name.

He'd do, my demon sent. Snorted.

I'd rather not think about him right now, I sent.

Suit yourself, my demon sent. *But I'd prefer to think happy thoughts riding to my death.*

I paused with my hand on Max's spiked shoulder and sighed. *I guess... I can't go like this, can I? I have to tell them.*

They'll forget anyway, my vampire sent. *But they'd want to know.*

As one, I reached out to them, to the souls I knew so well, the hearts I loved with all of mine. From Gram to Charlotte to Ethie and Quaid, from Sunny and Frank to Sebastian and Alison. The coven, my parents, Sass and Jiao and Mabel with the drach. Piers and the sorcerers who listened intently as I dove into their magic and showed them where I stood while my sister embraced me with her power.

I love you, I sent. *Take care of each other.*

I didn't cut them off in time. Oliver had enough space to send me his heart. My sister her pride. Gram her quiet embrace, the one I couldn't bear in person. Sass his grief. And, in the last instant before I let them all go, there was only the sound of my mother.

Weeping.

I thought it was done, that I could go then, accept the gray and do what I needed to. But he wasn't finished with me. And I knew it the instant he appeared, felt his soul next to mine. Bit back the pounding sorrow that rose at his presence as I turned and embraced my son.

Gabriel hugged me tight, whispering his love in my

ear in a voice beloved to me. Not his voice, not the sweet, kind boy's voice I knew. But deeper, older, vibrating with the earth and time.

I leaned back, looked up into Liam's face with my son's soul behind his eyes and found a smile despite it all. Moisture shone in his gaze, wet his cheeks as Creator, my son, kissed me gently on the forehead.

Mom, he sent.

"Creator." He wasn't alone. Mia Dumont stood off to one side, face pinched as she avoided looking at Trill while Zoe waved with her fingertips, hugging herself then, teeth gnawing her lower lip. The wind rose, whipped at their hair until my son gestured and sealed us off from the gathering storm. I knew that storm, didn't have to be told who and what was coming. He'd already warned me, hadn't he?

Gwynn and the Wild Hunt. *I'll see you soon*, I sent into the sky.

"If there was any other way," Gabriel said. "Even I, in the end, have no choice."

I nodded, held his hand just for a moment. Just to be in physical touch with my son one last time. Creator. But my kid. My sweets. "Used to it," I said.

"No one else is up to the task." He smiled at me with his father's mouth. "And as for the guilt the pair of you carry around about who's to blame and why we're here, I want you to take this with you." He exhaled and smiled up at Max. "If it's anyone's fault, it's Hers." Max grunted softly. "That's right, my friend. It's Creator's. And mine, now. So, it's time you both understood and accepted nothing you've ever done is outside the fate you've been created for."

Max seemed to deflate slightly, but not in a bad way. "Thank you," he said.

Gabriel patted his shoulder and tilted his head down, meeting my eyes again. "I should have let you go," he said. "You don't need the distraction. But I had to see you again."

"I'm glad you did." I hugged him one last time, the armor giving way to allow me to hold him close. "I love you, sweets."

"So proud of you, Mom." He released me then stepped back as lightning struck the barrier he'd created overhead, casting sparks down the dome of it while the sky turned to black.

Nice to go to our deaths with a clean conscience. I snorted in surprise at Max's jovial words.

I guess, I sent. It was so hard to leave my son but I did it, leaping with magical support onto the drach's wide back again, settling between the spikes of his armor and resting the sword I brought winging to my hand across my thighs. *Let's go save the Universe.*

One last time. His power embraced me, integrated mine into his until we felt as one. *It has been the greatest of honors to know you, Sydlynn Hayle.*

I blinked away tears while he rose, parting the veil, the armor flexing and forming a helmet to protect my face. How odd, it seemed transparent, keeping my vision clear though I felt the fullness of it engulf my face. I didn't look back as we dove into the veil and, with a push of black sorcery around us, split that power into shards of rainbow light.

And plunged, screaming our battle cries, into a new Universe where the armies of the maji waited for us.

THIRTY-SIX

Have you ever fought an endless battle against those as powerful as you are with no victory in sight?

I clung with magic and all the will I could muster to the straining neck beneath me, the sword in my hand no longer weightless, though I was grateful for its continued assistance in that department. How long? I had no idea, only that surely an entire lifetime had passed while Max belched smoke and fire and I swung that sword at the seemingly limitless number of maji mounted on drachmor who attacked us over and over again. The air around me, superheated by their answering flames and droplets of acid and even clouds of cutting ice crystals pounded against me, against my giant friend, battered my helmet, though the living metal never once failed me.

Weariness pulled at every muscle, at my power, but there was only the battle and survival, the wash of heat and the push of death ahead and behind, beneath and above and from every side. I have no idea, honestly, how we survived, though perhaps Max and I had spent so much time fighting before now neither of us knew how to quit.

I rocked in my seat when a ball of green lightning slammed into my side, driving me part way over Max's neck. Only the ridged spikes caught and held me, my own magic diverted to block the last of the attack.

This isn't what I remember in the dream, I sent to him, feeling desperate at last.

Nor I, he sent. *But we have no choice, Syd. We must keep fighting*. He grunted and swerved, his flying skills unsurpassed. Maybe if we'd faced even half the number we did he would have been master. But the maji, dark and light, didn't offer respite, refusing to back down, their drachmor mounts, while weaker seeming and less agile than my friend, were countless.

We were going to die all right, before we could do what we came for.

My armor flexed in response to a hammer of dark sorcery that crushed my right thigh, but I couldn't help the scream that tore from my throat regardless. Pain was such a foreign thing to me, had been for so long that facing my end woke a very human response.

Fear of harm.

No time for cowardice or base responses. I had to

focus. And launched my own attack as we spun and wheeled beneath a small pack of sinewy drachmor with their multihued bodies and furious light maji riders.

Three of them tumbled from their mounts and fell toward the barren earth beneath us, the gray sky cloudless and lacking a sun. I hadn't time to worry about why this Universe felt so unfinished, but it wasn't hard to figure out, really. It wasn't meant to be permanent, was it?

Max roared his own pain, fire slicing through the thin membrane of his right wing. I lurched in response, feeling it as I know he felt the ache in my thigh, sending healing energy.

Thankfully it was the edge, he sent. *But we can't do this much longer.*

Should we run? I hated to suggest it even as I gasped for air, knowing we were both near the end of our endurance, as remarkable as our combined power was.

Max didn't reply. He didn't have to.

There was no running for us.

I caught a flicker of motion on the ground, the transparent one way visor of my helmet augmenting magic, making it easier to spot. *Down there.*

I see them. Max dove, falling beneath the layer of drachmor and maji who swarmed toward us, smothering us with their numbers. I think our rapid descent shocked them, Max folding his wings and letting us fall. My stomach climbed into my throat, the sword in my hand light again for a moment as gravity lost its control and we plunged like a burning meteorite, flames gouting from Max's open mouth, toward the army on the ground.

Something struck my back, driving me forward, but the armor absorbed it. Still, I could feel it weakening, knew if we were going to have any chance of success we had to stop being on the defensive. But how did one lone drach and a multiple personality woman turn the tide?

Drachmor flooded the air just above the gathering on the ground, forcing Max to heave a huge wing stroke, carrying us upward again. I could feel him straining, knew we were both stretched to the limit.

I fear we've failed, he sent, sounding calm, composed.

Sucks, I sent, patting his shoulder with my free hand. *Fate can bite me.*

Indeed. He chuckled, pouring on speed as he spun and headed back the way we came. *One last plunge, my friend.*

Let's make it count. I leaned into him, sword over my head, knowing we'd failed but not having any other choice.

No choice at all.

Until the sky overhead burst apart, the skin of the new Universe separating in a jerk and a giant, pulsing cloudbank rolled in. I gaped in shock, weariness making me slightly delirious as I cheered the arrival of the doom that was the Wild Hunt.

There was no sign of individual riders, just the

hounds, massive and red-eyed, bulking larger even than the drachmor and Max, galloping next to the storm front. The maji retreated with haste, disoriented and scattered, their fear driving them back while Max finally backwinged, magic holding us in a hover as we caught our breath and watched Gwynn ap Nudd and his riders appear from the leading edge.

"PLAYERS," his voice boomed through the air. "TIME FOR PARLEY."

I shuddered at the weight of his voice, the way thunder rocked through the small Universe and shoved against my very bones. Max obeyed immediately, wing strokes carrying us with casual slowness to hover again and wait.

Two forms rose from the ground, one on the back of a huge, black dragon that would have been recognizable in pop culture. Not nearly as big as Max, mind you, but big enough. The other joined us astride a thin, silver drachmor, blue eyes icy cold, faint trails of frozen mist drifting from her lips.

I didn't care so much about their mounts as I did who rode them. Funny to see Trinol, the leader of the dark maji, mounted on the lighter while Zeon, the puffed up and arrogant idiot who led the light maji riding the opposite.

Spoke volumes, really.

But they weren't alone. Thanos sat behind Trinol on

the silver beast, one hand rising to me in greeting as if he hadn't just watched his people and the light maji try to kill me and Max for the last however long. Impulsively, I waved back. And why the hell not? I was going to die soon. Might as well go with a smile and a cocky attitude.

As for Bellanca, she observed from her side saddle perch behind Zeon, aged face as dark as the hide of her mount.

"What are you doing here, Sidhe?" Zeon's arrogance knew no bounds, clearly.

Gwynn's giant shape didn't register emotion. "The Wild Hunt has come for the end of days," he said. "When this clash reaches its ultimate conclusion, it is our task to ensure the Universe's destruction."

Zeon flinched, shook his head, his robust Santa Claus act falling away as doubt crossed his face. Bellanca hissed at him, whispered something in Zeon's ear. What lies was she telling him?

It doesn't matter now, Max sent. *We can't stop what's coming.*

But, I sent, *at least it seems we'll have a chance to stop it after all.*

Fate, Max sent. *We really should learn to trust it.*

Like that would ever happen.

"Our conflict will create a new future," Zeon said then, faith restored by whatever she'd told him, the pompous ass. "We will renew our Universe and form it in the image Creator intended." He jabbed a finger at me, all self-righteous and stuff. Dick. "And erase the abomination from the face of history!"

He was talking smack about my son again. Oh no, he did *not*.

"This conflict," Gwynn interrupted with a boom of thunder so loud he had to stop and wait for the echo to end before speaking again, "will end everything."

Silence fell. Aside from the panting of the hounds and the distant whine of growing hurricane force winds barely held in check behind the giant, black dogs, no one said anything for a long time. Were they getting it yet? Was there a chance, maybe, the maji might stop being asshats and sort this out before Max and I had to throw our lives away to stop them?

Dear elements, were they actually going to be smart for once?

I should have known better than to hold out any hope. After all, hadn't Trill said the maji weren't supposed to exist at all? They had to go, one way or another. Either they took all of the rest of creation with them...

Or Max and I made sure they didn't.

"I command you to stand down." Zeon's smug expression didn't last. Not when Gwynn burst into deep, rumbling laughter that triggered the howling of the hounds. They emerged at last, the rest of the pack, looming now, bigger than Max, filling the sky with their pacing black bodies, their red, burning eyes like suns overhead. Panting breath stirred the wind and I knew at last where the clouds and the storm of the Wild Hunt originated.

In the damned souls of the black dogs.

"THIS!" I stabbed at the air with my sword, screaming to be heard as lighting crackled and impacted the tip, augmenting my magic for a moment. I'm sure it lit us up because every head swiveled toward us, even Gwynn's. "This is what Bellanca and Zeon are leading you to." I let my sword drop, pushing at the helmet until it retreated, leaving my long hair to swing around my shoulders, ponytail lost ages ago. "Not a new creation. Not what Creator intended. Death and destruction and nothing." I sagged on Max's back, shook my head, knowing this was a waste of time and breath and energy but having to try. Because it was in my nature to never give up. "Don't let everything Creator made end because of their madness."

Zeon shook in his place, howling like a crazy person, like a werewolf gone revenant. "THIS IS YOUR DOING!" He threw his arms wide, power crackling around him while the black dragon twitched in surprise. "IF THE UNIVERSE ENDS, I BLAME YOU, SYDLYNN HAYLE!"

"There will be order," Bellanca said, much softer but with power to augment her reach. There was magic in her words, manipulating and penetrating. And the maji listened to her. I watched them turn as one, heads swiveling in her direction, their fate as sealed as mine. "The Universe will be restored and we will rule all as was foretold."

They are lost, Max sent, sad and weary. *They have always been lost, Syd.*

Because they were never meant to be. I nodded, sighed. Clenched my fist around the sword in my hand.

"With you leading us?" Trinol's words shocked me and, in that moment, triggered the vision at last. Because now I knew. Now I understood as he nodded to me. "The dark maji know the truth. And we will not stand for the yoke of your control, Zeon. It is we who are the destined ones, tied to sorcery by fate and by choice. You rejected your own magic and cling to ours like children who lost their favorite toy." Disdain, outrage from the dark maji who muttered and parted from their light counterparts. Here was the division. Here the division had always been. "The Universe we create will be of our making, not yours."

Zeon roared at him, incomprehensible as Thanos's mind touched mine.

This was inevitable, he sent. *Both Bellanca and I foresaw it, have known the end was coming. You couldn't have stopped it, Syd. But you can end it.*

Understood. The armor replaced my helmet, so the end

wasn't just yet.

Not yet.

Even as Zeon and Trinol's magic clashed and the Wild Hunt howled overhead, Max's massive form heaved, lifting us high above into the pack. A strike from Bellanca's hands just missed while the two massive armies of the maji faced off below and time

slowed

down.

THIRTY-SEVEN

I'd been here before, many times, in my dreams. But it wasn't a dream anymore. This time it was real. The armor sat heavy on my shoulders but I barely felt it now. I welcomed its presence. It saved me as I took the now expected hit to the chest from the distance, Bellanca still trying to kill me despite the massing armies below, while Max wheeled and dove to protect us from attack. The pressure of building power pushed against me from without while the wrongness expanded from within, squishing me between the two. The Wild Hunt flew all around us now, howling a steady, bone jarring squeeze of their own.

The heat of it burned through the metal and scorched my skin, bruising my damaged body, crushing my chest so tight I had to fight for breath. I forced my lungs to inflate out of sheer spite, screaming a soundless yell of defiance, voice already parched and cracking, failing me.

But I would not fail.

My magic pulsed, as weary as I was but refusing to quit while the massive wings of my drach friend swept us forward, his power as unrelenting as my determination. We were together in the end, as we knew we would be and I would not falter for he was with me.

We would reach them before it was too late. I already knew it, had died time and again. And embraced what was to come.

The glowing, white sword of light hung over my head, weightless again, brilliant, shining a beacon in our fore, casting shadows over the sharp, violent spikes adorning his once smooth, scaled shoulders. He was a weapon from the tip of his snout to the sharp edged blade of his tail, all of his creation now made for war. Designed by Creator to do what must be done.

We both were, now.

My love, Gwynn sent as the storm howled overhead, waiting for the end we would bring. *I pray you, prevent me and mine from our final purpose this day.*

We're doing our best, I sent back before Shaylee could answer. *Take care, Gwynn.*

I clenched tight the sword's hilt in my gauntlet, sweat running from my hot palm down inside my suit of living metal as my mount's massive head arched backward, fire spouting in a cascade of heat and ash blowing past my cheek. I inhaled fire, choked on it, searing my insides. That hurt didn't matter, was part of what had to come and wouldn't stop me. Nothing would.

Another blow, this one to my head, carried away the helm that guarded my face, the hit powerful enough at last to sheer away the living metal, its defenses almost depleted. But it was okay, I knew I'd make it no matter what was to come. At last, we were here, in the right time and place, as all things had been meant to happen. I shook off the blow, hair flying clear, ears ringing with the rush of impending death. I embraced it, sucked it back like a draught of joy. We were almost there, the building juggernaut of destructive force between the armies hurtling toward each other narrowing by the instant.

Almost too late. But Fate wouldn't let us fall. Not now. Not ever.

Bellanca tried. Her magic reached for the veil, for our Universe with the edge of the bubble. So close. But this time she was the one who wasn't enough.

White sorcery severed her connection. And I laughed in her mind as my power did the deed.

She howled at me, but it was too late for her, for the maji, for all of us. I was still laughing when he reached for me.

Syd, he sent.

Max, I answered.

And that was all.

We soared into the barest crack that remained, gathering together the brilliant, powerful magic Creator Herself intended for us, for everyone in the Universe, calling on the white sorcery that was life and goodness and the future. Blood magic, that immense power that I had once thought evil. Blood magic was the key.

My blood. Max's. Both of us bleeding not just crimson life but the sizzling purity of Her perfect magic. And, in the end, the blood of the maji would be their undoing.

I felt it then, understood their flaw, their lack. They did not accept white sorcery because they couldn't. Blood magic, true power, would forever be lost to them, even if they won. Which they would not.

Not.

The bellow of my companion was the trigger for the power that burst from us, the sword over my head erupting into a massive outward explosion of white sorcery that devoured everything, fed by the blood of the maji. I reveled in it even while I accepted my true destiny. Doombringer. Light One. Wild Card of Creator.

Peace engulfed me as we died in the crushing press of the violent clash of their magic and ours, taking the maji with us into death.

THIRTY-EIGHT

Wait.

Something was wrong. I felt the shift, felt myself detach from Max in the final instant.

WAIT!

No, not to come so far just to lose now.

Sudden, crushing pressure, choking, dying. It was supposed to end quietly, gone in a flash of an instant, not drained, empty, broken.

Falling.

I fell, hurtling toward the ground below, slow motion all over again while the two armies above me clashed together around a bright, white light.

Max. A shining star, his magic devouring the maji, burning him up. *I only needed your strength and your heart*, he sent as illumination flared so bright I was blinded by it, eyes burned, crying out in pain. *Not your death. Live, dear Syd. With my thanks.*

NO! I fought and writhed, the armor on my body struggling against me as I tried so hard to return, to end my plunging fall, to go back to Max. This wasn't how it was supposed to be, I was supposed to die with him, to have my ending.

The blood of the maji was on *my* hands. Not his.

Live, he whispered. *For both of us.*

I hit the ground hard, feeling bones crack and shatter, my insides shaken and bleeding. I wept tears of blood, the armor desperately feeding me power, keeping me alive while my blind eyes tried to see, heated shockwave of a nuclear explosion devouring me to the distant sound of thunder—

I opened my eyes, gasped for air, sat up abruptly in the moist, damp darkness. No, not full darkness, but dim and quiet. My hands ran over my face, my body no longer sheathed in metal but just a t-shirt and jeans, right sneaker untied, the languid laces seeming to mock me.

What the hell just happened?

The cavern in Wilding Springs. I knew this place like my own back yard. I half rose, spinning sideways, confused and disoriented, still in battle mode, body broken, right? Dying no matter Max's attempt to—

I saw him then, caught my breath before leaping onto

the giant head resting on the floor of the cave, diamond eyes closed, flesh smooth and soft as I remembered it. His massive wings folded over his back, body still.

Too still.

MAX. I screamed his name in his head, knew I was too late, begged the Universe for one more moment.

One diamond eye fluttered. Fixed on me. And his soul sang. *I love you.*

The light left that shining eye even as I watched him go.

He rose from his body in human form, the song of the drach filling the cavern when Max died. The cave sang with him, echoing back the words I knew so well in a language I'd forgotten how to speak, the beautiful melody supposed to be soothing but just making me angry. So angry. I was supposed to die with him. And now he'd left me behind.

I fell over his snout, hugging him and sobbing, feeling the black ribbon slip from my wrist. Looked up long enough to find we weren't alone, that the shining, multicolored collection of drach souls I'd known for so long had come, dancing and singing in utter joy around Max's smiling echo.

He waved to me, morphed into a sparkling diamond strand and joined them, pure happiness, wavering around my head for a moment before he rose with them and, giggling and singing still, they left me there with the rapidly hardening drach body he used to wear.

I choked on tears, staring down with deep and abiding grief at the black ribbon that had been Max in the other Universe, now puddled at my side. With a sigh, it convulsed, spinning itself into a tight, shining ball without a seam to be seen. I lifted it into my hand, the warmth of it pulsing in my palm. Kissed it gently and held it tight as I once again collapsed on the now rock hard form of Max's drach body and shed my soul wrenching despair into the dark stone.

I don't know how he found me or how long I lay there, weeping desperately like a broken child. Nor did I fight him when Oliver lifted me into his arms and carried me away, leaving my friend behind.

THIRTY-NINE

Home. What an odd thing to be in Wilding Springs, at the house with the family around me and nothing changed. Everything though, really.

Oliver didn't let me wallow. He carried me right to the back yard and held me in his arms while I finished crying—I never thought I would, was surprised when I ran out of tears at last—and just let me talk about Max, about our history and all the times I wished I'd told the lord of the drach how much he meant to me.

"He knew," Oliver said, soft and gentle.

Maybe.

Mom and Gram emerged from the house first, saddened but hugging me with relief. At least they hadn't forgotten Max after all. I really couldn't have born that, if the Universe had allowed his amazingness to be erased after all this time. He was as much a part of the makeup of everything as the veil, the eternal son. I caught myself over and over not believing he was really gone.

I met Mabel that afternoon, knowing she and the other drach would want to see him and cried some more, Oliver's arm around my shoulders, Sass holding a weeping Jiao, as the drach sang and sang and sang until hours had passed and the sun had set. She finally came to me, embraced me, kissed my cheek.

The small, black stone that had been his other soul twitched in my pocket, reminding me I carried him. When I pulled it free, Mabel gasped.

"What?" I offered the warm, smooth ball to her and she accepted it—no, *him*—with reverence.

"I don't know," she said, diamond eyes sparkling with tears. "But it feels of him, doesn't it?" He did and I itched to take him back while forcing myself to retreat from the small bundle of soul now silent and withdrawn. "I will guard and protect him for you, until such time we find out what purpose this serves."

I let her take him, with whispered promises she'd care for him while his presence I instantly missed.

I sighed and rubbed my wrist where I'd carried his soul for so long. *Bye, Max.*

The next few days revolved in a blur of what seemed like coincidental endings I knew better than to attribute to anything but fate. Piers and Demetrius, now firmly ensconced as leader and second of the Sorcerers League, finally got around to killing Liander Belaisle.

"She's not done." Belaisle had to have his last word for me, didn't he?

"Bellanca." I knew who he talked about, found it hard to care as I observed him behind the glowing white bars of his magic cell in the bowels of the Scottish castle. Needless, it turned out. He'd been drained so far his magic had gone dormant. The final insult to the fallen hand of Dark Brother. I couldn't bring myself to celebrate and, from the hum of the prison, Piers wasn't taking any chances the former Brotherhood leader might be faking.

Belaisle paced in a circle, perfect suit gone, goatee scraggly, face lined and now, at last, a hint of madness showing. Piers had, more than likely with purpose, dressed my old nemesis in a torn coverall stained and patched several times. The original color was long blended into the grime ground into it. Belaisle plucked at the sleeves with disgust as he spoke again.

"You know she escaped the last battle," he said. Turned sneaky, conspiratorial as he gestured me nearer his cell bars. "I can help you track her, you know."

"If I save your life." I shrugged. "Bellanca is no longer a threat, Liander. And I'm so tired of you I could kill you myself. But I won't take Piers's joy from him."

I stared at him for a long time. History pulled at me, wound backward in my mind. Here stood the soul I'd hated so long, who had caused so much death, so much destruction. Who I'd feared and fought most of my adult life.

I turned and left him there, empty and ineffectual now, powerless and screaming after me to come back.

I didn't bother staying for his execution. He just didn't matter to me anymore.

As for Eva, Piers was determined to kill his mother, too, but I talked him out of it, holding his hand in the highest tower of his castle, looking out over the Scottish moor on a cloudy, cold day that smelled of snow.

"Enough death," I said, still weary. "Enough."

Prison then, relegated to a cell on the coast of Ireland. Let her rot.

Charlotte's massive hug and kiss shocked me when I saw her again.

Don't ever, she sent, fierce, furious, *try to die again. I'll kill you myself.*

Yes, ma'am, I sent, grateful for her love. *Danilo?*

Will survive, she sent, pushing me away, blue eyes full of her wolf. "He's right. He deserves to serve penance. And this is his choice."

At least he seemed to be holding his own against Konstantin's soul. My short visit revealed a toothy smile from the former wereking and an acquired facial tic that had to be the Black Soul sorcerer battling for control. But Danilo waved off my questions with a deep, snarling laugh.

"We're doing fine," he said. "My little friend and me."

Okay then.

It was nice to see Mom in Hong Kong. She seemed to be enjoying herself, far more than she had as the North American leader. If anything, she was thriving and Dad just smiled and shook his head.

"She's different since the… incident," he said in a soft aside as I waited to talk to her while she dealt with business. The sun shone into her office, the glass walls showing my favorite view of the harbor, calm and yet the air seemed filled with the zinging excitement of change and progress. "Good different." He sighed with a smile. "I can barely keep up with her on the best of days. Now?"

So death and rebirth had supercharged Mom. Oh boy.

I found Karyn just as happily doing her thing at Harvard, her strong hug and murmur of welcome genuine.

"There's been some dissent," she told me over coffee, an early snow making the Yard outside her window glisten. "But I'm handling it."

I had no doubt that was the case.

Mom's decision to convert all witch councils to the new North American model—all covens having equal voices—had been met with a bit of resistance. As in "over our dead bodies" resistance. But between her and

Karyn, I knew the two of them could handle things in the witchy part of the paranormal world.

Those two were going to single handedly change everything for the better. And I was going to stay out of their way.

I missed Femke, though. Probably always would. I hated to think we'd drift apart now, that she'd have her own path, something out of the way and quiet. We'd stay in touch for a bit, out of courtesy and friendship. But without the big things to tie us together…

I had no illusions I'd lose track of her. And wished her a happy life free of my kind of trouble.

I was surprised, the morning of the second day, to find Charlotte in my kitchen with a drooling and near comatose Jean Marc Dumont in her possession.

"Not my doing," she said, handing me a note. "And from what I can tell not a trick, either."

I unfolded the heavy parchment and read while she watched.

Consider this gift a peace offering. Staying out of your business.

It wasn't signed. But the trace of dark sorcery on the page told me what I needed to know.

"The Russian Mafia seems to have fallen on hard times," Charlotte said. "From what my sources can tell," Iosif Greshnev, obviously, "their sorcerous support seems to have abandoned them."

So, the Black Souls had decided to treat me with

respect at last? I loved having bad guys on the run. But, did I dare let them go?

I folded the note and handed it to her. "Good for them," I said.

"Apparently," she said, "Iosif has taken over control."

Of the mafia? Well now. Though, the mafia man had his sorcery woken, hadn't he? His rule would stand watching. "What are you going to do with wingnut?" I grimaced at the line of saliva stringing from the edge of Jean Marc's lower lip. A long, narrow cut still oozed pus down the side of his face, his normally close cut hair shaggy and filthy.

Charlotte didn't seem to notice. She shrugged, grinned at me. "Might keep him for a pet," she said.

Seriously.

I knew when she left she'd never let it go, that the Black Souls continuing existence was an honor issue for her and the werenation. Not to mention her mother's betrayal. I was sure Olena's location had to be a priority for my friend. And, if it came to a fight, I'd be there for her. For now, though? For now, I'd take a truce over more battles.

I was sad to discover the disappearance of Iepa. When I finally pulled myself together long enough to search for her, I wasn't surprised to find her gone, but it still hurt my heart. But when I went to visit Zoe and Mia and found they had their own houseguest, Liander

Belaisle's warning about Bellanca didn't seem so irrational or like his desperate attempt at wishful thinking.

Thanos didn't explain how he survived, refused to talk about it, and the two Fates stopped me before I could demand physically and magically that he tell me.

"He's under our protection," Mia said.

Zoe had the good grace not to meet my eyes.

Fine. Screw them. I left Sanctuary in a fury. Max died to ensure the safety of the Universe and here these two idiots were protecting one of the very people who'd put us in danger in the first place. Being Fates for so long must have somehow protected Thanos and Bellanca from the end of their race, altered them enough. Well, I'd make sure the next time I had dealings with them in private they'd find out what staying behind was going to get them.

If they survived the conversation. Oh, and if I ever found Bellanca in Zoe and Mia's presence? Creator would be needing another set of Fates.

So unfair how the good guys seemed to lose even when we won.

At least the death of Batsheva Moromond was final and over with. Sebastian confirmed it for me, though her loss made me wonder where, in all these endings, were our beginnings? That was easy enough to see, though, when I allowed myself to. In the giggles of Payten's twins.

Weird to have her and Quaid living in Wilding

Springs, just next door. To call them both family. And, even weirder, to discover Sassafras and Jiao were now officially together, that they, too, had their own home at her insistence, living like just plain folks.

He blushed a lot I noticed, those first few weeks. Made me happy for the first time since Max died.

Turned out the only drachmor to survive were Jiao's family, the ones who'd originally stayed behind in our Universe. I wasn't sorry to see the others go.

And, oddly enough, Sashenka Hensley reached out to me. Not in any kind of overly friendly way, just a magic infused letter with a thank you for saving her from Bellanca. An overture of forgiveness? I wasn't sure I was ready for that. But it was Tallah who was the bad seed in her family. I could understand that Shenka might have fallen into something she couldn't handle. Mind you, I wasn't about to run off and be her bestie again.

Still, it lightened my heart a little to know she didn't hate me anymore.

My sister, on the other hand, had a few choice words for me when I visited her on Demonicon.

"Don't you ever," she began.

"Oh, but I will," I said, crossing to her, hugging her hard. "And so will you. Because that's who we are."

She grumbled and she swore while the power of the planes swirled in frustration. And then, my sister laughed. Hugged me back. Because she knew I was right.

I kind of wished I wasn't.

As for my daughter... Ethie still wasn't talking to me, not when her father chastised her for her rudeness, not when Payten calmly told her she was being selfish. I missed her hugs, her kisses, her enthusiasm. Her brother.

Gram lived at the house, though she was more and more in Scotland with Demetrius. Yes, she was still coven leader. I considered taking the power back to free her up so she could be with her husband full time, but she rejected the idea.

"You need to rest," she said, kissing me. "Girl, just stop for once and put you first."

I'd talk her into it eventually.

Didn't help that Ethie hated Oliver, though he took great pleasure in spending time with her, to her frustration and exasperation and his amusement.

"I'm not purposely trying to torture her," he said to us one afternoon while she flounced off in a fresh huff and Payten tried to apologize. "I just can't help it." He laughed, gray eyes glinting as he smiled down at me, arm around my shoulders where we sat on the couch in their living room. "She reminds me so much of you."

Didn't I know it? Temper, temper.

One loose end tied itself up in great satisfaction. My tentative inquiries into Sonya O'Dane and Hortense Spaft turned up blank looks and confusion. As for Everonus, he greeted me with cool curiosity when I mentioned the original council. His genuine reaction to the contrary told me that part of my life, at least, didn't linger.

Hard to say goodbye to the last of Liam. But it would seem he and his family never existed. And the Gate cavern beneath Wilding Springs was gone. So…

So. Closing that book. Though I could have gone to Aoilainn for answers, I chose to leave it alone.

Instead, I found myself thinking more and more about my own future rather than lingering in the past, looking for things to do, to occupy my time in a world that suddenly didn't need me. I was supposed to die with Max, regardless of how much everyone would miss me. That was truth. And, as the days passed and calm and quiet settled over the Universe, I increasingly found myself frustrated, cranky and asking the sky, "Now what?" Like I'd get an answer any time soon.

It wasn't fair to blame him, maybe, but I did anyway. This was all Gabriel's fault.

And so, the day she called to me I had to admit I was equally delighted and shocked to find Ameline Benoit still existed in the maji chamber below the vampire mansion. And I ran to her like a child searching for a long lost joy.

FORTY

I didn't bother troubling Sebastian with my appearance, instead stepping out of the veil immediately in the chamber itself and threw my arms around the stunning young woman who greeted me with a smile.

"I thought you were gone," I whispered to her soul that hugged me, as solid as any physical form.

"As did I," she said, sounding puzzled. "I felt the last battle. I was there, Syd."

"I didn't know." I wiped at tears, still smiling to see her. "It's been days. Have you been here all along?"

"No." She looked down at her hands, frowning now. "I feel oddly. Like this isn't the way things are supposed to be anymore. Syd." She looked up then, smiled faintly, sadly. "I think it's finally time for me to go."

Grief, still fresh, hit me with a fresh blow. She'd been my nemesis once, hated and reviled. But the real Ameline, the woman I'd grown to love here in this place, she I wouldn't willingly part with.

"You're right." I spun, Ameline's soft gasp in my ear telling me she was as surprised as I to find Trill standing on the other side of the round chamber, watching us. I circled the slab in the middle of the room, denial in my very soul, scowling at her and knowing I would fight her to the death to keep Ameline with me.

It was the principle of the thing, you see.

"I'm not here for you," Trill said before tilting her head to look past me. "Hello, Ameline."

"Hello, Trill," her soul said. Sighed. "It's time, then?"

No. No. Absolutely no way, not happening.

"It is." Trill gestured, a whisper of magic bypassing me before I knew what was going on, sliding over Ameline while my heart broke one more time. "You knew the end of this existence was coming."

Ameline shivered as the power passed through her then nodded. She was changing already, her face altering, form shifting while she spoke in answer. "I've known," she said. "I couldn't remain like this forever."

"No," Trill said as Ameline's body finally stopped morphing and I gaped at her, sudden understanding stopping everything. I couldn't be right, could I? Was I seeing things? Did Ameline look to be about my age, still gorgeous but, but...

Real?

"Creator isn't cruel," Trill said, sounding sad. "You've lost enough, Ameline. You all have." I turned to find Trill staring at me. She smiled then, shrugged. "Now is the time to bring back some of what was given up."

"What does that mean?" Only then did Ameline seem to realize something radical had happened, that a fundamental change had occurred. She looked down at her hands, touched her cheeks with trembling fingers. "What have you done?"

I laughed, crying, too. "She's alive." I looked back to Trill and laughed again. "You brought her back." Could she do so for Max as well? Dear elements, even Liam?

I could tell from the deep seated sorrow in Trill, despite her own smile, I wasn't going to get everything I wanted. "I'm sorry for what you endured," she said. "Knowing that it was necessary does no good. But maybe this renewal will heal you somewhat." She faltered. "And help you forgive me."

I shook my head, turned at Ameline's next gasp, ready to reassure the former soul made flesh. And froze.

He was perfect lying there, his small body stretched out on the slab, blond hair with tints of red over long, hanging to the stone. Pink cheeks held a ghosting of freckles, his t-shirt askew, jeans torn at the knees. And when he exhaled softly, smiled with his eyes closed as if waking from a dream, a sob escaped me.

I found myself at his side, embracing him while he

woke, feeling his little arms wind around my neck when Gabriel hugged me.

"Mom," he said. "Hi, Mom."

"Sweets." I choked on that word, kissed his face, stroking his hair until I couldn't bear it and had to hug him again. "What? How?"

"Thank you for trusting me," he said, gently pushing me back so he could spin sideways and hop down from the slab. He smiled at Trill and waved a little. "We're good. You're all set."

"You did a great job," she said. "Tough act to follow."

I gaped back and forth between them, Ameline, too. "I don't, I don't understand." I was babbling, fair enough, but the beloved kid I'd thought I'd given up as Creator was here with me again, not a trace of that power inside him though the gigantic presence of the Gateway remained.

So confused.

What the hell?

"Our new Creator needed to act outside of fate," Gabriel said. "So it was necessary for me to take Her place until this was over."

Who?

Oh. My. Swearword.

Trill's hands rose and fell, a bittersweet smile lifting her lips. "I know," she said. "Don't much look the part, but I imagine I'll grow into it."

Trill. Dear elements.

"I've known for a while," she said. Cleared her throat like it was hard to talk about as my mind spun backward and reassessed every single thing that happened, every moment, every judgment and action and conversation. Her pain, her frustration, her decisive trust despite my accusations and fury.

Trill. Trill was Creator.

"From the moment I was compelled to steal the heart." She seemed to want to say more, to explain, but just laughed. "I wanted to tell you, but I couldn't."

I nodded. "I'm sorry."

"So am I."

I tucked my son against me, unable to believe I had him with me again, knowing it would be a long time before I trusted he wouldn't vanish into thin air on me.

"As for you," Trill said, addressing Ameline who stood, stunned and still unbelieving, staring at her. "It's time you shed your past completely, Ameline Hayle." Her dark eyes met mine. "As it should be."

I grinned. "Sold," I said.

Ameline wept, came to me, shaking and nervous. It was my son who smiled up at her, who refused to let her argue or deny her right to that name. After all, she'd been a Hayle in the Dark Universe. We'd call it a win.

Too much, it was all too much and I was sure my

heart would explode any second now. I looked down at my son and blurted what I wanted him to know. "I remembered you." He knew that already, it was a silly thing to say. "I would never have forgotten."

My son smiled up at me. "Did you wonder? Why those three did, too?" Max. Jiao. Oliver. I nodded, couldn't speak further. Gabriel glanced at Trill who nodded before he winked at me. "Max had to remember, because he caused it all. And Jiao was tied to his magic because she was his apprentice."

That made about as much sense as anything else in my crazy life. But didn't explain the last of the three. "And Oliver?" He was Order, was that it?

Tears shone in Gabriel's hazel eyes. "Because," he said, voice cracking as he wavered, small and oh, so dear with that tender smile on his little boy face. "I knew I had to leave you. And I didn't want you to be alone."

I couldn't speak. Or move. Not even when Gabriel turned, wiping at a happy tear that escaped, to grasp Ameline's trembling hand.

"Come on, Auntie Am," he said, leading her toward the staircase. "Mom and Trill have more to say and you need to go home."

FORTY-ONE

I almost protested him leaving me, but he just waved, pausing long enough to kiss Trill on the cheek before he and Ameline ascended the stone steps, out of sight.

Silence fell, though the pounding of my heart filled the space well enough it seemed.

"I only have a little time left," Trill said. "And I'm finally able to talk about it. So ask."

I laughed, couldn't help myself. "Was it worth it?"

She seemed surprised by that question, before she tossed her dark hair back, eyes glittering with good humor and acceptance. "Was it, Syd?"

"Of course," I said.

She smiled.

"It's not over." I hadn't meant to say that, but it came out anyway. Blurted from deep within me while the girls held still. They'd been quiet, all three, since Max's death and this was the first time I'd caught them interested in the world outside.

Trill sighed, still smiling. "It will never be over," she said. "Until it is."

Right. "The Wild Hunt?"

"Back in the realm," she said. "Until the day the Universe really ends."

"Not today," I said.

"No," she said, gentle and kind. She was changing, too, shifting out of the young woman I'd known all along, face taking on a certain maturity. Subtle, this alteration, but enough. I wasn't talking to Trill anymore. "Not today. Or tomorrow. But yes, some day." She came to me then, hands on my cheeks, our heights matched though the young woman I knew was shorter than me. She kissed me softly on the forehead, the infinite sadness of eternity in Her eyes when She leaned away. "Oh Syd," She whispered. And yes, it was She. Creator. "Know I love you, that you are my daughter and that I am so proud of all you have accomplished. I could never have asked for more from you. My dear, dear Sydlynn Hayle."

Tears found their way down my cheeks, my heart healing as She embraced me with power. Speechless, I simply nodded.

"The day will come when I call on you again," She said.

"I'll be ready," I said, voice cracking with emotion.

She nodded. "At least this Creator will be a little more chatty." And laughed.

I laughed with Her. Hugged Her. And stepped away, ending up in the back yard in Wilding Springs, alone, arms extended into empty air. I let them fall, darkness surrounding me, hugging myself then, crying alone but in happiness, to the sound of laughter from within the house. I listened, hearing music, multiple voices. A party? How appropriate. I finally felt like celebrating. But I didn't get to go inside, not yet. I felt him before he walked out the back door, triggering the motion sensitive light, casting his tall, broad body in a halo of illumination while he strode toward me.

Oliver embraced me without pause, hugging me close, kissing my temple as he rocked me against him.

"Gabriel is here," he whispered, joy in his voice.

I laughed and cried against his chest, only capable of clinging to him and nodding. If only he knew the gift Gabriel had given me, making sure Oliver remembered everything.

He finally let me go, wiping at his own face, beaming a smile as he turned me toward the light. "I love you," he said, fire sparking in his gray eyes.

I touched his cheek, the harsh buzz of a half day's beard against my skin. And had a thought while I stood there and considered love and the future. "You know what's weird?" So random, my brain. "I just realized you never told me your last name."

He frowned just a little. "Yes, I did," he said. "It's Opal, for my mother." And paused. Paused a long, long time. Before sighing, eyes guarded while truth burned in my heart.

"And," I said.

He squared his jaw, inhaled. "Dane. For my father."

Oliver. Oliver Opal Dane. Oliver O—

O'Dane.

I couldn't breathe, needed to desperately, needed to say something, to finally accept what I'd known all along. That Oliver, he was—

"I'm not him." He spun away from me, shoulders rounded forward, scowling at the ground, big body shaking.

What? Yes, yes, he *was*. He was Liam, my Liam, but who Liam was supposed to be. Had he been born in the Dark Universe and had sorcery instead of Sidhe magic, had the chance to fully embrace all that he was meant to become—

When Oliver turned to me again, there was so much hurt in him I had to stop my mind running, freeze it in place and just listen, damn it.

"Don't, Syd," he whispered. "If you do, if you try to make me him, I'll leave. And I'll never come back." Green glints in his eyes flared and died. "I'm not Liam."

"But you knew," I said, stumbling over my words.

"You knew you could have been. That he's you, but with sorcery, with—"

Stop it. My vampire's sharp order cut off my babbling. *Look at him. Syd.*

Just look. My demon joined in. *It's not Liam.*

It never was. And couldn't be. Shaylee sounded sad. *But, he's better.* She flinched. *I didn't mean it that way.*

I stopped her floundering attempt to make amends. *I get it,* I sent, really looking at him.

And seeing Oliver as himself for the first time ever.

He flinched when I approached, looked like he was ready to run. I didn't let him, reaching out with power and love and my arms and drew him to me, cheek against his chest while he hesitantly, then with more passion, hugged me back.

I let him feel how I felt, shedding the connection to Liam, the need to have my love back. Because I knew the truth now.

What was it Zoe said to me the day she told me to go to the Dark Universe? *When you meet him, you will know him. You must trust him. He's not only vital to your fate but is exactly who you have been looking for.*

Now I understood.

Oliver. I whispered his name in his mind. *I've been waiting for you.*

From the way he kissed me, I'd been in his dreams, too.

FORTY-TWO

Well now. The end again. Imagine that.

Oliver moved in for real, and I had to admit I liked having him in my space. He looked great on Egyptian cotton and even better in my shower...

Ahem.

I had to admit, though, I kind of lived in constant worry he'd make the massive mistake of asking me to marry him at some point. Not that it would be a disaster, but... yeah. Disaster. Two husbands were enough, thanks. I was rather enjoying this whole soulmate bonding thing without needed some kind of outside indicator we were meant to be.

We were. I had no doubt whatsoever of that. And, thankfully, my guilt over my previous two loves hadn't surfaced. Because I guess finally finding him made the past just part of the process.

Awesome.

Besides, he seemed to know better than to bring up the whole holy matrimony thing. Maybe Order soldiers didn't get married? Knowing his mother killed his father to protect him, it was likely Oliver equated wedded bliss with murder and mayhem.

I knew exactly how that felt.

My darling Gabriel was my son, the dear, sweet boy I remembered, without any massive change to his personality or demeanor, despite what he went through. Mind you, I did notice a few small alterations. He seemed a little quieter, more contemplative, even a bit older in his understanding and processing of certain things. Matured. If that was the worst side effect being Creator and carrying the weight of the Universe on his shoulders was going to have, I'd take it and thank the gift horse that brought it to keep its damned mouth shut.

Of course, Gabriel was still the Gateway. I guess nothing anyone could do—not even the new Creator— would alter that fact. And seeing as that power was a huge part of who he was, I saw no reason to cry over it. He of all people understood the importance and consequence of using that power for the right reasons. I would not pressure him by not trusting he knew what he was doing.

Watching over his shoulder, on the other hand...

Funny how his reappearance was like a lightbulb moment for the rest of those in my circle. One second they had no idea who I was talking about and the next they looked at me funny when I asked if they remembered him. Quaid was the worst, of course. If that man made one more snide remark about how I chose to raise my kid—*my* kid, not his anymore—I'd be smacking him hard enough he'd be the one people forgot.

Grrr.

Now, don't get me wrong. Everything going right for the first time in a while wasn't something I was complaining about. It was especially lovely to have Ameline in the family, after everyone got over the whole second coming routine. When Gram finally decided she'd had enough and gave the coven back, I had every intention of asking the former Benoit—now Hayle—to be my second. Freaky but true.

Still, I think I'd grown so used to the other shoe dropping it was taking me time to settle this round. When I'd married Quaid so many years ago, I was naïve enough to believe I could have a happy ending and that would be the finale. But life goes on, doesn't it? New challenges, new days, new tests. Maybe not life and death, end of the Universe, oh my swearword we're all going to die kinds of things. But asking for nothing to happen and for sunshiny awesomeness is actually, well.

Kind of boring.

Trill had already informed me she'd be calling on me again, so I knew better than to be complacent. And was finally willing to admit to myself I liked being in the thick of things. That's what I was made for. Of course I wasn't about to go stir up trouble or anything. But that eight years of dull predictability I'd called my happy ending? Yeah, I was so over that. About as much as I was over being anything close to normal.

So, this time of joy and peace and melding with Oliver, of enjoying my son and daughter—as much as she'd let me—and the love of my family and friends I would chalk up to Creator's gift to me for being a good girl. Meanwhile, I would bide my time and wait for the day She called on me again. Without complaint or guilt or regret.

This was who Sydlynn Hayle was meant to be. And I was done arguing that fact.

I used to wish for happily ever after, and wondered where mine went. But, you know what? I've decided I'd rather be happily right now.

Ever after can take care of itself.

MY DARLING READER

Here we are again, saying goodbye to Syd. I had no idea when we first met just what was in store for me. Had I known this book would mark forty releases in this single Universe, I think I would have jumped for joy. And knowing there are many, many more volumes to come in the Hayle coven's story makes me immensely happy.

Is Syd done? I'm not sure. I never say never. For now, however, her story is through. So, what next? There are other lives to visit, adventures to explore. Ethpeal's past in the **Hayle Coven Enforcer** series, the **Hayle Coven Inheritance** with Ethie, Gabriel and a few other characters I won't share for fear of spoiling the surprise. I'll also be completing the **Helios Oracles**. Due to major spoilers on Zoe's part, I was unable to write *Sanctuary* and

Phoenix until the **HCDestinies** were complete.

In case you missed them, jumped from *The Last Call* to *The Outcast*, there are other series already waiting for you in Syd's world. They will fill in for you the events between the end of the **HCNovels** and the beginning of the **Destinies**:

The First Plane Trilogy (Meira)
The Planeless
Second Seat
Ruler

The Lychos Cycle (Charlotte)
Weregirl
Revenant
Lychos

The Helios Oracles (Zoe)
Foresight

And, our darling silver Persian, ***Sassafras***, has his own book, self-titled. As well, Syd's great-great-great grandmother, Auburdeen Hayle, has a Victorian era paranormal steampunk trilogy you might enjoy:

The Blood and Gold Trilogy
Smoke and Magic
Fire and Illusion
Steam and Sorcery

I also have **many, many more books** (!) in other worlds you might like to visit. From horror to dystopia and post-apocalyptic, contemporary and action adventure, mystery and magic await...

For now, look for news of all my new releases coming right in your inbox! I'd love for you to sign up for my newsletter:

http://smarturl.it/PattiLarsenEmail

You get the inside scoop on all new releases, things I love and, on signing up, a couple of free books as my thanks to you.

Thank you so much for reading, for loving Syd, for sticking with me through all the delays and frustrations as I worked out the best path to take. You are fabulous and awesomesauce, Sydtasticly stupendous.

Best from Wilding Springs,
Patti

Like what you read? Find out more at
pattilarsen.com

Don't despair! There's more of the
Hayle Coven Universe ahead.

Here's a look at the
Daeva and Drach novella

REENA

The depths of Demonicon enveloped me in their cool darkness, my footsteps softly hollow on the polished stone floor. I resisted the childish urge to extend my right hand and run it over the roughened stone of the corridor as I often did when I was young, the wonder of this underground city more enticing to me than ever the surface of our world could be.

I was born for spaces beneath, for the shadows and the silence. Raised in secret by the Daeva of this plane to lurk in places other demons shunned, to seek out answers to queries they had no idea were even questions. To uncover the truths often wished left buried by those in power.

I bowed my head in recognition to a team leader on my way past, his scowl as familiar as the halls I strode. My shoulders remained erect, however. He might not approve of me or my unusual parentage, but the council long ago allowed my inclusion in our particular order and he hadn't the power to naysay it.

I was accustomed to their stares, their judgments, my fellow Daeva. It was part of the reason my hip length black hair hung in dreadlocks. I wore my pale, pink skin proudly, not bothering to disguise its human tint. Why I shrouded my large eyes in black makeup, dressed like a human teenager tuned into death metal music. Let them stare and whisper and judge my black boots and corsets, more familiar in the court above than in the reserved ranks of the Daeva. My mother chose to bring me here, to Demonicon, to be born and raised and I was grateful for her choice.

Any other demon family would welcome me. All but the mighty Daeva and their pure bloodline issues. Mother didn't care. She did what she wanted, always. I considered myself blessed to take after her.

Even though she managed to go and die on me. From what I understood, the group that shattered the stone effigy she used to cross to their plane and took her life were still in existence. One of these days, when I was free to act on my own, I'd make sure to take care of that injustice.

"Reena." I slowed, though I maintained my forward motion, as a pair of feet fell in time with mine, a slim set of shoulders swaying next to me. I should have felt her coming, but knew better than to judge myself in that regard. Raethnn had been around longer than most, millennia of practice carrying her between shadows in ways I was only beginning to understand.

"Mistress." The leader of the Daeva council was the only reason I remained here. I was quite cognizant of her support, though not surprised. I would never openly use the term, but my mother's mother had my back for my entire life and I would remain grateful. For her support and her teaching.

Raethnn's long, skeletal fingers slid over my wrist, making me shiver. Make no mistake, her touch betrayed none of the weakness her physical body seemed to reflect. Power unlike any other I'd ever felt bumped me gently before she retreated, black nails scratching softly as her hand fell. "This assignment troubles me."

I was just on my way to a meeting. One she was meant to chair, from what I understood. But, though she was the defacto leader of our people, I knew it was sheer will and strength that kept her there, as was our way. And cleverness. More to be grateful for.

"Should I turn it down?" Doing so would instantly damage my standing. Unlike other demons, we didn't aspire to plane climbing, but to our own system of loyalty and success carefully tracked by those who thought such things mattered. But if she told me to decline, I would obey immediately. No questions asked.

"No," she said, "just…" Her crystal white hair shone crisp in the low light of the embedded glowdisks, sharp voice deep and precise. "Care and caution."

"As always," I said.

Her eyes glittered up at me, deep wrinkles hiding her faint smile from all but those who knew her best. I was honored to be one.

Raethnn pushed on, speeding her stride ahead of me as the meeting door loomed in the distance. I slowed on purpose, to put further distance between us, knowing she preferred it and agreeing with her. There might have been a time once I wished things were different, that the maternal feelings I had for her could be fully realized. But to show too close a bond to her could leave me open to either attack by her enemies—not that I cared—or advertise apparent weakness that I needed my grandmother to protect me.

No. The skills, training and sense of worth she'd instilled in me over my eighteen years had been more than I needed to handle the Daeva's criticism of my birth. I'd shown them over and over, with each assignment I accepted, just what being Raethnn's granddaughter really meant, but of my own actions and ambition. Let them wish it were otherwise. A fraction of their ages, I was already better at this vocation the Daeva claimed than the majority of my brethren.

Most likely the main reason they cared for me so little, bloodlines be damned. It wasn't the first time, though, my human heritage had been more a help than a hindrance. I knew very well I didn't think the way most of my fellow Daeva did. As I entered the meeting room, that much was increasingly apparent. Ten faces looked up, most frowning at me, Raethnn's expressionless from her seat at the head of the table. I was last in, naturally. It was pure heaven to saunter to the final empty seat at the end of the room, slide into the chair furthest from her—a seat meant for the lowest, but one I flaunted as a place of power with my half-smile around at the others. They all saw me as a freak, as someone to be looked down upon with disdain. While they matched each other perfectly in dress and appearance, not a scrap of creativity among them.

No wonder I'd climbed so far so fast. They'd spent so long down here in the dark, they'd lost their willingness to take risks.

Human dad, whoever you were, I'd find you and thank you someday. Unless you were one of the people who took away my mother. Then, I'd have to kill you.

"Ruler is engaging in one of her non-standard city tours this afternoon." I crushed my grin of glee. I cut my teeth as a child on the streets of the capital, Ostrogotho, following our old Ruler, Ahbi Sanghamitra, and monitoring her in the guise of a simple wee one. Ahbi's predictability had left me annoyed even as a girl. But our new Ruler, Senne Hathenemeira, was her opposite, often shifting plans at the last minute or taking impromptu visits outside the city whenever the hell she felt like it. I was a whim kind of girl myself and, knowing our Ruler's young age, I'd always felt an affinity for her, a kinship of bold sisterhood. Not to mention her own heritage matched mine, though in her case it was a witch mother and a demon father that mixed her blood.

I would love to meet her someday, a secret desire, though I knew that likelihood was a dream. She was Ruler, First Seat and all powerful no matter her lineage, and I was just a fledgling Daeva assassin trying to find her way in the world.

Still, a girl could dream.

The group muttered their unhappiness while I pondered the chance I might get close enough to have Ruler notice me in some small way. I knew Ahbi had seen me, that clever old demon as formidable as my grandmother. But our new Ruler seemed less aware of the world around her, as though she carried its full weight on her shoulders, too heavy to see up close the details that might keep her safe. Considering her sister, Sydlynn Hayle, had saved the Universe several times and our own Ruler herself presided over the near fall of Demonicon, she was allowed her distractions. I had made it my mission, though no one asked me to or even knew I did it, to monitor her young daughter, Zuzameirhaylynn, while Ruler toured. Just as a private precaution.

"Assignments." Raethnn began listing them off, as usual the most important—immediately in front of the caravan—going to the most venerated. I ignored Phygon's grin in my direction as his name was called. The tall, though soft bodied demon had a few centuries on me in age, but acted like a bratty kid. Still, he had support on the council and, unlike me, was more than willing to use his father's position to bolster his own ranking and gain prime assignments. In other words, the ass kissing sack of useless had set himself up to never, ever fail.

I hated him so much I could taste it.

"Reena." Shocking to hear my name so early. Yes, I was doing well in rankings, a regular on this high-powered squad now, but I was typically the last one called. I met Raethnn's eyes and did my best not to show my surprise as she went on to the muttering unhappiness of the others. "Surveillance of suspect targets in lower Ostrogotho."

I almost groaned. That meant no following of the caravan after all, my usual assignment, and bottom of the barrel as most dangerous. But, from the angry outcry from Phygon, this new post was a good placement, enough to make him speak up.

"Hurthisa is much more qualified—" His face darkened to a deeper red than usual as my grandmother gestured for his silence, a push of power behind it sealing his throat. I wished she'd leave him that way. Bulging eyes and lack of breathing became him.

"Do you accept, Reena?" Her gaze returned to me while Phygon struggled in her grasp. I pondered the question, partly out of spite and partly because of her warning in the hall. Did she switch me out or fight for this? It was impossible to know.

I finally nodded and she released Phygon who gasped as his torso fell forward.

I didn't hear the rest of the assignments. I was too busy worrying. Overthinking things often kept me on my toes and out of trouble. But I'd been known to obsess to the point of explosion.

No time to work out if Raethnn had helped me or I was on the trajectory she'd warned me about. We departed immediately, splitting up as we reached the surface. I hung back as was my way, though I had the right to walk among the others. No one said anything, but they didn't have to. I already knew they were waiting for me to screw up.

As I slipped into the street through the heavily damaged doorway that hid the lower entrance to the Daeva underground, my brain spun even as my instincts took over. There had been enough unrest on Demonicon since Senne gained Ruler's Seat we'd been on the alert about assassination attempts and attacks on the royal family from, not criminal elements, but the damned Family itself. When Ruler faced down the evil Planeless cult leader, Xeoniteridone, her enemy aided by her own grandfather and Second Seat, she was forced to allow the Node holding our planes together to collapse. At least, that was what I was able to ascertain from Raethnn and sneaking around during private meetings so I could overhear what was going on. With the help of her sister and some strange white power I'd never seen before—or since—Senne collapsed the Node before rebuilding it again. I was fortunate enough (yes, I considered myself fortunate despite the desperation of the situation) to be one of the Daeva present when Senne faced down the Planeless leader and was still in awe of her power and poise.

I'd never tell my grandmother, but as much as I admired her, I did everything I could to make sure no matter what I engaged in, I'd never be ashamed to stand before my Ruler and speak of my accomplishments. That meant Ruler—and Demonicon—came first for me, not the almighty Daeva.

But it seemed not everyone was as impressed with Senne's actions and subsequent successes. In fact, the entire Ruling Family, initially grateful for rescuing their sorry behinds, immediately turned back into the seething cesspool of wretched they'd always been and, emboldened by Senne's more lax nature and distraction with Universal problems, had begun braver and more open attempts to remove her from the throne.

Demons. I shook my head a bit, dreadlocks swinging together, as I crossed to the other side of the street, boots thudding on the stone walkway, dodging down an alley. Regular demons were cracked. No one hated you more than your own blood.

What the Family didn't know was the Daeva had Ruler's back. I would like to see them try anything out in the open and with me or any of my people present. Had, actually. And observed the inevitable satisfying outcome of their power loss and retreat with their tails between their wobbly legs.

I positioned myself down the street from the caravan route, power open, scanning for trouble. It wasn't long before I felt Phygon's magic approaching, sloppy and pulsing. So obvious. I wanted to jab him to remind him of the import of his role, but he wasn't alone. Deragors lingered with him and, though he had no love for me, he was at least good at his job and would keep the idiot he was saddled with from screwing up too badly.

Again I wondered at my assignment. It was plum, after all. In other words, out of the line of fire. Since when did I earn such a position and, did I really want this for my life? Give me risk and danger any day. Any day. This standing guard against something that probably wouldn't happen went against everything I believed in.

I needed to talk to Raethnn. Maybe this was what she meant. They would elevate me to get rid of me. It made total sense standing there, chewing my bottom lip, letting my human/demon mind work over the scenarios unwinding before me. This was their plan, it had to be, paranoia told me. Raise me up until I was off the street and unable to "embarrass" them by being in public, doing what I was born to do.

My heartrate increased, blood heating up. Over my dead body.

Rough with growing anger, mind carrying me into the myriad of ways this could go horribly wrong for me for the rest of my life, I was too late to do anything about the sudden crack in the veil that opened right in front of my face. I only had time to catch a gasped breath as something tumbled forward through the gash and into my arms.

MATHIAS

Dust puffed up from the soles of my boots as I crossed the compound, keeping my head bowed to the brightness of the sun, though the feeling of lowering my eyes was as familiar as the crackling heat of the Texas afternoon. Looking up had never been an option for me.

The bunkhouse fell behind me, long and low and in need of paint, the bachelor quarters kept apart from the main house and worship center. Gray, weathered wood blended into the soft gold of the sandy ground, scraps of withering grasses valiant in their attempt to grow despite the raging summer and lack of water. Hardy, they were called. I guess that made me hardy, too.

Father said living separate from the women, without much in the way of amenities, kept our minds pure. The only TV outside his private quarters was lucky to pick up the two local stations. More fundamentalist Christian bible thumping than I cared to watch—the preaching going against Father's teachings though he never tried to stop us from watching—and a weather station on rewind—hot, hot and more hot. With a side of thunderstorms and frazzling ozone to shake things up a bit.

Father refused to allow the other males of the compound to interact too much with the opposite sex outside of prayer times, for our own good, he said. But I knew better. I'd seen enough of the world beyond the compound walls, snuck enough peeks at life without the heavy hand of Father and the First Race Faith to understand his motives were purely selfish.

Whether in the dark forests of New Hampshire or the cold of Alaska or the humid everglades of Florida, compound after hiding place after refuge from the laws of ordinary man, my life hadn't changed all that much, thanks to my father and his view of the world.

Even if I caved, even if I was the good son Father demanded me to be, I knew it would never be enough. He kept all the women—and the freedom to be who he was—to himself.

Typical, from what I understood, from the few times I'd been able to break away and do some exploring in our latest town. Even had a nice guy running the local coffee shop in nearby Avlin show me how to use the Internet. An amazing world out there and I was trapped in here, behind the tall, chain link fence wired with enough electricity to kill a human being and the guns of the loyal men who protected us from the outside world.

A cult. I shivered despite the heat, feeling a headache begin behind my eyes, forcing my jaw loose, my expression calm no matter where my mind took me. That was the word I learned the last time I escaped, almost two years ago if the old calendar in the kitchen I'd been using was true. Florida, all mosquitoes and bogs and alligators. That same calendar came with us in our hasty move to Avlin and the burning nothing of Texas, just ahead of the authorities Father claimed wanted to break us and imprison us in their evil way of being. I was running out of months ahead, displayed as tiny and insignificant at the bottom of the panel with the happy kittens playing on top. As tiny and insignificant as I felt.

I knew better than to show emotion, to give Father a reason to challenge or push me. A lifetime of abuse—mental, verbal, emotional, physical—hadn't broken me. But it taught me a thing or two about trust and love and loyalty.

My boots thudded on the wooden steps as I ascended to the long, wide porch of the worship center. Almost late, most of the rest of the family long gone inside. I usually held back, the lack of air conditioning sweltering, though the heat barely affected me. I just couldn't stand to be inside any longer than I had to be.

With them.

With him.

I caught movement from the corner of my eye and paused in my slowing progress to look up despite telling myself not to. I almost smiled at the surprise of finding her sitting there. She raised one hand, rocking slowly in the wooden chair at the end of the porch, the normally creaking furniture silent under her skirted behind. The shining black crow perched on her shoulder, a constant so familiar he was part of her, a streak of white running over his forehead. He rocked with her, chattering softly in her ear, though she appeared to ignore him. I wouldn't have been surprised to find she understood everything he told her in his crow language, though. Viviana had always given me the creeps, though she'd been one of the only people in my life to be kind to me I could ever recall. And that was good enough for me these days.

So, benefit of the doubt. If not trust. No, never that. Not for anyone.

"Mathias." Viviana's voice was deep and rough, her lined face smiling, though the coldness of her gray eyes showed little. Curling black hair streaked with white—an eerie match to her pet crow—tucked behind a pale blue kerchief she used to control the puffy mass. Her thin body seemed unaffected by the heat, her button up blouse and flowing skirt faded and dusty.

I nodded to her and paused, knowing I should go inside. I was going to be late if I took the time to talk to her, but wanted to steal at least this tiny moment of liberation. Besides, Viviana was the only person I knew who Father didn't bully. Or, at least, didn't succeed in bullying. If I was with her, he might let my tardiness pass.

"Hello, Viviana," I said.

"'Thias," the crow croaked.

The old woman laughed, a sound as dusty as the hot afternoon. "Good boy, you remembered, Henry." She stroked his feathers. "He likes you."

Couldn't say the same, but I just nodded again. Not sure why I was nervous of Viviana, but I did what I could to stay on her good side. Anyone who could keep Father at bay had to have something up her sleeve. A scary something. As far as I knew, she was the only one who came and went from the compound. Not a member of the family, just a visitor.

I'd often wanted to ask her just what her story was, but didn't have the courage.

"Saw your mother earlier." Viviana's tone remained the same, but something about her words made me tense. I didn't like it when people noticed my immediate family. "And those young sibs of yours." Her gray eyes met mine, smile still in place. "Your daddy makes pretty kids."

I bit the inside of my cheek to keep from scowling. "You staying long?" Easier to change the subject with a soft tone than to stir up trouble. Life lessons learned.

Viviana laughed like I amused her. "When are you going to get up the balls to leave this place, boy?"

I choked on my next breath, chest heavy, the world going black around the edges as panic punched me in the gut. She laughed again at my expense while I shook my head and tried to deny what I'd been contemplating all along. He couldn't know. Father would kill me this time.

Twice before I escaped death when he caught me and brought me home. But I had no doubt this time if I didn't make it out permanently, he'd make sure I didn't see another day.

Unless I kill him first. That thought whispered through my head, silenced the second it appeared. I wouldn't think about that. I wouldn't be like him.

Viviana was standing beside me before I saw her

move, her fingers settling on my wrist. For an instant electricity raced over my skin, burning like a brand. I gasped and jerked away from her, rubbing the spot where not a mark showed. At least on the outside. She turned and walked off, heading for the entry to the worship center where I could hear Father speaking, already building up in his sermon, deep voice escaping the walls and into the cutting heat.

"Going to be late for worship," she said over her shoulder, disappearing inside while the crow stared at me with his shining black eyes. I panted into the dust and despair of the Texas summer, chest heaving, hands sweating, fire burning around the edges of my mind. For an instant impulse took me over. Run. Run now. Just go while they sat inside listening to Father rant on about how the First Race was the only race, that ordinary man was in our shadow, that he was the greatest, a god, rising to destroy all who opposed us.

The same old litany of a madman who controlled a flock of fifty. Including me.

I *could* have run. I could have left right then and there. Never looked back. Set my sneakers on the path to Avlin, use the credit card number I stole from Father's room to buy a bus ticket, go somewhere, anywhere but here. Change my name, do it right this time. Escape him for good.

Except, there were three lives in the balance. Three

lives he threatened the last time he caught me, dragged me home. Beat me until I could barely breathe, bleeding on the dusty floor of the worship center while my mother wept and my siblings watched in pale silence.

Three lives Father threatened that night. So, it wasn't just my own I feared for. Would he really kill Mother? Winda and Blaise? I didn't know. But I couldn't risk it. And they wouldn't come with me, would they?

Father had won. With a heavy heart and my entire being dying for release, I forced my feet forward, my hand to rise and grasp the handle of the doorway. To enter the worship center and face my future.

The only future I'd ever be allowed.

He was waiting for me, the echoing silence eerie as I paused to allow the darkness to envelop me. I was lost in it a moment, not realizing he'd fallen quiet until I stumbled into a chair and looked up. Past his bare chest, the muscles he used to intimidate exposed as always when he preached, over his corded neck and broad jaw. Into my father's eyes.

So much rage. I felt the mirror of his emotion flare in my own chest and needed to look away. But couldn't. My skin stung and burned while something new—and yet familiar—churned in my stomach, woke for the first time, it felt like, stretched and grew and sighed. While I stared my father down with a mix of horror at my own boldness and a fresh perspective that shocked me more than my stillness.

Mathias. What are you doing?

"BOY!" My father did nothing without fury. He raised one arm, covered in small, scale-like tattoos meant to make him look like a reptile of some kind, pale eyes flaring, bald head pulsing with a vein of anger. "Show your respect and bow before me!"

I felt it, the weight of his command. Familiar, commonplace. I was in this position often enough, a target of my father's displeasure, seemingly a daily event despite my usual attempts to avoid it. I needed to step back and let him have his moment, his dominance, or risk a beating or worse. But I couldn't. I just couldn't today, for some reason. The back of my hand continued to tingle with heat and pinpricks of faint pain where Viviana touched me. Only now my chest heaved, on fire, while my head exploded with flames. And defiance I'd never dared before and honestly had no control over.

"No," I said as I climbed steadily and with purpose I couldn't command to my feet. I'd lost my mind at last, it would seem, cracked under the pressure of my father's control. Gasps around me proved it true. Yes, I'd spoken after all, no dream. The dread on Mother's face, on Winda's, was no match for the hope and triumph on my brother's. But Blaise had no idea what I'd done, what speaking out this way might mean for him. I needed to stop, beg forgiveness, sit down. But again, I just couldn't.

Father's face twisted, froze. Something in the way he looked at me changed. I caught movement, and couldn't help but turn my head in slow motion, watched Viviana take a seat, smirking, her crow hopping from one foot to the other in obvious agitation. Then, with deliberate but detached curiosity where terror should have lived, back to my father who stormed toward me suddenly, appearing to grow as he approached, a physical wall of fury hitting me before he reached me.

"HOW DARE YOU CHALLENGE ME!" His words preceded him as much as his rage, striking me like blows.

There was a time I would have fallen to my knees under the pressure. Instead, I found myself raising my head further, shoulders back, fear dying in the roar of fire in my soul. It might be my last moment on this earth, with my hand in flaming pins and needles and that thing in my gut forcing itself into my throat as it roared in answer. But I'd take it for a chance to be my own man at last.

"Go to hell," I said, calm and clear, as the world around me burned and the woken fire in my belly burst outward to flush my skin with its heat.

No death blow, no pummeling fists. Instead, Father stopped in his tracks, gaped at me. And then lunged.

I knew from the hate in his eyes what he intended to do. He outweighed me by at least fifty pounds of muscle, his bare chest rippling with it, with old scars. Father knew how to fight. And I was just eighteen. Whatever had come over me, however, wouldn't let me go and I felt the rush of those flames consume me. Father disappeared as a giant tear appeared in the air before me, edged in fire, blackness beyond turning to a skyscape unfamiliar. I stumbled in fear, the overwhelm of whatever was happening to me fading in the face of this unbelievable shift in reality.

It drew me, like a magnet to iron, pulling me forward into a soft amber sky, toward a towering cliff of black glass. I cried out as Father surged around the edge, lunging for me, but too late. Instead, I fell face first into the gap in reality.

Straight into the arms of a red faced, amber eyed and black horned devil woman.

ABOUT THE AUTHOR

Everything you need to know about me is in this one statement: I've wanted to be a writer since I was a little girl, and now I'm doing it. How cool is that, being able to follow your dream and make it reality? I've tried everything from university to college, graduating the second with a journalism diploma (I sucked at telling real stories), am part of an all-girl improv troupe (if you've never tried it, I highly recommend making things up as you go along as often as possible). I've even been in a Celtic girl band (some of our stuff is on YouTube!) and was an independent film maker. My life has been one creative thing after another—all leading me here, to writing books for a living.

Now with multiple series in happy publication, I live on beautiful and magical Prince Edward Island (I know you've heard of Anne of Green Gables) with my very patient husband and multitude of pets.

I love-love-love hearing from you! You can reach me (and I promise I'll message back) at patti@pattilarsen.com. And if you're eager for your next dose of Patti Larsen books (usually about one release a month) come join my mailing list! All the best up and coming, giveaways, contests and, of course, my observations on the world (aren't you just dying to know what I think about everything?) all in one place: http://smarturl.it/PattiLarsenEmail.

Last—but not least!—I hope you enjoyed what you read! Your happiness is my happiness. And I'd love to hear just what you thought. A review where you found this book would mean the world to me—reviews feed writers more than you will ever know. So, loved it (or not so much), **your honest review would make my day**. Thank you!